SACRAM

SACR

D0098762

NIGHT WHEREVER WE GO

NIGHT WHEREVER WE GO

A Novel

TRACEY ROSE PEYTON

ecco

An Imprint of HarperCollinsPublishers

This is a work of fiction. Names, characters, places, and incidents are products of the author's imagination or are used fictitiously and are not to be construed as real. Any resemblance to actual events, locales, organizations, or persons, living or dead, is entirely coincidental.

NIGHT WHEREVER WE GO. Copyright © 2023 by Tracey Rose Peyton. All rights reserved. Printed in the United States of America. No part of this book may be used or reproduced in any manner whatsoever without written permission except in the case of brief quotations embodied in critical articles and reviews. For information, address HarperCollins Publishers, 195 Broadway, New York, NY 10007.

HarperCollins books may be purchased for educational, business, or sales promotional use. For information, please email the Special Markets Department at SPsales@harpercollins.com.

Ecco® and HarperCollins® are trademarks of HarperCollins Publishers.

FIRST EDITION

Designed by Alison Bloomer

Library of Congress Cataloging-in-Publication Data has been applied for.

ISBN 978-0-06-324987-5

22 23 24 25 26 LBC 5 4 3 2 1

NIGHT WHEREVER WE GO

CHAPTER ONE

IN THE COMING YEAR OF our Lord, the 1852 *Farmer's Almanac* predicted four eclipses, three of the moon, one of the sun. It said nothing of torrential rain. No prophecies of muddied fields or stalks of cotton so waterlogged and beaten down the bolls grazed the earth.

By the time the hot Texas sun made its return, glaring its indiscriminate and wanton gaze, it was much too late. The cotton wouldn't mature, instead choosing to rot right there, the bolls refusing to open. It held back the white wooly heads that were so much in demand, and instead relinquished a dank fungal smell that remained trapped in the air for weeks.

The day we were ordered to clear the field, we prayed for a norther, those horrible howling winds that scared us plumb to death our first winter in this strange country. But we knew better. Texas weather was an animal all its own, and we had yet to figure out what gods it answered to.

With no plow, we had no choice but to break it up by hand. We took to the field with pickaxes and dug up the roots, and patch by patch, we set them aflame. It was easy to get too close, to underestimate the direction and sway of the growing fire. We spent the day that way, leaping from one blaze or another, our long skirts gathered in our fists while black plumes of smoke darkened the sky.

The smoke remained long after dusk. It was still there late that night when we shook off sleep and stumbled out of our lumpy bedding to peek outside through the gaps in the cabin's chinking. All the while, we debated whether to go crossing at all. There was a lot of complaining and grumbling about tired limbs and feet, about bad air and threatening fog, about howling dogs, hungry lobos, and angry haints lying in wait. Yet, no one wanted to be left out.

We yanked loose the rags and moss stuffed into the cracks and crevices, but even then, we couldn't see much. Everything appeared to be still and dark. Ahead, a haphazard row of sloping outbuildings stuck out of the ground like crooked teeth. The high brilliant moon made monstrous shadows of them, dark shapes we stared at for long bouts until we were sure there was no movement.

The wind stirred and we could hear the wild swinging branches of half-dead trees just beyond the farm, the knobby limbs that clacked all night. We listened past them, for dogs, for wolves, for any sign of the Lucys.

Opposite the outbuildings was the Lucys' house, a wide double-pen cabin nearly three times the sizes of ours. From our doorway, only a sliver of their house was visible, but it was just enough to gauge their wakefulness by the solid black reflection of their windowpanes, the lack of firelight seeping from the cabin's walls.

The Lucys did not like us moving about at night. Often, they threatened to lock us in after dark. We imagined only the fear of fire kept them from doing so. After all, burned-up property was akin to having no property at all.

A quick word about the Lucys, if we must. To most, they were known as the Harlows, Mistress Lizzie and Master Charles of Liberty County, Georgia. Or really, she was of Liberty County, Georgia, and he was one of the many who came to the Texas countryside claiming to have no past, in hopes of making the land yield some invisible fortune he believed he was owed. But to us, they were just the Lucys, sometimes Miss or Mrs., Mister or Master, but typically just Lucy, spawn of Lucifer, kin of the devil in the most wretched place most of us have ever known.

One by one, we slipped out of the cabin and around the corner and farther still, past the Lucys' property line. There were six of us total, trudging single file into the forest. Junie led the way, followed by Patience, Lulu, Alice, and Serah, while Nan, the eldest, brought up the rear. We slipped deeper into the grove of dead trees, the large oaks and elms skinned of their bark, in various stages of atrophy. This was believed to make clearing the land easier, but it seemed to us wholly unnatural, another sign that the land of the dead maybe didn't reside under the sea as we previously thought, but was somewhere nearby, in some neighboring county in Texas.

⚞

WHEN WE BECAME WE, Texas country was still new, only a few years old in the Union. Navarro County was known as a land of wheat with dreams of cotton. Corn was the surer business, but men like Mr. Lucy came to Texas with cotton on the brain and dragged us along to make sure the land would yield. He had been unlucky before, we knew from Junie, because she had been with the Lucys the longest. She had worked for Mrs. Lucy before she was a Mrs., then was carried off to Wilkes County, Georgia, where she worked field after worn-out field as the couple's debt grew and grew. And she told us how they packed up and left in the dead of night to outwit angry creditors that threatened to seize what little he had left. By then, all Mr. Lucy had between him and sure ruin was thirty worthless acres and three slaves. They took to the road in two wagons stuffed to the gills with furniture, clothes, crockery, and seeds, the Lucys fighting all the while, their two small children screaming in fits. Harlow droned on about a vision from God, about a land of plenty, while his wife called him a fool with foolish ways, her pitch increasing with every mudhole, every windstorm, every feverish river of dirty water. God's favor would surely shine upon them, Harlow assured her. But when their two male slaves were seized and held at the trader's office in New Orleans for outstanding debts, Junie wondered if Lizzie was right all along. She knew she had only been spared a place in the trader's pen because on paper Junie belonged to Lizzie, a dower slave held in trust for Lizzie's children.

Junie never told us much about the two men who had been seized, if they were kith or kin, and if that was the reason she didn't work in the house for Miss Lizzie anymore. Instead, she told us about the tavern in New Orleans where they stayed for a couple of nights. How she sat on the back steps outside the kitchen, eating a bowl of bland rice, while the men's voices, drinking and carousing inside, carried out into the alley. How she was listening for Harlow's voice, to hear how he might go about retrieving the two men and how long that might take. He was sitting at a table a few feet away from the door, downing beer with his uncle Pap, a Louisiana merchant. And she wondered how long Pap would continue bragging before he offered to pay

Harlow's debt, but that offer never came. Instead, Pap told him, start fresh. Take what you have left and invest in women. They are cheaper than men and more versatile—can not only pull a plow and clear land, but can cook and clean, too. And best of all, they can breed, increasing a master's profit year over year every time a child is born. "But be careful, boy, about using your own seed," the man warned. "Out there, you'll want hardier stock and while half-breed gals fetch top dollar down here, outside Orleans, you can hardly get two nickels for 'em."

At the markets in Louisiana, Harlow asked us all the same questions. Had we born children before? How many? And had those children survived? In the back rooms of the auction houses, where they pulled dresses up to the neck, squeezed breasts, thumped hips, examined teeth, more questions were asked about the history of our wombs. Our previous owners or the brokers that negotiated for them were asked about our health. Were we without venereal disease or tumor? Were we verifiably sound and would a doctor certify to that fact? Harlow was teased about his need for certification, while the rest of the planters assured him they could read a slave body like a book, could determine with their bleary eyes and grubby, callused hands all one needed to know.

Alice, Serah, and Lulu were acquired there, along with Patience and her young son, Silas. Nan, having been in Texas prior to the war with Mexico, was picked up in Houston. Too old to be a breeding woman, he was told, but a good cook and doctoring woman, which he figured he would need out in the wilds of the upcountry, where the land was supposed to be better albeit remote.

But like us, the land proved finicky. Nothing grew sure or full under one bout of unrelenting sun after another. Cotton buds fell off the plants, the bulbs never growing full size, or

they rotted with too much rain. The corn planted early survived, while the late corn withered. And so far, not a new babe
born among us.

———✗

WE HURRIED ON DEEPER into the woods, dodging brittle limbs
and swarms of mosquitoes, while listening for snakes and wolves,
only slowing down once we reached the live part of the forest,
where the grass and moss softened our footfalls and the heavy
green leaves gave us cover. It was darker in this part, harder to
see, but harder to be seen, with a refreshing coolness that nipped
at our necks and feet. After a long day pressed with heat, the
coolness pulled down our songs, had us singing under our breath,
praise-house songs, feeling-good songs, the kind we knew before
ever coming to this place.

For each of us, these songs were different, as all our before-
heres were different, and some days, it's too much work, untan-
gling them. We borrow and steal in good measure, sometimes
throwing all our before-heres in a pot and making them available to the whole of we. She who can't remember her daddy
may borrow the memory of mine. Tell me about your ma, one
of us would say, what she sang to you at night, how she braided
your hair, what kind of dress did she make you for church, what
kind of sweet did she give you when you couldn't be soothed by
nothing else. But, of course, there were things each woman held
back, things she deemed too valuable for the pot or the opposite,
things too likely to spoil it whole.

We finally stopped when we reached The Tree, a large split
oak, growing in two opposite directions, one reaching sky-
ward, the other stretching out, wide and low, as if trying to
reach the sea.

BEFORE THE CROSSING COULD happen, there was a small matter that had to be handled. By this time, Serah knew the drill. She plopped down on the ground while the other women spread out around her, some kneeling and others sitting in the tree. It was important that all of their heads be higher than hers, a clear demonstration of her guilt.

Serah twirled a leaf between her fingers, a practiced blank expression on her face, as she listened to the details of her crime. Yes, she was in "hot water" again, but not because she was a troublemaker. That was solely Alice's purview, let Serah tell it, but more so, because at nearly seventeen, she was the youngest and still unschooled in the ways of life. She didn't yet understand how to manage white folks and their questions, and how often what was being said aloud had little relation to what was being asked or the request being made.

Nan, the elder of the group, dropped a bucket near Serah's leg and tipped it upside down with her walking stick. This was the signal that it was safe to talk, that the bucket would trap the sound and make their dealings under night sky unknown.

"I still don't get," Nan began, "why you opened your mouth."

"I didn't. She asked me," said Serah.

"You could've said you ain't know. Why didn't you?"

Serah stopped her twirling. She could hear the impatience in the old woman's voice, could picture fresh lines of irritation creasing her forehead. She hated being the cause of it. She respected Nan. Didn't want to be the kind of useless woman Nan thought little of, because Nan was one of those women who could do most anything. Nearly every farm had one. Not only could Nan cook and sew, but she could pull a plow, fell a tree, deliver babies, make medicines, and as such, had little compassion for able-bodied young girls, like herself, who could barely haul water. "'Cause Lucy was in a foul mood, waving a poker in my face. You know how she can be."

Stifled tittering broke out among the group.

"Alright, women, what say you?" Nan said, opening up the floor, but the rest of the group just yawned and waved their hands, ready to get the whole subject over with.

"We ain't talk punishment," said Alice, the only woman with a stake in the matter. It was Alice who had actually done the deed in question and had already been punished by the Lucys for it. She had stolen a cut of bacon from the Lucys' smokehouse and, in a panic, hidden it under the cookhouse steps. What Serah was guilty of was the telling. As the youngest of the group, she was still liable to make a wrong move and not necessarily understand why.

"Fine," Nan said. She motioned for Junie to hand over a small sack of corn seed she had been carrying. Nan then emptied the sack onto the ground next to the bucket. "Alright, your punishment is to pick up each and every seed of this corn."

Nan tipped the bucket over and picked it up. "See this," she said, reaching down and feeling for a notch in the wood with her fingers. "It should reach here. If it don't, we'll know you ain't finish and send you back. But the longer the seed is down, the harder it'll be. You ain't got long before the mice and squirrels come calling."

Alice made a whistle-like sound through her teeth.

"What now, Alice?" Nan said.

"She got the easiest one. She should get the hardest. Something smaller, like rice or benne seed."

"You see any rice or benne seed 'round here?"

"No, but in Carolina—"

"This look like Carolina to you?"

"At least make her kneel in it first," said Alice.

The small germ of anger Serah had been tamping down threatened to rise up, her face growing warm, a snappy insult flashing across her mind.

"Oh, shut up, Alice," Junie said, from her place underneath the tree.

"Don't pay her any mind," Nan whispered to Serah, squeezing her shoulder.

Serah nodded, inching closer to the pile of gray seed, its normally pale yellow color darkened from yesterday's tarring. In this country, they didn't push corn into the soil naked. Instead, the seeds were soaked in a mixture of hot water and sticky black tar, then laid out in the sun to dry, in hopes of staving off squirrels and raccoons who'd eat the seed before it took root.

She could smell the tar as she picked faster, her face over the bucket, strangely soothed by the soft tapping sound of the seed hitting bottom. She could feel Alice watching her, the woman's arms folded across her chest, while the rest of the women chatted among themselves, already done with the matter. She knew Alice could be what the women sometimes called a "miserable spirit." Everybody had the propensity to be one, but Alice was of those who embraced the feeling of it, felt more alive in the thrall of it. And if Serah understood anything about the prevailing wisdom of dealing with such folks, it was to handle them with care.

⚓

CLEARLY, THE ROAD TO becoming a we was not a honeyed one. The sun of Texas felt different to each of us. It made us crazy for a time and that crazy was called many things—homesickness, grief, drapetomania. What forged us together was more than circumstance. In some ways, we were more different than alike. None of us the same age or born in the same place. Some of us knew the folks that birthed us and some of us didn't. Some of us were born Christians, others came to it roundabout, if at all. Some of us practiced Conjure and practical magic, others steered far clear. Some of us had born children and lost them, while others were little more than virgins. We were bound together by what tends to bind women like us together. Often, that doesn't make folks kin. Makes them trapped. And that can make them hateful toward one another, unless it's redirected and harnessed toward something else altogether.

⤙

THE OTHERS BEGAN WITHOUT waiting for Serah, Nan, or Alice. Serah could hear them praying on the other side of the tree. Someone was singing, a throaty drawn-out hymn that sounded like a dirge, more vibration than song.

And it remained that way, low and thrumming, until Nan checked the bucket and emptied the corn seed back into the sack. She tied off the bag and handed it to Alice, and then carried the bucket over to the women singing, where she placed it inside the circle of women and turned it over. Serah and Alice followed her, joining along the outer edge.

Nan moved around the circle, dotting foreheads with oil as the song grew louder. The vibration grew so strong, it felt as if the group was being pulled deep inside it, made weightless, now swaying and rocking, like leaves in a strong wind. Junie moved into the circle and the women locked hands around her.

Serah watched as the woman spun and danced and cried. Moonlight shifted through the trees and lit up Junie's hair, braided and tucked at the base of her head, the long, crooked toes of her bare feet, the faded brown trousers rolled over at the ankle. Junie was the only one among them who wore pants, a set of Harlow's old trousers she wore tied around her waist with a thin rope. And that was often how Serah thought of her—the one who wore pants. It was a holdover from Serah's arrival, this need for categorization, to understand this new world and the people inside it by their habits and tics, their wants and weaknesses. Junie slowed down, turning her tear-streaked face to the light, before stumbling out of the circle and taking her place back along the perimeter.

Patience went next, inching her way into the circle with small steps. She didn't dance or shout. Instead, she just stood there, in stillness, with her eyes closed, her hands clasped together, a strand of rosary beads dangling from her wrist, whispering a prayer. She was the only Catholic among them, but she didn't seem to mind it. If others used their faith to separate themselves from others, she wasn't one of them. She needed the gathering part, she told Serah one day.

When Serah's turn came, she entered the circle, unsure of what to do. She didn't feel much like shouting or dancing. She liked the song enough, liked the sound of the women singing, but she couldn't drop down into it, the way the others seemed to. She wasn't a Christian, but the other women didn't know that, and didn't seem to care, really. This was just a means to open the door. It was your business whose help you sought—whether it be Jesus or the moon or your dead.

She spun around, repeated a prayer she heard others pray, whispering the words over and over while she waited for something to happen. She wanted to feel whatever it was that made the other women so joyful, whatever made them rock on their heels or fan their arms with glee. She wanted to know for herself what created that dazed, wide-eyed expression they often gave her afterward, like they were still somewhere else, and hadn't yet returned to the constraints of this world. She danced and she rocked, but nothing happened past her own self, past her own muscles moving as she directed them to. No Holy Spirit descended upon her. No burgeoning warmth washed over her.

At the edge of the circle, Lulu began shouting, her eyes closed, and fists clenched. The women recognizing the presence of Spirit moved to encircle Lulu, making it safe for her to move deeper into the sacred realm. Just like that, Serah's time in the circle was up, where she thought if anything was to be felt, if any spirit was to make its presence known, it would be there, inside the heat of the women.

Serah rejoined the outer edge of the circle, where she watched Lulu go deeper, jumping higher and pumping her arms, as if on the verge of flight. That seemed fitting. That if anyone would be a vessel, it would be Lulu. Not because Lulu was more righteous or upstanding than any of the others, in fact, most would say the opposite. It was more because there was little veneer between her and the world. Lulu was guileless. She'd say the meanest thing possible directly to your face with no shred of sass or anger in her voice, then get up and make you a cup of tea. She was fully a product of the moment itself, with little regard to the seconds before or after.

And still the sight of Lulu shouting and dancing made Serah feel worse. Locking hands like this was one of the few times Serah felt of the women, when she felt like they were something more than just a gaggle of strangers fastened together. But she found this night, she could take little comfort in it. She knew it took time to figure out a place, to learn its climate and its ways, what flora, fauna, or predators it might kill you with. So, it made sense that it took time for her gods and her dead to find her here, to cross the many miles of land and sea, not to mention, if there were protocols necessary to tangle with the gods here already. Kiowa gods, Cherokee gods, German gods.

However, the presence of Lulu shouting in front of her said different. This woman crying and dancing so freely made it clear to Serah that other people's gods had no problem locating them. So, if it wasn't Texas, with its strange air and stubborn fields, its plagues of pestilence and grifters, then surely, it had to be her. It had to be something wrong about her or in her that kept them from coming, that left her in this strange place with little to no aid in this world.

CHAPTER TWO

DAYS LATER, OVER THE DIN of pickaxes and hoes, we could hear Mrs. Lucy shrieking. One sharp cry, followed by another long high-pitched wail. No one cast an eye in the direction of the sound. We went on pushing oat seed knuckle-deep into the earth, as if the sound of Mrs. Lucy going into labor was the most natural thing in the world.

The shrieking kept on, at turns growing louder, then fading out, only to start up again.

"Think Nan need a hand up there?" Junie said, after a while.

"She'll send Silas if she need us," Patience replied.

We knew Nan would tend to the birth despite Mr. Lucy's incessant railing about finding a suitable doctor to tend to her this go-round. Everyone knew it was all talk. This part of the country was still desolate, with few neighbors to speak of, and even if he had a connection to a bona fide doctor willing to make the journey, it was unlikely he could afford the fee.

The boy Silas ran up, waving his bony arms. He was a thin whisper covered in dust, his shirttail skimming his ashy knees. "Nan want you!" he cried. "Come now."

"Want who, baby?" Patience asked him.

He shrugged, one naked shoulder poking out of the neck of his shirt. She stood up and crooked her index finger at him. *Come here.*

He stared at her for a moment but didn't move.

"I said come here," Patience said.

The boy ambled over.

She sighed. She shifted the shirt so it centered around his neck. "Boy, you are a sight." She licked her thumb and cleared his face of sleep and crust, while he squirmed.

"Who she ask for?" Junie asked him.

He shrugged again.

Patience pinched his shoulder. "Open your mouth when somebody speak to you."

He gave Patience a defiant look and pulled back from her. "Didn't say. She just say come now and bring hot water."

A flash of anger crossed Patience's face. He saw it and ran, back in the direction of the Lucys' house.

"Get back here, Silas!" His legs slowed a moment, so she knew he heard her, but he kept on anyway.

He was skinny and fast, but Patience was faster. Years of worry had made her wiry and taut, and she leaped over to him, in a few quick paces, her skirt gathered in her fist. She grabbed ahold of his shoulder and pinched it hard, turning him toward her. His small face twisted up and he let out a ragged breath. She bent her face close to his. "Don't you run from me. I'm your mother, not them. You listen to *me*, you hear?"

He nodded, his eyes wide.

She wrapped her arms around him, but he was stiff as wood

in her arms. He pulled back from her and leaned his head in the direction of the Lucys' house.

"Alright," she said, dropping her arms. He turned and ran away. She watched him until he reached the edge of the yard, a flicker of disappointment flaring up in her chest. She probably wouldn't see him the rest of the day, and this was how the one moment she had with him went.

She went back to her place on the row and crouched back down, wrapping her fingers tight around the handle of the pickaxe she'd left lying in the dirt. She slammed it into the ground a few times, until she could let the air out of her body slowly and then slower still. She wasn't sure when it happened, the moment when her boy became more theirs than hers. Initially, she didn't protest too much at the idea of him being a houseboy. She figured he'd spend most of his time helping Nan, and that seemed alright, as he was a frail child, often too sickly to follow them around in the fields all day. Most of the time, she worried about harm coming to him in that small evil house, how quickly and often he'd become the target of all the discord that flowed between the Lucys. Every time she got an evening with him, she checked his back, his legs, his arms, for lash marks, for bruises, but she got fewer and fewer evenings with him now. He slept in the Lucys' house, to aid with the Lucys' children, and getting him back to share a meal became harder and harder to come by. "He can't be spared now," she was always told.

And worse, he didn't even bother to sneak away to see her anymore. There was a time when he did, dipping by the loom for a moment to make her laugh or swinging by the cabin, while they were finishing up their sewing. Now, if he came at all, it was because she begged Nan to send him, for a few minutes when he wouldn't be missed. Now, when he came, he'd make it plain how much he didn't want to be there. He no longer liked the ashcake she made in the fireplace, singeing her fingers in the process. He didn't want the small corn-husk dolls she made him. He no longer liked sitting in her lap and listening to tall tales or singing with her. At first, she thought he was just worried about being punished, so worried he couldn't relax, but soon, it became clear to her, that wasn't it. He no longer felt at ease, so far away from the Lucys. He missed them now, it seemed, much like he used to miss her.

Patience ran her fingers over the gaping hole she made. She pushed the dirt around, making a mound and pushing the seed down inside it. It was early, the position of sun in the sky told her, but she felt so tired she thought the sun must be wrong. "Bird, you go," Patience said suddenly, from her place at the end of the row.

"Why me?" asked Serah.

"'Cause you still slow as sorghum syrup . . ."

"Like molasses."

"Slower . . . like cold tar," said Alice.

The women chuckled. "Now, you go on."

Serah groaned and headed off after Silas.

Patience watched her, hoping the girl might tell her something more about what she saw inside the house. All this time, Nan had been telling her not to worry, but it didn't ease her mind any. Instead, she suspected that Nan was holding something back, not in a malicious way, in a protective way. But if her boy was in danger, Patience wanted to know. Even if it didn't seem like there was much she could do about it. What was being somebody's mother, if not that? Sensing danger and putting your body in between it and your child. Maybe she couldn't sing him songs at night anymore, nor wash his face and hands in the morning, but maybe this she could still do.

SERAH DID NOT RUSH in the hot, humid air. Silas ran on ahead, only slowing down once, to peek over his shoulder at her. She waved him on. "Go 'head. I'm coming."

She peeled off in the direction of the well, where she filled two buckets with water. It took her a few minutes to link each bucket to the opposite ends of a shoulder yoke and balance them proper across the back of her neck. Gingerly, she inched toward the yard, with a close watch on the rim of each bucket, only spilling a cupful before Lizzie let loose another wild, piercing shriek.

When Serah reached the cookhouse, a small building with a large hearth and square table, she transferred both buckets into a large iron kettle and got a fire going.

Nan appeared in the doorway, her face shining with sweat, a long white apron cresting over her ankles. "Why you doing that out here instead of in the house?"

"Oh. I didn't think to—"

"Girl, I declare," Nan said, sighing in exasperation. "Hurry up." She turned and walked away.

Serah ladled hot water into a pitcher, wrapped a cloth around the handle, and carried it into the Lucys' house. She was blinded for a moment by the sudden darkness, an unfamiliar earthy scent washing over her.

"In here," Nan said, calling her from a bedroom at the end of a long wide hallway. Inside the room, Serah placed the pitcher down on the floor next to Nan, without looking at Mrs. Lucy, drenched in sweat on the edge of her chair, a thin slip scrunched around her pale thighs. Serah averted her eyes and headed back out of the room.

"Where you going? Get back here," Nan said, rubbing the pregnant woman's stomach.

"To fetch more hot water," said Serah, though she had no intention of returning to the dank dark room.

"I need a hand. Get behind her."

Serah forced herself to move closer. She didn't even want to be in the same room. The whole process stirred up a wild anxiousness inside her. Whenever women grew big with child, their bodies growing alien and monstrous, she found herself watching them with suspicion, though she couldn't place what it was she found frightening about them. Maybe it was the deep wide bellies, so heavy they could tip a woman over on the row, sending them headfirst into the stalks. Or the sight of them unclothed, a new taut round world affixed to their bodies. Or the muck that descended from them when the babies came spilling out, one after another. Or the incessant need of the thing once it arrived, the swaddled bundles lying underneath a shelter of leaves at the edge of a potato bed, the constant sound of crying and mewling they emitted throughout the morning, only growing louder as the day went on. She couldn't forget how the births turned the women on her old farm in South Carolina adrift, made them wan and stiff-legged as they chopped and weeded, sometimes with the babe hoisted on their backs. They spent the evenings sewing and fighting off sleep, while the child fed or cried, or cried, then fed. But the worst part was the artless rebellion of their bodies after too many births, how their spines tipped forward, or their uteruses descended lower and lower, suddenly trying to meet the air, and how some never healed right after the fifth or eighth birth. How one woman was banished altogether, sent to the woods to live in a cave after her inside parts never mended. The woman lost all control over her bodily functions. Rivers of piss and shit dribbled with such frequency and without warning that all the time, she was afraid to eat or drink, the smallest excretions causing her great pain and great embarrassment.

Ever since then, Serah looked askance at the whole birth enterprise. And while she was surprised Lizzie of all people rekindled this anxiety in her, it just confirmed how little she wanted to do with the entire process. She had no desire to be bedside while the woman shrieked and squirmed. She didn't care to witness the elaborate protocols doctoring women, such as Nan, were insistent about following, in hopes of helping a new soul transition into the world proper. And most of all, she didn't want to be in the thick of it herself, with a trapped soul inside her, sucking her dry and tipping her organs about, or later, nursing at her breasts or cradled in her lap, where eventually it'd be taken away, the moment she allowed herself to love it.

"Rub her back, will you?" said Nan.

Serah ignored the parts of herself that wanted to run elsewhere, that would instead be grateful to be cast back outside in the sticky heat, sowing winter oats with the rest of the women. Instead, she did as she was told and rubbed the woman's back in slow circles, her fingers damp from the sweat-soaked slip. Just how long would she have to do this?

Lizzie let out a loud moan, her body sliding down off the chair. Serah slipped her arms underneath the woman's armpits and felt the woman's weight sink down into her. Lizzie's hair was now plastered to her head, her breathing slow and wide.

Serah looked down at the lolling head, the neck no longer able to support it, and she found herself looking for the seam of the woman, as if there were just a few tired stitches holding Mrs. Lucy together.

"My first lying-in, I had six women in the room with me," Lizzie said. A sudden wave of pain seemed to hit her then and her head snapped back into Serah's chest with a thud.

Nan sat opposite the two, now squatting on a makeshift

stool, waiting to catch the baby. "Mmhmm, who was there?" she said, pressing a warm compress on Lizzie's swollen stomach.

"My ma, both my sisters, Mrs. Kenneally from the farm over, and Mother Amy from the church . . ." Lizzie breathed.

The child seemed to be crowning now and Nan motioned for Serah to hold the woman firmly, lest she sink down when the child slid free. Serah tightened her grip and closed her eyes.

"Send for them, won't you?" Lizzie said, her voice breaking.

Nan began pressing low on the woman's abdomen. "C'mon, Mrs. Lizzie, push a little bit more."

"It was a storm that night and they all had to stay over. There wasn't even enough room for them all, but they wanted to be close to me and the baby—"

A long low moan stopped the anecdote, then a surge of water spurted out from the woman, splashing Nan's arms, so high it soaked her rolled-up sleeves. Serah was startled, but Nan barely blinked. She just reset her footing and urged the woman on.

Within seconds, the baby emerged, the small slippery body coming so fast, Nan almost lost her grip. "I got you, honey," Nan said, gripping the child firmly and placing it in her lap. She cleared its mouth with her finger and wiped it off with a warm, damp cloth. The pale red creature drew breath and screamed.

"Is it a boy?" Lizzie asked.

"Yes, yes, it is."

"Well, that's a relief," Lizzie said, a slow grin spreading over her face. "Let me see him."

Nan wrapped the child up and held him out to Lizzie.

Serah looked down at the wrinkled infant, its mother slumped over and leaning toward him, and couldn't resist the urge to extract herself. She slowly began trying to pull her arms free.

"Where you going? We have to wait for the afterbirth," Nan said.

Serah strengthened her hold and a few minutes later, the dark purple mass slipped down and out, Nan catching it in a waiting chamber pot. Serah could see it, wet and jiggling, the long pink cord extending from its center. Nan set the child down and tied off the cord. She then cut it, firing the end with the flame of a lit candle.

Serah had never seen an afterbirth up close. She just knew there were many folks who attributed a good deal of their misfortune in life to this moment, to the separation of their body from this quivering mass. She didn't know why exactly, only that it needed to be buried at the base of a good tree and it needed to be close by, where one could look after it and visit it, when necessary. She didn't know what the fallout was when one couldn't do that. The afflictions people named were all different—water in the lungs, sickness in the head, a deadening of an arm or leg. Almost anything could be attributed to the mishandling of this sacred thing and one's untimely separation from the tree or hollow where it was buried.

"Here, take him, while I get her cleaned up," Nan said, holding out the mewling, crying child to Serah.

Serah hesitated, before taking the pale pink babe in her arms. She looked down at it, the blue veins crossing its face, the tiny, pursed lips, the heavy eyelids snapping open and closed. He looked harmless, not unlike a sleeping chick. *Oh, what damage will you come to do in this world?* she thought. And because she was holding him and could feel the child settling into her arms, she wondered if they could speak this way. Perhaps she could make her thoughts travel down and out her fingers and into his small soft body. She could plant these notions inside him while he was still wet and forming, like setting seeds in damp soil.

I should dash your head in right now, she threatened, grinning at the child suddenly. *How many lives could I save just by doing that? But you'll be different, won't you? A righteous man in the hell-carnival?*

The child began screaming.

"Bring him here," Lizzie called out from the bed. Serah handed the baby over and watched as Lizzie put the child to her breast, but he couldn't latch on, couldn't draw down the thick yellow milk of the first days.

"Here, take him," Lizzie sighed. Serah took the squirming child back in her arms while Lizzie sat up, squeezing her breast, trying to coax milk out. "I thought this time feeding would be easier," she said. "I didn't have much milk with the first two either, but our old house girls had plenty. We never wanted for milk when they were around. I didn't think much of it at the time, but you know that Roberta had a baby every time Mother did."

Serah felt stuck under the weight of this small pale boy. Nan had disappeared with her tools, motioning for Serah to stay put until she returned.

Lizzie continued pressing on her left breast, until a thick smear of fluid trickled from her nipple. "Ooh, give him here."

Serah gave the child back to Lizzie. He opened his mouth to scream and Lizzie slid the glob into the child's mouth. "Well, Roberta was a married woman. I suppose if I want plenty of milk round here I got to get y'all husbands," Lizzie said, chuckling. "Young Master Will, we got to get these gals married off, now don't we?"

It was all too close. Serah surveyed the room, looking for a task that would get her out of that house. She grabbed a sack and began stuffing all the soiled linens and bedclothes into it.

The baby opened his mouth again and Lizzie jammed her nipple inside, just as a wave of activity bubbled up from the front part of the house. The sound of Lizzie's older children bursting in, now stomping and screaming in the front room. "Go get them," Lizzie said.

Serah stepped out of the bedroom and went down the hall, where four-year-old Louisa was chasing her older brother, five-year-old Ollie, around the table. "Stop it!" Louisa screamed, as Ollie whooped and yelled.

"Both of you stop that running and hush up," Serah said as Ollie ran toward Serah, taking cover behind her legs. "Your ma wants you," she said as she steered the two children into the bedroom.

"C'mon and meet little William," Lizzie said. Louisa and Ollie inched toward the bed as if afraid. "C'mon, he won't bite."

Serah grabbed the sack and beelined for the door as the children crowded around the bed.

"Gal, come back when you're done," Lizzie yelled after her. "You know he won't sleep through the night."

❤

BEFORE NAN COULD GET dinner started, she needed to get cleaned up. She placed her tools in a pot of water and set them to boil. Any unused herbs needed to be set aside for inspection—that nothing got wet or damp, lest it would mildew and rot.

In a small room off the backside of the cookhouse, she kept her few belongings and the rolled-up pallet where she slept most nights, when she wasn't needed overnight in the Lucys' house. Only on special occasions—such as crossings and holidays—did she wander down to the quarters and sleep some portion of the night alongside the rest of the women.

On a small bench, she poured some warm water from a kettle into a bowl and stripped out of her clothes. With a rag and a small slice of soap, she washed herself, with particular care around her fingers and under her nails. In the corner of the room sat the waiting chamber pot with Lizzie's afterbirth in it. The wriggling purplish mass looked like it might slither away at any moment. She watched it from the corner of her eye as she washed, as if whatever came out of a Lucy could surprise her, if she wasn't careful. She chuckled to herself at the thought.

Now, in a fresh set of clothes, she felt better. The grit and sweat of Lizzie's labor off her, she felt like she could breathe. She pushed the soiled heap of clothing to the side. Scrubbing them would have to wait.

She walked over to the chamber pot and peered down at it. She had already inspected it once, but she did so again, just to be thorough, just to make sure it was whole and hadn't come out piecemeal, otherwise, she'd have to go back and wait for Lizzie to pass the rest of it. A fragmented placenta meant all kinds of danger.

But this one looked healthy and whole. The only concern now was the matter of disposing it. She had to admit she was puzzled. She hadn't delivered many white children, and the few she had were the offspring of indentured immigrants, Irish mostly, half of which were deemed "fallen" due to their relationships with Black men.

For the Black mothers she normally cared for, there were very specific protocols for each stage of delivery. All kinds of things that needed to be done to usher in the new spirit, and to keep bad spirits at bay so they couldn't do harm to the child or mother. Normally, she might bury the afterbirth near the trunk of a tree; other times, she'd salt it and burn it, and protect the ashes for the first few weeks of the baby's life. The burning would take hours, but Silas could watch over it, and set the ash aside, if she explained it to him proper.

Yet none of that seemed necessary. She picked up the bowl and walked out of the cookhouse, and over to the far side of the yard, past the smokehouse and around the barn, to the small pen, where the few hogs the Lucys owned were rustling about. Fat and noisy, they grunted and squealed. A spotted black one moved toward her, sniffing for food. She stood and watched them for a moment, before flinging the bowl's contents over the railing. She watched as the greedy hogs ran toward the bloody material and devoured it.

For all the years she had been midwifing, she felt a tether to the children she had delivered. The ones who survived and ones who didn't. They stayed with her, a genteel chorus that lived in the corners of her life. She didn't mind it, really. The alternative seemed lonelier. But she wanted no binding connection to this one. She'd see him and his mother every day, and that seemed plenty.

All those detailed rituals she usually did were there to help protect the child and mother, but in her estimation, Lizzie and baby William needed no such thing. And if they did, she damned well wouldn't be the one to provide them.

CHAPTER THREE

NEW COTTON WAS UP THE first time we saw Zeke. We were eating our midmorning meal of ashcake and coffee, passing a tin cup of the bitter hot liquid around from person to person. This was but another complaint we had against this wily country. Here, *coffee* had come to mean nearly any vile warm drink one could think of. It could be made of anything—pecans, parched corn, even walnuts—and yet, they still called it coffee and served it at every meal.

We only had a few minutes more to eat, so we almost didn't notice the man trailing behind Mr. Lucy like a shadow. On occasion, Harlow rented builders and masons, men we only saw in passing, erecting one leaning structure or another, so the man's arrival didn't trouble us. We didn't wonder after the man, who he might be, or what task he was brought to execute.

Instead, we concentrated on Mr. Lucy, still some distance away, his eyes obscured by the brim of a large hat. We couldn't hear him, though we could see without looking, his head cocked in our direction, his mouth moving, a likely river of instructions and invectives streaming from his lips. All spines straightened, all antennas leaned toward the two men as we shifted our bodies in the opposite direction, palming the last bits of ashcake, draining what was left of the foul now-lukewarm coffee, before heading off in the direction of the potato slips.

Later, when we made lore of this moment, we'd say the opposite. That we saw a monster coming, that the sky darkened, and a lone rooster crowed and flapped its wings, even though the sun was long done rising. Anybody claiming to be a seer would say they felt his presence, that the moment they saw the man, they knew something awful would come to pass.

⤙

WE DIDN'T SEE THE two men again until dusk. By then, we were sticky with day, our blouses soiled with sweat, our hems ragged and crusted with dirt. We were in the yard again, in the midst of our evening work. Patience was wrestling with the crank, grinding the corn needed to make our dinner, while the rest of us readied a sack of cotton for spinning. We plucked husks, seeds, and lint from the fiber, then carded it—combing the material with long wire teeth until it lay flat and pliable.

We could still smell what Nan had cooked the Lucys, a pungent dish of roasted meat that made our mouths water. We prayed she'd saved some bit of it for us, even if it was just the gravy, flavored with bacon grease. It was her we were listening for, so when Mr. Lucy and the man pushed into our circle, we were sorely disappointed, still wrapped up in our fantasies of corn pone drizzled with gravy.

Mr. Lucy motioned Patience to shut down the crank and sit.

It was then we got our first good look at the man. He was about a head taller than Mr. Lucy, a broad strapping figure, the way we figured Moses might have looked when he parted the Red Sea. He had sleepy brown eyes and a scruffy beard that obscured his mouth. Almost immediately, we began to anticipate the tasks he could take off our hands. He could split rails or help us clear the land on the other side of the farm, where our tiny garden plots were plundered mercilessly by the wandering roots of thirsty trees.

If any of us thought him handsome, she made no indication to the rest. And maybe secretly, for a lone moment, we were gladdened by the idea of him, someone to play the lady for, to adorn ourselves in perfumes and baubles, and carry on harmless, ongoing flirtations. This was true for those among us who enjoyed men. We would have been happy to tease one another about him, to make him believe we were half in love with him and entertain ourselves with silly jealous bouts where we'd force him to choose one of us. And those among us who found men scary or altogether more trouble than they were worth would find our games comical and take bets on which woman might best the other, and it is they who would get in between the two parties, if the game grew sour and someone really got attached to the man in question.

"This here's Zeke," Harlow said. "He gone be with us a while. Help him out, will you, like good Christians should. He'll stay in the barn."

We nodded. The man's face was a blank, his eyes looking past us.

"Nan's cooking up a meal for him," Harlow went on. "Patience, you take it up to him when it's done, hear?"

"Why me? He got two legs."

"Gal, don't mar my peace," Harlow said, glaring at her. "You want some heat on your back?"

Patience didn't answer, and the two men walked away. She went back to the crank, where she muttered under her breath about being chosen for the task. "I ain't his mother. I ain't suckle him." She cranked the mill faster now, the creaky gears drowning out all sound, all voices, making it suddenly too hard to hear one another.

———

IT WAS DARK BY the time Patience approached the barn with Zeke's dinner. She stood at the edge of the doorway, peering into its black insides, the dank smell of wet hay rushing toward her. She listened for the man but didn't hear him, only the rustling of a few pigs in the pen adjacent to the barn. Far off, somewhere a dog was howling.

"Hey, mister," she called out. He stepped forward, so sudden and quiet-like he startled her. The moonlight was dim, and she could barely see his face.

"What was you doing in there?" she asked.

"Resting."

"Oh." That struck her as curious, that he seemed to be there without a task or assignment. "They ain't give you a pine knot?"

"Yeah, but don't need it. Dark suits me fine."

"Hmph," she said. Another curious thing. "Here." She shoved the tray of food at him—corn pone with gravy and two slices of ham covered with a clean piece of homespun.

He didn't take the tray, or even seem interested in its contents. He smiled weakly, a small gap between his two front teeth. "It smells good," he said, "but I don't really like to eat until after."

"After? After what?" She tried again, pushing the tray toward his barreled chest until it touched. "Here."

"Come in. You're supposed to stay awhile." He grabbed hold of the tray, putting his hands on top of hers.

Patience jerked backward. The tray tilted, warm gravy spilling onto his hands and shirt. "Dammit. Sorry," she said, uprighting the tray. "Take the food and I'll see if Nan has something else you can change into."

He fanned out the shirt. "It'll dry." Again, that weak, strange smile passed over his lips. He stepped closer to her. "Don't be scared of me. I hate for gals to be afraid of me," he said, looking her in the eye so intensely, she dropped her gaze. "I'll be gentle as I can," he murmured.

It hit her suddenly what he was saying, and she dropped the tray, jumping back when it hit the ground, splashing onto her skirt. He looked at it for a moment, as if only slightly disappointed.

"Never mind all that. C'mon in," Zeke said.

"You a traveling nigger?"

He nodded.

"And you supposed to be a kind one? That it?"

"Yes, miss, I tries to be." And there was that strange smile again, the cautious pleading gaze, like he wanted her to acknowledge this kindness in him, that here he was talking to her plainly and reasonably, instead of dragging her into the barn like another stockman might.

But she was too stunned to care about all that. She stepped backward, watching the man closely as she put more and more space between them. They stared at each other for a long moment, before he turned away, disappearing into the barn.

She spun and ran full speed into the hazy darkness. She was tempted to run as far as she could, but the problem was, that wasn't very far. She had a better idea than the other women what lay at the end of most attempts—more land, little food, and an

infinite number of white men with guns. And what she understood more than most about all those white men with guns in
this strange and new country was how arbitrary and varied their
cruelty could be. Yes, it could be glittering and wild, but more
often, it was ordinary and banal and monotonous.

It was this ordinary type of cruelty that disappeared her husband, Jacob. She thought of him as she ran through the yard
and back to the cabin full of women. "Damn you." It was Jacob's
fault. That she was still here alone, running from a dark barn
in the dead of night from a man the Lucys brought for the sole
purpose of mating with her.

She thought herself a widow and if anyone asked, she said
Jacob had died, though she had no earthly idea whether he was
alive or dead. It's not that she wanted to wish death upon him if
he was still breathing. It was just the easiest way to finally wrap
her mind around the fact that he wasn't coming back. It was the
waiting that had almost done her in. That made the days impos-
sible to get through, that made her feel as if she was on the verge
of imploding.

She came to this place a wife, newly separated from her husband. And while the couple had lived most of their married days
apart, with her fate being tied to the whims of a wealthy widow
on a farm in northern Louisiana, and he being a freeman, working
the ports, he came up almost monthly, offering the widow free labor in exchange for being allowed to visit his wife and their young
son, Silas. When the widow died and Patience and Silas ended up
here, Jacob followed. He showed up some months later, not long
after they all arrived in Navarro. Harlow was cordial at first. Got
Jacob to help him build the first two cabins and even raise the
barn. And it seemed like maybe the couple could have a similar
arrangement akin to their life in Louisiana, but as time passed,
Patience and Jacob realized that was less and less likely.

Jacob still couldn't afford to buy her and Silas's freedom, as that price tag was always a goalpost in motion, but worse than that, freedmen weren't allowed to be in the country long. Texas had a law against them. Without a petition or a white man to vouch for him, he couldn't stay without risk of being jailed or re-enslaved.

Patience begged Harlow to vouch for Jacob, but he refused. Said he didn't believe in free niggers.

"Tell you what, though. I'm not unreasonable," Harlow said to her. "Jacob could sign himself over to me. And that would solve it. The law couldn't touch him, then. And nothing would change. He'd be here working on the farm just he like he been doing."

For days, Patience couldn't even bring herself to mention Harlow's proposed solution to Jacob. Every time she looked at him, the words burrowed themselves deeper into her flesh. It wasn't long before Harlow told Jacob himself. Gave her husband an ultimatum with a ticking clock in the middle of winter. And for days after, she and Jacob fought like they never had before.

"Over my dead body," she told him.

"Ain't up to you. It's up to me."

"I swear you do this, you gone have to marry one of them 'cause we through."

"Woman, you gone quit me when I'm trying to stay with you. You really are touched."

"Maybe. Still don't make what I say any less true."

That was the thing about husbands. You know them better than they know themselves. And she knew Jacob wouldn't survive it. He didn't have the kind of soul that could parse it for long. In short bouts, he managed fine. After that, he had to take off for a long haul on a fishing boat, or a gig managing horses for a stagecoach, or upriver somewhere, where he'd haul freight for any of the companies shipping goods back and forth. Too long here and he'd die.

Besides, didn't he know how fast he'd come to hate her and Silas under this new arrangement? How soon he'd see his family and the coffle as the very same thing. His being there for so long had already changed things between them. She had begun to think the distance they had before suited them better. After all, wasn't love served best in tiny bits, when one could eat it whole, when she could wear her good face and he his, when she could starch her one good dress and do up her hair for the short time they'd spend together—a period so short they never had to watch the other get beaten to the ground or cut real low? Hadn't they been better for it? To never have to look at the other with pity or shame.

By the time she reached the cabin, she was out of breath. She pushed the heavy door wide open, her breathing so ragged she couldn't speak.

"Somebody after you?" asked Alice, sitting up suddenly.

"No, no," Patience said, shutting the door closed.

"What then?" Junie asked, squinting as she broke a piece of thread with her teeth.

Patience didn't answer. She sat down on a stool for a long moment, then immediately stood up. She paced around the front door, pressing it shut over and over again. She wandered over to the lone shelf that held that week's rations and began moving them around. The small sack of corn now on the left, the gill of salt now to the right.

"Pay, what is it?" said Lulu.

Patience shook her head. She squatted next to her own pallet and yanked out all the stuffing—moss, corn husk, hay, old rags—and then, one by one, began stuffing it all back. "He a breeding nigger." She laughed, a high-pitched terrible laugh.

She shook her head again, the stark, outraged laughter growing choked in her throat. "Y'all hear me? Lucy done brought us a breeding nigger."

———✦———

THE NEXT DAY, PATIENCE fished her rosary out from its special hiding place and put it around her neck for protection. She wouldn't speak to us, only to it. All day we heard her whispering as she fingered the beads. "Mother Mary, never was it told that any asking your help was turned away. Mother Mary, I run to you for my protection." Those of us who consulted other earthly sources of help were at a loss. None of us wanted to get close enough to the man to collect the required skin and hair or fluids needed to do darker deeds. And maybe foolishly, we hoped it wouldn't come to that. That maybe Patience's prayers would be answered, that the Lucys would grow to see the error of their ways.

And by dusk, we thought maybe it was so, as we hadn't seen Mr. Lucy or Zeke all day. We went about our evening routines, casting lots to determine who would grind that night's corn and who'd have to stand over the hot fire to bake it.

"I don't care what that dice say, I ain't doing it. I did it yesterday."

"So . . ."

"That's your own fault. If you threw better . . ."

And while laughing at us, Patience did a dangerous thing. For one lone second, she forgot about them, the whole ordeal slipping to the back of her mind. Like tales of his namesake, Mr. Lucy could sometimes just appear. All of a sudden, he was there, standing behind her, and without a word or syllable even uttered between them, he snatched Patience toward him with one hand, striking her with the other. In his fist, there was a bundle of reedy branches and ragged green leaves. He struck at her bare skin, her arms, neck, and face. He let go and she sunk to her knees.

"Do it. Or tomorrow will be worse," he said, walking away, disappearing as suddenly as he came.

We helped her up, took her to Nan, who applied thick salves to the nasty, stinging welts that sprung up on her skin. The Lucys were often reluctant to use the long-tail whips so common across the South. Not because they objected to the cruelty of such methods of correction, but mostly because it wasn't economically feasible. Black snake whips and cat-o'-nine-tails flayed the skin, did damage to the muscle, put a person down for days, weeks even, depending on the number of lashes. Not to mention, it could affect resale value. Those were luxuries a yeoman farmer couldn't afford, with only a handful of folks in the fields.

PATIENCE TOOK A NAP and woke up hours later, the heavy numbing effect of the salve wearing off. She blinked at the stars, staring down at her from the holes in the roof, the small gaps where the logs didn't meet all the way, the spaces along the ridge that leaked every time it rained.

She was alone in the cabin and she was grateful for the rare moment of quiet. Muffled chatter began to seep in from outside. She opened the door and the chatter paused to ask her questions she had no use for.

Was she hungry?

Did she need more salve?

Did she want some tea?

She didn't answer, didn't want questions or their eyes or their speculating. Whatever was waiting for her in that barn probably awaited them, too, but not today. She didn't know why that mattered, but it did.

She walked past them and continued up toward the yard. She thought about Jacob, about the dark woods at the edge of the farm, where she could lie out for a few days. Someone else would have to go in her place, and maybe that'd give her enough time to figure out a solution.

She knew just the place, a gully with a thicket of low-slung ash trees, and the memory of it stung her. It was the last place she saw Jacob. After arguing about the ultimatum for a week, Jacob went ahead and signed himself over to Harlow. She was angry about it, but Jacob convinced her he could handle it. Besides, they just needed to wait for the weather to break, he said, then he'd get her and Silas out of there.

Jacob was good at geography, had a bird's sense of direction, so his plan didn't seem far-fetched to her. But that winter was brutal and several months in the cold cramped cabin, with not only a sickly screaming toddler but four other women, changed his tune. He picked fights, with Patience, with the women, with Harlow. "You sure Silas mine?" he'd ask her, whenever he wanted to get a row started. The child was too sickly and frail, he'd claim. She must have been running around with someone else back then. She spent most of the season in a state of silent seething, clutching her rosary beads, and whispering the Pater Noster, which, for some reason she couldn't figure, only made him madder.

He got Harlow to agree to let him build a new addition onto the cabin, but the two came to blows before he could finish. Harlow got a fist in his eye and Jacob took off running into the woods. Late that night, she snuck out to take him a change of clothing, a blanket, and some food. She figured he was in the gully, where they used to go whenever they wanted to be alone, but she hadn't wanted to be there with him in a long time, and almost forgot how to find it. She found him there, shivering and tired. "It'll blow over in a few days," she told him. "Lucy can't afford to lose you."

"We should go now," he said, clutching her arm, wrapping his body around hers.

"We can't. Silas won't make it. Not in this weather." She couldn't see Jacob's face but could feel the coldness in his demeanor return. "You didn't see him on the trip here," she went on. "That cholera going round. He barely survived it."

Jacob didn't say anything for a while. He let go of her, brought his face down to hers, and whispered low into her neck. "Leave him."

The ground underneath her feet shifted; the trees in front of her grew soft and blurry, the branches melding into the dark sky.

"What?" she whispered, shifting her body backward in a futile attempt to see his face. A cold gust of wind sent the branches of the trees clacking. The sound of it felt like it was inside of her. The sharp edge of her heart beating.

"I ain't hear you," she said. *Say it again, you bastard.*

He didn't say anything more, just pulled the blanket around his shoulders, tucking it tight under his arms.

Maybe she didn't hear that. It was just this land playing tricks on her. Jacob would never say such a vile thing.

He rubbed his hands together. "How much food did you bring?"

She handed over the small basket she brought, filled with corn pone and a couple pieces of salt pork wrapped in cloth.

He stuffed a chunk of corn pone into his mouth. "It's not enough," he said, chewing.

"It's enough 'til I get back over here tomorrow," she told him.

"Lucy will cool off in a couple of days and you'll come back. You'll act sorry. He'll make a big show and then it'll be over with. And when it's warmer, we'll figure out a plan," she heard herself say, the words tumbling out fast and jumbled and high-pitched.

He nodded. "You say so."

"I do." She forced herself to kiss him goodbye. Her mind churning all the while, arguing with itself. *He didn't say that. Yes, he did. He didn't say it. You know he did. If he said it, he would've said it again.*

"I'll see you tomorrow," she said, pulling away from him.

He nodded again and she took off through the trees.

The next night, he wasn't there, and she found herself sur-prised by his absence. He must have moved to another hid-ing place, she figured. He'd be back around any day now. He wouldn't leave with those words between them. He wouldn't leave without making it right. But he never returned to the farm or the gully. With each day that passed, she was sure the next day would be the day when he'd return. Ask her forgiveness for all his misdeeds. Be the Jacob she knew, the Jacob who showed up after long bouts away. That Jacob was kind and warm, that Jacob was sweet and helpful. But she hadn't seen that Jacob in a mighty long time, and who knew which Jacob would appear if they ever crossed paths again.

She could see the barn up ahead, the ragged shape of it butt-ing against the cloudy night sky. Her face and arms still stung. The top half of her body was swollen and painful. The nettles created rashes that stung and itched, and she shoved her hands in her pockets of her apron to keep herself from scratching the wounds until they bled.

The air was humid, and though she couldn't see Zeke, she could feel him there, waiting and looming, with that crooked unsmiling grin. She felt foolish for trying to stop the inevitable. For what was coming anyway, like a wave rising up over the shore, like rain bursting from a cloud. Some things couldn't be stopped. And wasn't she silly for still trying. She hadn't been able to stop previous times, whether the men were white or Black, slave or free, whether they snatched her from behind and choked her until she suffocated, or just talked and talked and talked while they pulled her dress up over her face. And she hadn't been able to stop the country from eating Jacob, even though she tried.

She stopped at the cookhouse, where a covered tray lay on the table. She picked up the tray and moved stiff-legged to the barn. She made her mind blank as a sheet as she walked into the barn's dark maw, in much the same way her father had walked into the sea. She had never been told what body of water it was, only that he charged forward into the rising water, determined to walk back home. Mother Mary, why did you not bring me a great sea to walk into?

Zeke stirred when he heard her, a pine knot torch catching light. And she could see him in the dim flame, sitting up in a makeshift bed of hay, a soft expression in his eyes.

"You hungry?" she said.

"Starving. But I don't eat until—"

"Right," she said, putting the tray down on a bench.

She went and eased herself down next to the man on the pallet.

"You're very pretty," he said.

"Don't. Just get it over with," she said, lying down. The flame went out and she pulled up her dress.

She thought then about water, how it must feel when boats enter it, the sharp bows that seemed to sever the water in half but didn't. And she thought about Jacob, how he'd kill this man if he knew, but he would likely never know, because he didn't stay.

—✦

WHEN PATIENCE SLIPPED BACK into the cabin sometime later, we were still up sewing. We had just finished our allotments and had taken up hers.

"Go to bed. I'll finish," Junie whispered to the rest of us.

We shook our heads.

Patience lumbered past, and we all resisted the urge to touch her, to squeeze her arm or rub her back.

"Nan brought down more salve," Junie said, her voice sounding more like a question.

Patience didn't respond. She walked over to the pitcher on the table and filled a bowl with water.

We finished our sewing without speaking while we listened to Patience behind us, washing the man off of her.

Once she was done, she fished around her bedding, slow at first, then more frantic, tossing out the stuffing, as she had done the day before, but searching this time. Her fingers pulling apart the moss and hay. She shook loose her dress, the pockets. "Where my beads?"

We looked up.

"My rosary beads. Nobody seen them?"

We shook our heads.

"You had them the other day," Serah said.

"I know, but they ain't here now."

We tried to help her look, but the dark shadowy cabin made it hard to see much. We grazed the uneven floorboards with our fingers, checked the hard wooden shoes chucked in the corner.

Finally, Patience stopped. "Alice, you take them?"

Alice paused, scratching her face. "'Course not."

"'Cause if you took them, I won't be cross. I just want them back. Now."

"I said I ain't got them."

Patience walked over to Alice's corner of the room, where her pallet and trunk lay. Patience put her hand on the trunk and drummed her fingers on top of it.

Alice's blank expression grew steely as she rose from her stool. "Don't bother my things."

"Open it, then. Show me they not there. We all know you got a bad habit of taking what don't belong to you."

"So now I'm a thief and a liar?"

"Alice, even the mice in this room know the answer to that there question."

Lulu let loose a low whistle. "Back home, those are fighting words."

"Lulu, shut it."

Alice leaped toward Patience, but Junie grabbed ahold of her arm. "Leave her be," Junie said, with a hard edge in her voice.

"Let her go," Lulu said. "Patience a big girl. She can answer for all them choice words she spitting."

"Lulu, stop," Serah said quietly.

"No one's talking to you, Bird."

"How 'bout everyone shut it?" Junie said. "Let's not add any more dark to this awful day, alright?"

There was a general nodding and muttering, the tension in the room loosening a bit. Junie let go of Alice's arm with an affectionate squeeze.

Patience moved back to her bed. She shoved the stuffing back inside her mattress and lay down, pulling her blanket up over her head. Even in the dim flickering light, we could see her body shaking. Normally, one of us would go over to her and whisper soothing things, but this time, no one did. It was as if we feared the stockman's presence was contagious and whoever touched her would inevitably be next.

CHAPTER FOUR

BEING PAST CHILDBEARING YEARS, NAN was the only one exempt from spending a night or two with Zeke. However, she was responsible for certain hospitable tasks. It was she who showed him where to bathe, washed his clothing, and cooked his meals, serving him breakfast and lunch at the cookhouse daily.

And Nan felt bad for not realizing what he was the moment she saw him. In hindsight, she felt she should have seen it. There was a certain incoherence around the eyes she noticed that first day and, even now, was still trying to make sense of.

Some days, he ate on the cookhouse steps, and when he'd catch her watching him, he'd give her the strangest manic grin, his lower jaw twitching from side to side. The two halves of his face didn't seem connected, deadened eyes and an animated mouth.

Ever since Patience was struck for rejecting the man, Nan had been trying to find something that would help the women's cause. Before sunrise, she crept out into the woods, searching for roots and shrubs that might be useful. She didn't want to kill him, just wanted to make him ill enough that he couldn't perform.

By the time Nan reached the edge of the woods, the sun was just coming up. The dogwood trees were flowering, small red berries glistened from their branches. She could take back some berries that might cover the bitter taste of dogwood bark. Perhaps she could even make him a dessert.

In the understory, tall spindly plants with purple leaves swayed in the faint breeze. Pokeweed. It was poisonous, but the timing was all wrong. The trick with herbs was always timing. Harvesting a plant at the wrong time could be disadvantageous, even fatal. Choosing the wrong day, the wrong moon, could do a person serious harm. And she wanted to show a bit of restraint. After all, he had a family to go back to, he told her as much. Mentioned them with great care for some reason, and she thought it strange then, as she had barely exchanged more than a few words with him.

"You done?" was the only thing she could remember ever saying to him. But no matter what she said or if she said anything at all, he took her presence alone as an invitation to talk. Maybe he was lonely or just wanted this one woman to see him as whole, even if it was just the old lady cooking up vittles in a dark smoky kitchen. The impulse was a reasonable one, she supposed, but she didn't care for it, couldn't oblige him. She just wanted him gone, with as little harm done to the women down farm as possible.

There was some jimsonweed, a white flower surrounded by spiky leaves, but it seemed risky. It could sicken the man, she knew, but it was more likely to create an effect on his brain than his body. More likely to send him into some dreamy, hallucinogenic state where there'd be little telling what he'd actually do in that dark barn.

Some feet ahead, she spotted a chaste tree, its bright purple flowers just beginning to open. She wandered over to it, sensing some vibration calling to her. An unbelievable phenomenon she realized whenever she tried to describe it, but she had known it all her life—this ability to hear plants and trees whispering to her, offering her help. Young women came to her all the time, trying to develop remedies for one ailment or another, as if healing was just a matter of putting together the right recipe. They didn't understand the most important part of her job was listening. That most plants have dueling abilities, easily able to heal or kill you. And their effect on a body could change based on the makeup of that body. It wasn't like baking a pie, she warned whoever would listen to her.

She had learned this the hard way, after years of trying to ignore what her grandmother had taught her when she first began apprenticing. "The gift ain't just here," the old woman used to tell Nan, placing a palm over her eye. "It's here, too," her grandmother had said, motioning toward Nan's ears and heart. "Plants able to do most anything, if you listen to 'em."

Take the chaste tree for instance. In women, the seeds were thought to aid one's fertility, but in men, the seeds acted as a sedative for their lower parts.

She reached past the bright flowers, the fan of green leaves spread out, the thin reeds bearing clusters of black seeds. She took two seeds, crushed them with the edge of her mattock, and inhaled their sweet scent. Yep, these will do nicely. She carefully removed a few clusters of seeds and dropped them in her lap bag.

The sun rose higher, and she rushed back the way she came. She paused for a long second, in front of that dogwood tree she saw earlier, as it was still whispering to her. She put her hand over it and thanked the trunk in advance for its assistance, before peeling off a few pieces of its smooth gray bark. It was another sedative but, in the right amount, could cause nausea and painful stomachaches.

Then, she hurried back to the farm, a remedy already forming in her mind. She'd boil the dogwood bark for a few hours and use the liquid to make Zeke a soup. Then she'd crush the seeds and sprinkle them on top. She'd set it all with a nice piece of corn bread, just ripe for dipping.

Back at the cookhouse, she got the corn bread on the flames and the dogwood tea boiling. And when she saw the women coming in for their midmorning meal some hours later, she left them their coffee and bread without saying much. She didn't want to offer them false hope. The remedy would likely work, but it just as well might not. Bodies and medicines could be unpredictable.

—⤙—

When Lulu's turn came, she sat down opposite Zeke and emptied her pockets. On the dirt floor, she had laid out an assortment of valuables, one by one. Two silver shillings, a handful of seashells, a small mirror the size of a fist, a speckled barrette, one gold button, and a set of rosary beads.

"And I got a hog, too. I ain't seen him in some time, but can find him, if you want him."

Zeke looked at her puzzled. "All this for me?"

"One hand washes the other, right? They pay for a thing. I pay for the contrary," she said. "Understand?"

His jaw hardened. "I understand you best get those trinkets out my sight."

"I ain't mean you no offense." She held up an iridescent cone-shaped shell. "You ever seen the creatures that live in these? If I had a place this pretty, I'd never leave it." She was rambling now, her words running together as she picked up each object and explained its origin story. "This mirror belonged to my sister. She gave it to me when we parted. And this barrette, too. It's broken now, but I still keep it. Oh, and these beads . . ." She picked up Patience's rosary beads and rolled them in her palms. "These belonged to my mother. My inheritance. I'd hate to part with them, but . . ."

The man's hard jaw softened and his eyes wandered, as boredom overtook his face.

He let her talk awhile longer, before removing the rope from his trousers and lowering his pants.

She talked the entire time. Now contradicting everything she said before. New linkages arising. The shillings handed down from her father when he died. The beads from an uncle, a cousin. The mirror from an old mistress who had taught Lulu her figures. The barrette a gift from her oldest brother.

She had offered Zeke her entire life savings. A treasury of things lifted from all the different places and farms she had been. None of the stories were true, all the people she linked to the objects imaginary. When she first stole them, she had only intended to borrow them, but people noticed them gone before she could return them, and it became much too hard to give them back. The fact that folks missed them, wondered after them, only confirmed what she had gained by taking the items. The closeness born of the object. The gift with all that warm feeling attached. A lineage of kin, blood or otherwise, connected to it. That was the thing she wanted. That was the thing she took for herself.

She wasn't willy-nilly about it. She wouldn't pocket any old thing, and to her credit, she tried to do it less and less. But there were particular times when she couldn't help it. Whenever the world felt particularly dark or more lonesome than usual, the treasure of objects made her feel better. It couldn't be helped that an object's warmth soon wore off and she'd have to obtain something new to keep the good feeling going.

And so it was with Patience's rosary. The wooden beads connected by a frayed piece of twine radiated something unfamiliar to her. The kind of connection an orphan like her had never really known. On her last farm, folks called people like her lost, a no-name—a person sold away from her family so young they were doomed to remain forever unmoored. She had been sold four times and she wasn't an old woman yet. In truth, though, she didn't know how old she was—older than Serah for sure, but younger than Junie and Patience, and likely closest in age to Alice, who believed herself to be twenty-four or so.

To the whole of the group, she lied all the time about the friends and family she'd left behind. Aunt Carrie, who was the funniest, cousin Brendy, who could dance better than any of the neighboring folks. A trail of names from an assortment of farms, names and faces she mixed up now and then, fading as the years passed. Because no one else need know she was a no-name. If they couldn't recognize it, she wouldn't bother telling them. People sensed it, though, even if they didn't know what it was they were sensing. The sliver of desperation was familiar as the smell of rain coming.

She hunted for the telltale signs of it on her and had only recently accepted that there was little to be done about it. She was the kind of woman people disliked immediately, without the need for evidence. An instinct of some kind that remained no matter how much wooing she did. The cache of objects, though, never refused her. They remained perfect and arrested emblems of affection and warmth. What did it matter if that affection and warmth was originally for someone else?

And so, when the man set about his work, she cast him in the same light. She placed his hands where she wanted them. She imagined them a lover's hands. She told him how she much she'd missed him, reminded him how long it had been since they had last seen each other.

"Don't you remember that peach tree?" she whispered in the man's ear, now no longer Zeke but a man she had known two farms ago, or a woman at an outpost near Houston.

"Mmhmm," he answered.

The willful collapsing of memory never adhered to the moment perfectly. The grafting was always lopsided and ill-fitting, but if she squeezed her eyes shut and concentrated, the phantasm held up just long enough.

—⬩—

JUNIE HAD ALREADY BEEN working her own plan. She hadn't washed herself or changed her clothes in days. And after many hours chopping cotton under the July sun, the rank smell emitted from her intensified with every passing day. And to make matters worse, she started wearing an asafetida bag around her neck, to ward off a summer flu, she said. The smelly herb mixed with body odor was enough to give anyone a headache. The smell was so strong we slept with the window covering pulled back, the front door cracked, and the fire still going in the hearth, even though it was still unearthly warm at night. Usually, we kept the window covered and the door shut, with a chair in front of it, for fear of lobos or bears or men. But this time, we wrapped our weekly food rations tightly in a quilt and hid them underneath the floorboards. We used up half of that week's salt drawing protective lines along the window's edge and in front of the door.

Whenever we grumbled about the smell, she paid us no

attention, just hitched up her trousers and retightened the rope she used as a belt, her way of letting us know she didn't care nothing about our grumbling, and it wouldn't change her mind. She was stubborn that way.

The night Junie was sent up to the barn, she picked up the tray from the cookhouse and spit in it. She had to remove her cob pipe to do so, and a tiny bit of ash fell into the soup. Ah well. More flavor.

With one hand, she held the tray and with the other, a pine knot torch. It was a moonless night and the humid darkness felt syrupy and thick. She raised her torch high as she stepped into the barn, spotting Zeke sitting in the corner. He waved her over.

He appeared smaller than she remembered, a bit paler, too, his forehead damp with sweat. She put the tray down near him and sat out of arm's length, but close enough for her smell to overtake him.

"Ain't feeling too good," he said.

She continued to smoke her pipe, eyeing him closely, stifling a laugh when his eyes filled with water, and he coughed, the smell finally reaching the back of his nostrils, the rise of his throat. He coughed again, and she cackled.

"Say, gal, whose britches you got on?" he asked after a while, peering at her trousers with hazy, bleary eyes.

"They mine. You like them?"

"No," he said, making a puzzled face.

She laughed, his confusion coupled with sickness making her feel more at ease.

"They were a gift," she said. In truth, they started out as a punishment. All the women wore long skirts and dresses, no matter the season, no matter the task. In muddy weather, the hems grew black and soiled. When washing clothing at the creek, the skirts were cinched high around the thighs, but still got soaked by rising water. And Junie was no different until she and Lizzie got in one of their rows.

Out in the reaches of Texas country, Lizzie was horribly lonely, and she liked to summon Junie up to the house to lallygag with her about times back home, as if they were old friends having tea. Junie hated these sessions, but she put up with them, in hopes of securing a bit of news about her children back in Georgia. Whatever affection the woman claimed to have for her, she knew she should treat it like glass, a fragile endangered thing. But sometimes, she failed miserably.

The last time she did, she was too exhausted to hold her tongue and criticized Lizzie's jagged cutting of the cloth set aside for the women's winter garments. The cutting was a task Lizzie always insisted on doing herself, but since she didn't have to sew what she cut, she didn't realize how much extra work she created. Junie listened to the woman chatter on, while slyly trying to steer the scissors straight, but all she could think about was how exasperating it was going to be later trying to make the seams lie flat and the edges not fray. Finally, she interrupted Lizzie midstream and demanded the woman hand the scissors over. "A blind mule could do better," Junie muttered.

After that incident Lizzie took her clothing and left her only Harlow's old trousers and shirt to wear. Most women wouldn't be caught dead in a pair of britches for fear of being seen as mannish or ugly, fears some of them already had by nature of the labor they did. After all, when was the last time anyone had seen a white lady make a road or fell a tree? "Ladies" wore hoopskirts and bonnets. They sat in parlors away from the oppressive glare of the sun, where they sewed or spun. And maybe some of the poorer ones went out and fed the chickens or milked the cows or even churned the butter themselves, but there were certain things they would not do. And because Junie and the others washed the linens of said ladies, they knew that while their clothes and sheets may smell of flesh or musk or urine, they were hardly ever crusted with soil, mud, and the carcasses of dead bugs—all things she and the other women beat from their own clothing and linen regularly.

She didn't take back what she said to Lizzie, initially out of spite, and as time went on, she grew to like the trousers and wanted to keep them. She couldn't ignore how nicely they kept her thighs from chafing in the heat or kept the insects from attacking her ankles in the high grass. The skirt was a tent for things, what got trapped underneath often sank its teeth and claws into her flesh. But no more.

The women ribbed her about wearing the white man's pants. A talisman of his power, his evil. What could it do so close to the skin? It was likely to cause her flesh to rot, they teased.

Zeke moved toward his tin cup of water and drained what was left, putting it down with a loud clatter. His chin wobbled on his neck before pointing in her direction. "Did you bring me a drink?"

"No."

"Fetch me some water? Please."

"No." She returned his puzzled gaze, but her humor was lost on him.

He jolted up out of the barn and vomited, his body heaving and seizing, until finally he set down right there in the entryway, his head leaning against the doorpost, his mouth sucking air in greedily.

Junie stood up and slipped past him, so relieved she could cry. By the time she reached the cabin, she was whistling.

She pushed open the door and grinned. "He down like a rabbit in a trap."

Serah and Alice looked at her, puzzled.

"What you mean?" said Alice.

"He sick."

"How sick?" asked Serah.

Junie shrugged and stretched out on her pallet.

"But won't Lucy think you did something to him?"

"Doubt it, but if he do, maybe it'll put something on his mind. Make him realize this ain't the way."

"He think you did something, ain't he likely to kill you?" asked Patience, without raising her head.

"He can't get the harvest out of the ground without me. He know it and I know it," said Junie, pulling off her trousers. "Besides, that traveling nigger ain't dead. I know dead when I see it, and he not it."

———

IT WASN'T THE FIRST time Zeke had been poisoned. Since being sent out on this "traveling business" nearly five years ago, he'd been stabbed, burned, blinded, hexed, peed on, and called every name but a son of a God. Husbands, boyfriends, and fathers waited for him in the dead of night, and he didn't like fighting them, but when they came, he was ready. Not because he wanted to hurt them, not any more than he wanted to have sex with their women, but where else was he to put all these things thrashing about inside him?

When they swung at him, he swung back harder, cracked ribs, kicked out teeth, not because he was in the right. He knew if he was in their place, if any man touched his wife or his daughter, he'd do worse. But he had a job to do and the quicker he did it, the quicker he could get home to his own family.

He accepted that it was only a matter of time before someone killed him, before he was castrated or infected, made so sick he withered and died, and every day of every trip he went out on, he woke up wondering if that day had finally come to pass, unable to barely breathe until he returned home and hugged his wife.

That wasn't always so. When he was young and foolish and unmarried, it didn't seem such a bad job then. At least in theory. He was more social then, loved going to frolics and always had a few sweethearts on neighboring farms. And like most young men, he had a ferocious appetite for lying down with them. It seemed like the most natural thing in the world to him, not unlike eating or sleeping. But that changed when he was sent into one smelly back room or another and told to copulate with a crying, fearful woman as if he were no more than a bull or a horse.

And late nights, when he gathered with the men on his home farm to drink rotgut and gamble a bit, they'd press him for lurid details about the women he met, lust gleaming in their eyes. Just once, he wanted to tell them how he hated it, how all the looks of disgust and fear began piling up inside him, how they burrowed under his flesh like a nasty parasite. How he used to love the smell of women, but the musky scent of these scared angry strangers clung to him for days, made him sick. But he knew what the men wanted to hear from him, so he gave it to them. He boasted about all the women he bedded, how sweet the loving was, and the scores of children he gave them. He never told them how he begged his owner to stop sending him out, how he just wanted to be home with his wife, and how Master Simmons just laughed and shook his head. "Knew I should have never let you marry in the first place," the old man said. "You know, Jensen was just by here and he's taking quite a liking to your little boy. Now, I told him he wasn't for sale, but . . ."

This was the cost of keeping his family intact, having his wife and children all under the same roof. And if he only had to "travel" a few times a year, maybe that was worth it.

His face burned with fever, his clothes were drenched in sweat, his stomach roiled like a stormy sea. Someone had finally done it, he thought. And now he could put to rest the idea of stopping it himself. He had seen desperate men take to themselves with an ax, chopping off a finger or a foot to avoid being sent into the jaws of cane country. It never worked. Lying never worked either. It only ratcheted up the evil. He had tried it a few times when he first started out, when the woman was so upset, he couldn't bring himself to do it, and when the door was unbarred, he lied and said they had. He quickly learned it only made things worse, only created maniacal audiences—viewing parties of white men who sat alongside, tittering and ogling, clamoring and shouting like they were at a boxing match.

But maybe that was all over now. He flopped over, a cloud of dust rose up, filling his nose and mouth. He coughed and lay back, opening himself to the full weight of the fever. And when the old cook came in with vittles and medicinal teas, he waved her away. Harlow then dosed him with ipecac and castor oil, which made Zeke's retching worse for a spell before the fever finally broke. Once it subsided and he was finally able to stand again, he had to admit the feeling that washed over him wasn't relief.

—◢—

SOMETIME LATER, MR. LUCY told Junie to take Zeke his dinner and look after him. It became clear to everyone then that they hadn't succeeded in ridding themselves of the man or his task. Serah took to hiding out after that, disappearing into the woods for hours, sometimes a whole day, hoping she might be skipped in the process. She'd come back, hungry and wan and peppered with purple inflamed pest bites. Nan would feed her and grease the wounds, but at the first opportunity, she'd disappear again. So it wasn't surprising when they put the harness on her, a strange contraption with two irons bars across, one encircling the shoulders, the other, the torso. The two crossbars were connected by a vertical iron spine that towered up over the wearer's head, where a small bell was fixed.

The bell rang all day, and most of the night. Every time she moved and even when she didn't. She slathered wet mud inside it to make it stop, and that would help once the mud dried, but it didn't take long for the mud to dry further and flake off in large chunks, raining bits of dirt into her hair or down her dress.

She wore it nearly a week before they removed it, the sudden absence of the weight making her light-headed and nauseated. And even with it gone, she still heard the ceaseless ringing inside her, between her ears, bouncing around her chest.

One night, Mr. Lucy dispensed with the dinner ritual altogether and walked her to the barn himself. He closed both barn doors and locked her inside with Zeke, the darkening sky still visible through the slats. She banged on the door until she was tired while Zeke whittled on a bench. She slid down to the ground, her back against the door.

"Water?" he said, cocking his head in the direction of a pitcher on the floor.

Her throat was dry, but she couldn't bring herself to say yes to the water. It seemed like saying yes to the whole thing.

He stood up and filled the cup and set it down a few feet from her. His long shadow spread toward her, and she pulled her knees up to her chest to keep the shadow from reaching her feet.

He returned to his bench and continued his woodwork. "I know you hates me and I don't mind it. I don't. But whether you hate me or not, it all comes out in the wash just the same. I can get it over with and you never have to see my ugly mug again."

She heard the wind outside knocking against the cabin walls. An inevitability of a rising storm headed toward her. Neither Patience nor Junie nor Lulu had escaped it. And they were smarter than her, wilier than her. How did she think she could sidestep this thing when they hadn't?

She remembered when she and her brother Jonas were little. They were twins, her being the oldest by a few minutes. Often enough, they took up trouble together, but when their misdeeds were found out and the time came to pay for their sins, oh, how different they were. Jonas would walk right up to their father and take his beating, by sticking his hand out or turning his backside to the waiting hand or tree switch. Jonas would cry when struck, but not long afterward he'd be off, on his next bout of mischief, as if the earlier event had never happened, whereas she prolonged the spanking for as long as possible. She hid out for hours, sometimes a whole night, her father finding her in her favorite hiding spot. He'd pick her up and put her to bed next to her brother, but the next day, the whipping still awaited her. She'd be dragged back to the site of the alleged crime and whipped. And even though her father never hit her as hard or as many times as he hit Jonas, she cried twice as much. Was twice as angry and got spanked for still sulking about it days later.

She missed her brother, but it was hard to remember him without his teasing admonishments. He'd say whatever happened was all her fault, because she made what should have lasted a few minutes go on for days. She heard Jonas in her ear now, below the faint ringing.

And so, she didn't stop the man when he finally pushed her down into the hay. She closed her eyes tight and thought of Jonas on the other side of a whipping, gleefully throwing sticks in the air and watching them fall.

WHEN ALICE'S TURN CAME, she had already decided. She'd go into the barn one Alice and come out a different one. She had long harbored an obsession with molting animals—snakes, grasshoppers, and frogs that shed skin, leaving their old selves behind. Whatever happened in that dark room need not touch any other parts of her life. She could find whatever was to be found in the barn and leave it there when she left it.

She picked up Zeke's dinner and took it into the barn. She sat down, and when Zeke waved the tray away, she ate his until she'd had her fill. She was always hungry, and it was the first time in months she was able to eat as much as she needed, as much as she wanted. When she was done, she pulled out a small bottle of liquor she had swiped from the Lucys' storehouse. She hadn't shared it with any of the women and she didn't offer Zeke any either. She drank until she had enough, until the dark barn grew darker still.

That was the last thing she remembered. Every blurry thing after became part of this flaky, outer layer of skin she felt molting off her body. Every place he touched. Every patch of skin that met his.

It all would go, sloughing and molting away. Some of it went willingly, but some she had to help later with her fingernails or the sharp point of a twig, or even the dull edge of a whittling knife.

❧

AFTERWARD, WE ALL FELT at sea. Like Zeke was some strange illness we all caught and couldn't rid ourselves of. Some felt it in the body—congested lungs, rheumy eyes, and stomach pains;

while others felt it in the mind—a thick brain fog or the opposite, a compulsive agitated spinning.

Being so close to one another only made it worse, only made the grime inside pulse and spin and pitch. Whereas by one's lonesome, the muck would settle and harden, without another person kicking it up all the time.

"Stop all that jawing."

We found ourselves splintered then, unable to unstick ourselves nor pull anyone else from the rising, tightening mire. We were incapable of that for a while. All of us except Nan. But we hated her for being spared, then hated each other for not having been.

"Pass me by with all that."

That's how we spoke to each other then, in an exhausting state of seething. Made only worse by the fact that we were stuck together, like appendages of the same hand.

CHAPTER FIVE

A WEEK LATER, AT THE mouth of the creek, under the moon's half-closed eye, we threw in everything but our bodies. We had requests and we had offerings. We had leaves, fronds, and husks marked with sharp rocks and yellow clay and we had stolen apples, wild purple flowers, and fragrant buds of honeysuckle.

We waited for the water to take what we gave it, counted on its ebb and flow to absolve us, to wash our sins and carry them away, toward another town or dam, to be eaten or shredded by beavers or waterfowls, but minutes after throwing everything in, we could see our requests just lying there, floating, a thin soup over a shallow rocky bed.

No matter how many sticks we used to push it down below, a mirror of the muck inside us remained on the surface of the water. We could only watch for so long before clouds of mosquitoes drove us away.

From the creek, we went to The Tree to pray, but couldn't

shake the muck of the river. It felt personal, the muck solidify-ing. It seemed as if it was determined to hang around. Praying felt like a last resort. Some say, it should've been the first. And sure, some of us had been up to it all the while separately, but when gathered together, the power of the thing was supposed to be magnified. But the more desperate we felt, the more impos-sible it seemed.

And whereas usually it was just Serah who felt outside of it, unable to follow the thread deep down into its center, where all the joy and light was supposed to be, this night, it was true of nearly all of us. First, Junie wouldn't sing the song and Nan had forgotten the oil, and Patience led the prayer at whisper level, her voice getting lower and lower as she went on. No one wanted to hold hands or lock arms or get trapped inside the closed circle. No one wanted to close their eyes, even.

The night sky felt full of beings—water spirits and unteth-ered dead, gulls and dragonflies and murky stars—but it also felt empty, like the land was seeping and stretching out beyond its initial borders. The desert to the west, the swamp and gulf to the south. To the east, more dead trees and cleared land, and farms like this one aiming for Eden. And north, miles and miles of what? We couldn't fathom where the end of it might be and where we were in the midst of it all.

No one felt like praying. We wanted to be inside the prayer and song, the deep vibration and sweaty fist of it, but couldn't muster any of the necessary stuff to get up inside it. Some of us understood that these were relationships one remade over and over again. All the time, one was seeking alignment with God, with her Dead, with the trees and animals alike. All these rela-tionships required sun and tending to, but the youngest among us didn't understand the back-and-forth. What did it mean to be saved or spared or favored if only to be thrown out again later? It seemed hard not to be undone by such thirst, how often the spirits needed to be fed, praised, or worshipped. And how at times like these, all that effort felt fruitless.

———

"DON'T LOOK LIKE Y'ALL much for doing this," Patience said, shifting her knees up under her. We were all sitting by then, tired of trying but unwilling to give up just yet.

No one said anything.

"Alright then, I'm going to bed," Patience said, pushing herself up off the ground.

"Wait," said Nan. She poured out the contents of her sack in front of us. A pile of roots, clippings from the cotton plant. "Here. Divvy this up among y'all."

"What we supposed to do with it?" Serah said. We all knew the plant well, the knobby thinness of its stalks.

"If you don't want a baby from that breeding man, take it, chew it but don't swallow it. You'll need to do it for as much as you can, long as you can . . ."

Quiet fell over the group. Serah reached over and started separating the knobby roots into small piles of equal size, one for each woman.

"Don't include me. I don't want them," said Patience.

"How come?"

"'Cause I don't to want to lay eyes on that nigger ever again."

Serah stopped arranging and sat back on her heels. "You think Lucy will bring him back?"

"Why wouldn't he?"

"Lucy too cheap to bring him around again," Junie said. "All week they've been fighting about money. Miss Lizzie didn't even want Zeke here."

Patience made a sucking sound. "I hate it when y'all act simple."

"Watch your mouth," said Junie.

"You ever seen them put a bull to a heifer? They put them together over and over again," said Patience. "And if they don't get a calf, they try a new bull. They don't just stop . . ."

No one moved or spoke. The humid air settling thicker now, as if her words had sucked up all the good breathing air. It was hard to swallow, to think, to hear anything over the blood inside us now rushing up to punctuate her speech.

"The only way to make it stop," Patience went on, "is to let a babe come."

The words felt like a kick in the stomach. Something about the thought laid bare felt not just appalling but dangerous. It didn't feel like a careless thought or even just a likely possibility, it felt like a prophecy. And from the one woman who swore she didn't believe in them, didn't believe any who said they were born under the caul and had the ability to see what others couldn't. And maybe that's why it felt more solid, more akin to fact than fraught speculation.

Junie reached toward the pile of roots and pulled them toward her. "I won't have another . . ."

"Even if?" Patience asked, staring at Junie now, the question hanging in the air.

"Even if. Zeke's lucky he still catching breath. May not hold true next time."

Serah turned her face away. She didn't know who or what to listen to. Everything they said made sense and no sense at all and both possible futures were terrifying. She pressed her fingers into the dirt, the soil underneath cool and moist on her fingertips. She hoped her dead would rise up and speak to her through the soil. She figured all she could do was hold off the horror that seemed the closest. Zeke might come back, but he might not. A child born of him, though, would be here longer. Serah reached over and pulled a pile of roots toward her.

Patience shook her head. "Simple as can be, I declare."

Alice nodded in agreement with Patience.

Nan, who had been quiet this whole time, leaned forward and spoke. "Make up your own mind, but I think y'all have a better chance of the man not returning if y'all all go the same way."

"How you figure?" asked Patience.

"If you grow big and the others don't," Nan began, "then Lucy think something probably wrong with them. Maybe they can't have any more children or caught some women's disease. But if none of y'all bear fruit, then he think maybe something wrong with Zeke."

"But he's had to give women plenty of children before, or else he wouldn't be the traveling nigger."

"Yeah, but maybe he all used up now. He had so many he spent up."

"Maybe." Patience was thinking now, we could tell. Serah slipped one of the roots in her mouth and began chewing. She offered one to Patience, but Patience just stared at her hand for a long while until, finally, she took it and put it in her mouth. And once Patience was in, Alice, Junie, and Lulu followed suit.

WE CHEWED THE ACIDIC roots for days and days. We kept them around, soggy ground masses tucked in the pockets of our cheeks. The constant chewing made our faces tired, our breath sour, our teeth yellow, but they dulled hunger, dulled the mind just enough to lower the worrying pitch. This we did, until the supply of Nan's clippings dwindled, and by the time the frenzy of harvest was upon us, we had already become so adept at removing one plant or another, in different parts of the row, across the entire stretch of it, that we built up an abundant store of the root, which we buried in the ground underneath the cabin floor.

And when Lucy hired on some workers to help with the picking, the pitch of our worry increased, as we worried the three men might be brought on for some alternative purpose. But we rarely saw them, we worked together in one group, and they another. And we held on to the fact that they were never introduced to us as one thing or another, that we were never even told their names or what farms they came from, as proof that they were just passing through and we should regard them as no more than a cloud drifting over. The men must have found us rude, for the few times they tried to engage, greeting us with smiles or clowning around for our pleasure, we turned away from them. Only Nan showed the smallest sliver of teeth when she fed them a hot meal, but the rest of us remained as still and indifferent as the trees.

CHAPTER SIX

Charles Harlow had gotten it into his head that he had finally found the golden key. He now knew the reason why he had such poor showings of cotton the last two years, even though the oats and sweet potatoes did well as could be expected. And he now knew why last year's visit from the stockman bore no fruit and produced no children, leaving Lizzie without a wet nurse to help pick up the slack when her body refused to produce more milk.

He returned from a trip to the mill in Leesburg with an empty dray, two pieces of mail with past-due postage, and a shiny new book he toted around like the Bible. *Affleck's Southern Rural Almanac for 1854*, it was called, and it included detailed tables tracking the movement of the planets and the moon for an entire year.

At a depot in town, the grizzly store owner showed it to him with infectious reverence. The old man flipped through the pages and showed him the drawing of the Man of Signs, a wavy-haired naked figure surrounded by curlicues and symbols, and bold black lines linking each body part to a zodiac sign. Aries, sign of the Ram, corresponded to the man's head, while Pisces, sign of the Fishes, corresponded to the man's feet. The store owner went on and on about how a farmer should live by this diagram and its surrounding symbols to know when to sow seeds and cuttings and when to geld, wean, or breed stock.

"Cancer is the best time for planting, but if you can't manage that, Scorpio and Pisces is second best. And don't geld in any sign above the knees, otherwise the animal will get sick and die," the store owner told him. It wasn't the first time he'd heard sayings of this kind, but before it seemed the superstitions of old drunken men, who pontificated daily on the weather, with their predictions of rain and high wind, and still never prospered, never owned the land they lived on or the poor half-starved Negroes they rented for one year or another.

When he married Lizzie, he learned his father-in-law swore by the epact, but when the man tried to explain it, in that bored patronizing way that seemed reserved for Harlow alone, he couldn't grasp it. He understood it on its face, a system of determining the moon's age in January so as to predict the moon's cycle the rest of the year, but the math was hazy, with its accounting of solar days and lunar days. And worse, he didn't understand how it was used, how Lizzie's father organized himself and his labors around it, and how the more questions he posed to the man about it, the more foreign and unknowable the whole thing sounded.

It's not like he was out there without a plan of any kind. He had a planting calendar and a weather journal and an assortment of farming methods knocking around in his head. And he had worked enough in various capacities on other farms, from overseer to seasonal hand, to know that no two farmers swore by the same method of sowing seed in the ground or getting a healthy yield. Whether one had some special fertilizer he swore by, pig shit or guano, or another only planted onions during the "blooming days," most seemed subject to the same luck or ill fortune, each bowing to the whims of the most powerful deity none of their kind could ignore—Weather.

The difference now was he had seen men savvy enough to sidestep misfortune when it came. At the depot, he'd hear them talking, those who cut the corn early to avoid a sudden freeze, while most everyone else lost their crops and spent the next couple of weeks replanting. The wise (or lucky) farmers said they owed their good fortune to the almanac, to consistent study and testing of its patterns. Only by doing that were they able to predict what the others couldn't.

"What about breeding?" Harlow said, turning back to the store owner. "Would the best time be in the sign of Scorpio?" He pointed to the sign linking directing to the naked man's loins. "Or would anytime from the hips to the knees be good?"

The store owner didn't know, he said, only that the sign of the Virgin should be avoided. "Is that what happened? You tried to breed them during the time of Virgo?" Harlow didn't know, making a note to check his records against the almanac when he returned home, but another farmer in the store overheard them talking and sorely disagreed, said the timing of the Virgin was one of generation and blooming and he should be free to breed or sow seeds in the sign of "the lady with the flower" as he desired.

The two men began to argue, until a third farmer piped up, saying they were both wrong as a boll weevil. That in times of the Virgo, things were likely to "bloom themselves to death," the flowers taking over the plant and stunting all growth.

He listened as the men nearly came to blows, each pulling

out one story or another as proof, none of which cleared up the matter. He signaled to the store owner to add the new bible to his bill, and he balanced it among the sundries and few luxuries he picked up whenever he came to town—tea, sugar, real coffee, whiskey, laudanum, and castor oil. With that, he hurriedly left the store.

Even though his last attempt had been a bust, it still seemed the best course of action to right the ship. To finally get back in the black. Sure, it wouldn't help him much in the short-term, he thought. He'd still likely have to mortgage Alice or Lulu to pay off the promissory note coming due on the land, but some years from now, if he was patient and diligent, he'd surely see a handsome profit.

With this in mind, Harlow scheduled the stockman's return for the month that followed, arranging for him to come when the moon was in sign of the Scales, which, on the drawing, corresponded to the zodiac man's hips. He'd have the stockman stay until the moon moved lower and lower, until it reached the sign of Capricorn, in the zodiac man's knees. That gave him a good span of auspicious days to work with, seven consecutive days total, to get it right this time.

❦

WHEN ZEKE RETURNED, WE were so angry with one another we couldn't agree on whether to poison him or conjure him, and whatever tricks we each had in mind for avoiding the deed itself were felled by Mr. Lucy, now lurking nearby, outside the barn or hiding within the dark recesses of it. Half of us spent the week in a dulled blind fury, and the rest, in some semblance of a stupor. Junie had stolen some of Mrs. Lucy's laudanum, and the strange liquid had a distancing effect that placed a welcome haze over that entire week. We looked for ways to extend it, asked Nan what sort of herbs we could forage that would do the same thing.

To add insult, we spent the days trapped inside. Rain fell for three days straight, and we worked in the loom then, the grinding motion of the spinning wheel making a burrowing sound that the walls only made louder.

When the seven days were over and Zeke was carted off to wherever he came from, we still hadn't spoken more than four words to one another. And still hadn't by the next time we were scheduled to meet in the woods at The Tree. Nearly an hour after the fires dwindled in the Lucys' house, we all made our way there. The fact that we all showed up was surprising and it was unclear who was coming to fight and who was coming to pray.

"Told ya," Patience said, and Junie nearly swung at her.

"We knew it was a possibility he'd come back at least once more," Nan said, stepping in between the two.

"With all due respect, old woman, if you ain't lain with that bastard," said Patience, "I don't want to hear nothing from you."

"Damn right," agreed Lulu.

"Shut up," Junie said.

"Fine," Nan said. "Kill each other, then." She stepped aside and looked at the two women glaring at each other. She dropped the bulky sack of cotton roots on the ground between them.

Serah picked up the sack. "We have to do it again now. As proof that it don't work."

"Why in the hell would I do that?" Patience said. "No, if I have one, he'll leave me be for a while."

"No, if you have *one*," said Alice, "he'll bring that water-headed nigger back after every harvest."

We were all quiet then, the thought settling over us like a suffocating blanket. The wind rustled the leaves overhead and a cluster of birds let loose a deafening cry, as if attacked.

Nan began to pray and the rest joined in. It became a teeming hodgepodge of all possibilities, calling forth all helpers and saints: God, the Son, the Holy Ghost; ancestors hemmed between realms, in seawater and ocean, in sky and above it; those already in the next world and those barreling toward this one; the sun, moon, and stars; haints, both walking and stationary, those residing in birds, and those residing in trees; and the gods of our parents, whose true holy names we were never told.

Every tradition now mixed together—binding evil with a blade of grass, burying hair and skin of the stockman in a makeshift grave of clay and dirt and snakeskin, tarrying under moon until we grew dizzy, finally ending in a frenzied ring shout–turned–dirge. By the end, we were all soaked, wet as if we'd been dunked into the creek's heavy gray water, but lighter. We had shaken something loose, moved it out of the way, and could now touch the edge.

Serah reached for the sack and passed out the woody dank roots to each of us. A holy sacrament now. We each took one and chewed it.

—◅—

By THE TIME WE were done making candles and soap, and the cold weather of winter began to break, there had only been one slippage, which we caught before it got too far along. Alice miscarried, and we sent the soul back over, saving it for a better time, a better place, though we knew it might not take kindly to what we had done.

Harlow then brought Dr. Lewis in to look us over. A young pale man with barely a hair on his chin and a leather bag of loose jangly tools. Back to the barn we were sent, where he examined us one by one. And for those who had spent any time in the back rooms of auction houses, this was little different. He thumped breasts and hips, made us lie facedown on a short makeshift table, with our shoulders and head hanging off the end. One could look down at the dusty ground, littered with strands of hay, while a cold metal spoon was forced between her thighs.

The dim room grew darker. And one by one, we felt ourselves lowered into the belly of that big whale of Jonah's, but Jonah himself, no-account bastard, was nowhere to be found.

The doctor rummaged around, poking and scraping, until finally he removed the spoon, stepping back and declaring himself done. Outside, he and Harlow spoke, but their words made no sense now, a new language they found between them. The doctor said we seemed "sound," and he was unsure why there seemed to be such trouble with this matter. They talked more out of earshot, but a few words floated down toward us. Feckless, the doctor called us. "Liable to eat their own."

We didn't know who Dr. Lewis declared barren until a few weeks later, when Mr. Lucy took Alice along to help with a mill run and came back without her.

CHAPTER SEVEN

SEASONS STACK ON TOP OF one another and time rolls by as if a single year and not two sandwiched together. We mark the seasons not by temperature so much as by task. Corn goes in before sweet potatoes; sweet potatoes go in before cotton. We rotate planting of the second half of crops with cowpeas or snap beans or oats.

We mourn Alice as if she's passed on. We take a few of her things to the tree—her comb, a pair of woolen stockings, a brass button—and leave them there, so she's with us every time we go crossing. Without her, we feel strange and unmoored. The feeling doesn't pass.

There's too much rain, there's not enough rain. We weed and scrape, scrape and weed. Lay some of the corn by and plant again.

That is, until yellow fever comes and lays us low in the summer of 1856, taking both Silas and Miss Lizzie's youngest, William.

⤚⤜

OUT OF FEAR OF contagion, the two children were buried together far in the woods, much to both mothers' chagrin. Patience didn't want her child buried anywhere near William. Though, in life, the two were often tethered, Patience hoped for Silas to be free of the Lucys in death.

Lizzie loudly made it known that she didn't want young William buried far away in the woods. She told anyone who would listen she wanted him buried close to the house, where she could visit him often and his father would have to bypass that whitewashed cross every day, another reminder of the folly he had brought upon her and her offspring since he'd brought them to this godforsaken place.

Still weak with fever, Patience prepared Silas for burial, refusing all help from the rest of the women. She knew this hurt Nan the most, as she spent more time with him than any of them, but Patience couldn't help it. "You already got all the time with him," she told Nan.

The old woman's face crumpled, but Patience pretended she didn't see it. She turned her back and waited for the woman to walk away, before she approached the boy's stilled wrinkled body.

Alone, she washed him, rubbed the small calluses on his feet with oil, cut his hair with a straight razor. The disease had made him tiny again. She dressed him in white, in a shroud Junie and Serah had made, with small crosses and cosmograms stitched around the hem. She made a pocket in the shroud and sewed her new rosary inside it. This one she had made herself with dried seeds and twine and so it seemed the most fitting to accompany him. She washed his face once more and then pulled him into her arms for the last time. He was so light it stunned her. It felt like gathering the air.

The burial was quick, the words too few, and even the few things they said made no sense to her. The Father taketh and giveth. Her boy would be welcomed in heaven as he was not welcomed on earth. The words gave her no comfort.

On the way back, she broke reeds and branches, trying to leave markers so she could find her way back there. She promised herself when there was an ounce more of strength in her body, she would gather the women and they would come back here and move her son. They would bury him elsewhere.

<hr />

THERE WAS MORE RAIN, more fever, and even a frightful battle with locusts in the spring of 1857. Nan kept a tally stick, where she marked the occasions, but the rest of us couldn't read it. And whenever we asked, she'd warn us that the two times the stock-man came were different, once before cotton-picking time, and once a ways after, and so if we were looking to the season for clues of an impending third visit, we may not find it there.

Mrs. Lucy gave birth for the fourth time. A baby girl they named Carol. A healthy miracle child arriving on a wave of pestilence. A sure symbol of forthcoming bounty, the Lucys exclaimed.

New neighbors sprouted up to the west and again to the south. Most were small homesteads like ours, but a huge one across the water's edge loomed large like a small city, with rows of small buildings dotting the horizon. We could sometimes hear their cow horn in the morning, or a jangle of different bells summoning folks for one thing or another all throughout the day.

The Lucys were at odds; she ecstatic, him annoyed. Excited by the prospect of friends again, Mrs. Lucy met all the wives, invited the women and their hands over for quiltings, and took

us over to their places for cornhuskings and sheep-shearing parties. Mr. Lucy, however, saw every neighbor as an affront, a wily
bastard who stole swaths of land out from under him, land he'd
been just on the verge of acquiring the second his fortune turned
around.

We no longer asked Nan about the marks on her tally stick.
Someone begged her, she wouldn't say who, to cover over any
nicks marking the stockman's visits. Now, whenever she's asked
to recount the days for us, from the strange freeze that rotted the
bolls or that time a hailstorm punched new holes in the roof, the
awful fact of Zeke is left out.

It was true we loved these new gatherings with these new
neighbors. A cornhusking was alright, but a frolic deep in the
woods was even better. A quilting was pleasant, but a church
meeting under night sky, packed together in a rickety dark praise
house not much bigger than an outhouse, made us all giddy and
light-headed. Some of us loved any excuse to be in the company
of these others. And we loved them most simply because they
weren't us—they offered up news from the world, stories and
songs we hadn't heard, dances we didn't know. A lot of them
were from Virginia or Maryland, others from Alabama or the
Carolinas or Indian Country, and others still were just a foot out
of Africa, smuggled into Texas illegally by way of Cuba. They
spoke various tongues and creoles, unfamiliar and musical, with
different country marks adorning their faces and chests, not to
mention different sects of Christians with newfangled crosses
and rosaries. Others were Muslims, who carried white prayer
shawls wherever they went and dropped to their knees five times
a day. But we were most excited by the spiritual professionals:
two bona fide Conjurers, each making mojos and protective
pouches for any who could pay, and one preaching mystic, who
said the Bible had been written on his heart, so we should hold

him in higher esteem than any of the traveling missionaries who rolled through the area once a season to bring us the Gospel.

This new community was full of quirks and beliefs that felt foreign and strange. We hadn't met them all and probably never would. And while some of us embraced that as means to enjoy these folks with a certain temporary abandon, others put up all efforts to remain at a cool shelflike reserve.

CHAPTER EIGHT

BEFORE SERAH MET NOAH, SHE didn't believe in following her impulses. She thought herself an expert at dulling any ragged urge that felt costly. So much so, by the time Noah became a secret she kept from the other women, she barely recognized herself. How quickly she became a wet ball of desires, wanting, and dreaming all the time. The nakedness of it made her ashamed, but that didn't stop her from willing daylight to speed by, from stepping gingerly over Patience's sleeping body and out of the cabin to go and meet him.

She first met him at one of those Saturday-night frolics deep in the woods, but she had seen him before then, in passing, patching the road with the other men or bringing in kindling when the women were quilting over on his farm. And from the beginning, he struck up a strange compulsion in her, one she found herself warring with. For some reason, her eye was drawn to him whenever he worked or moved about. Even when she forced herself not to look in his direction, she was still aware of him, could still feel his presence somehow a few feet away.

The whole thing struck her as dangerous for a reason she couldn't identify. Her senses kept track of the Lucys in a similar fashion, almost always making note of their line of sight, their physical proximity, a quick cataloging of their gaits and faces for temperature and mood. She felt a similar cataloging happening, but with a different edge entirely. She noticed it at the last quilting. He came in with a stack of wood and greeted all the women. He then set the wood down in the corner and attended to the dying fire in the chimney.

One woman teased him about joining the group, said he boasted to her earlier that he could sew better than her and that he should prove it. All the women laughed, and he smiled with a generous show of pretty teeth, revealing a man-made dimple above his right cheek, triangular like the tip of a sharp blade. He shook his head but soon succumbed to the good-natured joshing of the women.

He took the rag and needle the woman closest to him offered and sat down at the edge of the group. He sewed a few stitches while the women peered over his handiwork, commenting all the while.

"Not bad," said one woman.

"But not better than me," said the original challenger.

They all laughed. And his eyes swept over the group, catching Serah's for a second. She froze, midlaugh, her mouth still open, feeling caught somehow, but just like that, his sweep was over, he handed back over the rag and needle, and stood up. He waved goodbye to them all and quickly left.

And she tried to listen to the gossip that followed, how two women commented on how handsome he was and a third got angry at the two for noticing. She wondered then if the curious feeling he inspired was not hers alone, but something he stirred up wherever he went.

IN THE WEEKS BETWEEN sightings, Serah tried to forget the curious feeling. And by the time word arrived that some of the new people were throwing another frolic that Saturday, she had almost convinced herself that it was just a delusion now passed.

She was determined to go, although she heard it was becoming more and more dangerous. There were whispers of rollicking patrols shutting down parties and busting up prayer meetings. Near the property line, she swore she could hear the patrollers some nights. Eerie echoes of high-pitched laughter and drunken singing punctuated by the steady clopping of horses.

So successful were the patrol's outings that there was little chatter or vague invitations to any frolics at all the last couple of weeks. And she had been warned that this one would be harder to get to, more far-flung and deeper in the woods than all the others before.

Only Serah and Patience were willing to risk it, and so the two stepped out alone, late that night. The moon was bright, but the walk was long and the mosquitoes so vicious they almost turned back, only heartening when they heard the soft strains of a fiddle. The two headed on until they reached a small clearing, where the frolic was already in progress. The fiddle player stood at one end, an excited caller goading the crowd, calling out dances to a group of women, dressed in a brilliant array of color, their skirts and dresses dyed berry red, mustard yellow, or deep indigo. Some of them wore hoopskirts, set with twine and starch, so stiff they crackled. Bracelets of copper and wood jangled from their arms. Their hair was plaited and curled or tied up in colorful scarves. The smell of flowers rose up from them, ribbons of honeysuckle and gardenia dangling from their necks.

On the opposite edge, men gambled. A solemn throwing of misshapen dice, made of bone, dotted with gray-black tips. Cheers went up as the dice stopped rolling. Under moonlight, it was easy to mistake one side for another. Three marks for two. Five for three. And the men squinted and shouted and cussed.

"He cheating."

"Don't give *him* the dice no more."

Some men threw up their hands and went to dance with the women.

Two women were racing now, but the most easy-gaited thing you ever did see. They balanced cups of water on their heads and danced toward the edge, arms and legs light and delicate. Whoever spills the water first loses. Whoever gets to the edge without spilling the water wins.

On another side, men and women were telling lies and drinking, filling gourds and tin cups with a strong-smelling brew. Within seconds, Patience dashed off toward the barrel, returning to Serah with a cup full of the strong heady liquid. Serah took a few sips and coughed as the liquid burned her chest. A breeze overhead picked up the leaves and moved through them in a slow languid wave.

Patience drank the rest and dragged Serah out into the crowd by the elbow. Serah saw Noah then, crouched at the edge of the dice game, smoking a cob pipe and making bets. She mimicked Patience's hands and hip motions, but her eyes kept on drifting back to the game. It appeared to be his turn now. He took the dice, shook them in one hand and then the other, blew on them, kissed them up, and tossed them gently. The men shouted as the dice stopped. Some cheering, some cursing. And he rolled again, and then a third time, until the streak was over. He stepped back

from the circle, where a woman-in-yellow threw a long possessive arm around his neck.

Serah turned away, back toward Patience, whose face was
softer than it had been in months. The music sped up, a triangle
now joining the fiddle. And the two women laughed and spun.
Serah threw her head back and caught a glimpse of the night sky,
starry and bright, an almost-full moon hanging above them. A
balmy breeze blew across her face, and she stared at that moon.
Almost full to bursting. That's how she felt, a whole moon somewhere inside her had pieced itself together and now it was nearly
whole again, this weird airy fullness in her chest. A strange joy
tinged with hurt. The two women whirled through the air, spinning and dancing, the two laughing into each other's ears, each
other's chest.

They stumbled out of the circle of dancing, to the edge,
where they collapsed onto the grass. The fiddle slowed down,
and the dancers partnered up, shifting from quick step to slow
drag. Couples danced close; their bodies pressed up against each
other. And she spotted him there in the crowd, dancing with the
woman-in-yellow.

Patience headed to the barrels for another drink, while Serah
sat still, the party whirring around her, the moon lower now. So
large it seemed close, as if it were slowly lowering itself down to
meet her. If she just waited patiently, maybe she could touch it.

"Come on down," Serah hollered toward it. She laughed,
clapping her hands over her mouth.

"Come on down," she heard a voice echo. She turned to see
Noah grinning at her.

"That didn't work. Should we try again?" he asked.

Serah nodded and he dropped down next to her in the grass.
"Come on down," they hollered in unison, before breaking into
laughter.

"Shut up that noise," an older man behind them yelled. "Have the patrollers running through here any minute now with all that foolishness."

They murmured a series of sheepish apologies while trying to stifle their laughter, but the more they tried to contain it, the stronger it became, until they were both tired and out of breath.

They sat there for a moment, just breathing, before he finally turned to her again. "If you got it to come down, what'd you do with it?"

"I don't know . . ."

"You just don't want to say," he said.

"It's silly," she said. "You'll think I'm touched."

"I won't."

She raised her eyebrows at him.

"I swear," he said.

"I think I'd grab hold of it and follow it 'til I get back home. It goes everywhere. Why wouldn't it pass through there?"

He grinned.

"You think it's dumb?" she asked.

"No, the opposite. Wondering why I never thought of it."

They both laughed.

"Especially since they used to say Paw-paw flew home. I wonder if that's how he did it," he said. "But how would you hold on? Wouldn't you just fall off it once it went up again?"

"Maybe, but hopefully I'd be closer than I am now," she said.

"Would you have to go under first?"

"Under? Under where?"

He grabbed a stick and began drawing a shape in the grass. He drew a circle with a cross inside it. He pointed at the median line separating the top and bottom half. "Above—land, sky, us, and below—water, land of the dead."

He pointed to the very top of the circle.

"The sun," she said.

He pointed to the bottom.

She said, "The moon?"

He nodded. "The farthest point in the land of the dead, where the oldest ancestors live . . ."

"I'd have to go there? Through the entire land of the dead and come back round? Oh hell naw."

They both laughed.

"You afraid?" he asked.

"Hell yeah," she said. "And if you're not, you should be. Would you do it?"

"No, not until it's my time, but death don't scare me."

"Really?"

"No."

"You don't have to play tough."

"I'm not. The pain is scary, but if you're just going to the other side for a while"—he pointed to the bottom of the circle again—"where everybody is and then you make your way back over, it's not that scary. You could wind up somewhere better than you were before."

"Do you know if your people made it there? Like your Paw-paw?" she said as she pointed to the bottom half of the circle

He shrugged. "I don't know. He doesn't visit. Seems like he'd visit, if he made it over."

"Back home, I used to try to see my mother. I'd go into the creek and hold my breath for as long as I could. Hoping she'd come back to get me, but she never came . . ."

"Could you see anything?"

"No, not really," she said. "Most of the time, I was too scared. There was all kind of slimy things in the water. That's what made me stop trying. Water snakes."

He laughed.

"And not the tiny ones, but the really big ones." She opened her arms wide.

They were both quiet for a moment, the party still whirring around them. The woman-in-yellow was waving now. Serah pretended she couldn't see the woman from the corner of her eye.

"You think the moon gets lonely up there?" he asked.

"Sure. Everybody gets lonely."

"The sun ain't in hollering distance, but the stars are right there."

"The stars probably awful company," she said. "All that haughty twinkling. Wouldn't that get on your nerves?"

"Okay, what about the clouds?"

"They may be better, but they so some-timey, in and out with the wind, or smothering everything."

They laughed again.

"What's so funny? I want to laugh, too," Patience said, plopping down next to them. "It's not going to last much longer."

They both turned toward her. "The drink. I had to scramble for this little bit," she said, holding her tin cup triumphantly. "You want?" She offered the cup to Serah, before turning to the man. "Who you?"

"Noah from Carolina," he said.

"Hmph. Mr. Noah, if a raft was going by with three women on it," began Patience, "one wearing red, one wearing yellow, and one wearing brown, which would you save?"

"Huh?" said Noah.

"Okay, would you save the tall one, the short one, or the mid-ways one?" Patience asked.

He looked at Serah. "What she talking about?"

Serah shrugged.

"Mr. Noah, get on out of here. You ain't serious."

He stared at the two women, unsure if Patience was joking or not.

"Go on," Patience said, waving him away.

"Fine. A fellow knows when he ain't wanted," he said, standing up in mock disappointment. He winked at Serah as he backed away into the sea of dancers.

"Good, then you a better man than most," Patience hollered after him.

She turned to Serah, now watching Noah talking to the woman-in-yellow.

Patience let out a low chuckle. "Oh, not you, too."

"What?"

"A goner for any fool come grinning in your face."

"We was just talking," Serah said, taking the cup from Patience. "Besides, that girl in yellow's probably his sweetheart."

"No, *he* was just talking. You were doing something else," Patience said, smoothing her skirt and giving Serah an exaggerated flirty grin.

"What you mean? I don't do that."

Patience laughed. "And didn't seem like he asked any of the questions he would've if he was trying to court you proper. Did he even ask if you were unattached?"

"No."

"No questions about spun or woven cloth? Or boats rigged or not?"

"No. Should he have?"

"Bird, did he even ask if he could talk to you before he sat down here?"

"No."

"Well then . . ."

As Patience talked, Serah continued watching Noah and

the woman-in-yellow. They were dancing now. He was trying to make her laugh and the woman was trying hard not to be amused, trying hard to stay upset, but even Serah could see the woman was softening toward him.

Serah wondered what was between the two, if they were, in fact, attached somehow. And while she hadn't considered the conversation between them as anything more than frivolous banter, to have it confirmed as such spawned a growing twinge of disappointment inside her. She stood up and stretched her hand out to Patience. "We should go. Patrollers be through here soon."

Patience took her hand and stood up. The two women drifted away from dancers and the music, slipping back through the woods, where the moon shone bright and full, with nary a cloud in sight.

CHAPTER NINE

HARLOW'S RIGHT HAND ITCHED. NEW calluses forming on top of the old ones, causing the tough white skin to flake and peel. The culprit was likely the handle of his new plow. He had been out there behind it since sunup, lumbering after the two plodding horses, while the women weeded and hilled the cotton for the last time. Any day now, the bolls would start to open and the frenzy of picking would begin.

He rubbed his hands together. In the lore of old wives' tales, itchy palms meant money was coming. Hopefully, there was a grain of truth in that. He had already lost a quarter of the cotton crop to worms, so he needed the rest of it to yield proper. He'd bought the new plow on credit, along with sulfur, vinegar, quinine, saltpeter, rope, and ink, and would need a decent profit to finally get square with all the merchants he owed. Merchants who regularly showed him statements listing out his purchases and the total amounts due. Daunting sums that seemed to tick up and up every time he closed his eyes.

He walked to the house but didn't go in. He was stalling. He should go inside and eat something, and then hurry back out for another round with the plow. He left Junie with it, but he didn't trust her on her own for long. She leaned when she got tired, skimming too close to the crop. But his stomach was jumpy and he couldn't imagine food would make it any better. Once Ollie showed up, he'd be able to eat. Hours ago, he had sent his now-eleven-year-old son over to Levi Sutton's house with a note, suggesting the two men revisit an old conversation they once had about Sutton's interest in purchasing a swath of Harlow's land.

From the second the boy left, Harlow hadn't been able to focus. Ollie should be back by now, he thought, but he had told the boy to wait for an answer, and maybe Sutton wasn't there when he arrived.

Or maybe it was a stalling tactic on Sutton's part, he wondered, and somehow, he had already ceded his hand. Perhaps he should have waited until Sutton sent a response, then he could have been the one delaying. He could've waited a whole day before responding, as if he, too, were so unconcerned by the prospect of buying or selling a measly fifty acres.

He didn't care for his neighbor Levi Sutton much. The man was all airs and bluster, snatching up acreage for miles and miles. It was as if the man was over there building his own town. Beyond the acres and acres of cotton, corn, and millet, there was a big fancy white house, not to mention a maze with an actual orchard of all kinds of fruit trees and decorative rosebushes. Folks didn't even refer to it as Sutton's place, but instead, some haughty moniker, like Greenbriar or Greenwich.

He hated to sell any land to Sutton, hated what it might mean if Sutton had designs on more than just that one strip of land, but he tried not to think that far. Instead, he set his mind on paying down his creditors, on getting his financial affairs out of the red.

He sat on the porch, watching the horizon, waiting for the dust clouds of Ollie's horse to appear. And yes, he knew what was said about watched pots and all, but in his line of work, he watched pots all the time. There was little he didn't put his eyes on and wait for verification that it would do what it was supposed to—grow, yield, seed, sunder.

Where was that boy? Just as likely to have dawdled off the path, if he saw the slightest inkling of something interesting. The boy wasn't worth a gill of hard work. And if the farm didn't turn around soon, he wouldn't be able to set Ollie up with much of anything when the boy came of age in a few years.

The sun shifted from behind the clouds, its angry rays now beaming down on his head and neck. From where he sat, he could hear baby Carol wailing inside. When she was first born, about a year after they buried young William, he and Lizzie thought her a miracle child, but no one used that language to describe Carol anymore. The baby had come into the world with Lizzie's orneriness—a fussy, angry ball of constant caterwauling.

He pushed the front door to the house open. "Will someone shut that child up?" No one replied, but it didn't matter, for at that second, the baby went quiet. He stepped into the dim hot room, smoke lingering in the air, the hearth fire burning.

Dorcas, the new wet nurse, cradled the baby in her lap while Lizzie hovered over them. He could see, now that his eyes had adjusted, that the child had stopped screaming because her mouth was full, impaled by the woman's dark naked breast. The wet nurse had been with them nearly a week, and still, the whole business seemed indecent to him. A stranger, some other man's property, nursing his daughter. A trace of shame flickered inside him.

His gaze met Lizzie's. She narrowed her eyes at him. *Not now.* He walked over to them, where Dorcas lifted her head in his direction, without lifting her eyes. See, the fact that she didn't even have the decency to cover herself in a white man's presence said everything. He reached for the baby.

"Give her here," Harlow said.

"She not done yet," Dorcas said, pulling a cloth up over herself and the suckling child.

"That ain't no business of yours. Give her here. Lizzie will feed her," he said, grabbing hold of Carol's foot.

"The hell I will," said Lizzie, stepping in between them, pushing Harlow backward. "Ignore him, Dorcas. Let her have as much as she wants."

Lizzie steered him away from the wet nurse over to the opposite side of the room. "I've said all I've going to say about this. I got her with my own money."

It was true. Lizzie had done the unthinkable. After the last bout of breastfeeding, she declared herself done with it. No more arduous attempts at latching, at increasing milk supply with herbs and poultices, or nursing despite raw sore nipples and clogged ducts. No matter what she did, she could never produce enough milk for their children. The babes howled day and night, and here she was, having to rely on animal milk and pap, like a serf, since the women in the quarters had yet to bear fruit. This is what she spat at him, whenever he brought up the matter.

This time, though, she had secured a wet nurse herself. She rented a woman with "fresh milk" from an acquaintance in the next county over and paid for her services six months outright, without even consulting him about it. The wet nurse just showed up one day. He came back from the fields and Lizzie was sitting there with her in the front room as if nothing extraordinary was going on.

The couple fought about it for hours that first night, to the point of exhaustion, with him refusing to allow the wet nurse near the baby until finally the child's incessant screaming wore him down.

Even now, so many days later, he was still sore about it. "Is it *my* money that's feeding her? Is she laying up under the roof that I built?"

"Fine. I'll pay for that, too. How much you want for her room and board?" said Lizzie.

"That's not the point."

"Then what is the point?"

He slumped down at the table. He started to say something but stopped. He was tired of explaining himself. Tired of her insinuating that the mountain of debt was all his fault, as if he were a god that could control weather and pestilence. As if he could simply raise his hand and stop rain and drought, or wave away the presence of worms, weevils, or grackles. It was simply a precarious business. Had been since the Panic of 1837 and the great depression that followed it. It made paupers of men smarter than him, and she didn't seem to appreciate how close they had come. That it was he who kept the wind at their backs; he, who had secured the five hundred acres that they lived upon. Even after Alice's buyer sued him for failure to disclose her barrenness. He handled it, hadn't he? Mounted an appeal that got the refund amount cut in half. Sure, he had to mortgage Lulu and Serah to secure a loan to pay the damages and the exorbitant legal fees, but he took care of it. He retained the title to the land, and that was the most important thing. Without that, where would they be?

Maybe her father was the reason she didn't seem to appreciate any of it. The reason she thought she understood more about the workings of his business than he did. The reason why every so often she butted into farm affairs, giving her opinion when he hadn't asked for it, and worse, refusing to allow him to use her property as collateral. He suspected her father was advising her and, worse, sending her money that she wasn't telling him about, but he had no proof, and she wouldn't admit it.

"The point is," he began, "you brought a plumb stranger into this house without my say-so."

"I apologized for that already. It's not like I bought her. I thought you'd be pleased to have peace in the house again. And look, Carol's so happy. I think she's already gained a pound or two."

He sighed.

Nan burst in, heaving a big steaming pot of soup onto the table. Soup in *this heat*. If that wasn't proof Lizzie's judgment couldn't be trusted, then what was?

"I don't want to see no more soup on this table until I can see my breath out there, you hear me?" he said to Lizzie.

But his wife wasn't listening. She had drifted back over to the baby and was now busy cooing at the suckling child.

"Lizzie, you hear me!"

CHAPTER TEN

WHAT SERAH HAD WANTED BUT didn't know she wanted came just before Christmas. The air was cooling and the drop in temperature gave the last few frolics of the year new urgency. She felt it most when the fiddler traded off with Delilah, a statuesque woman with a haunted singing voice. She sang beautifully, but no matter the song chosen or the tempo, it all became a dirge. Call it moon sickness, the way Delilah could stir things up in everyone, a slow unraveling of whatever dark mass was swirling deep down inside. A catharsis of the worst kind emerged, as there were never more fights than when Delilah sang, never more old couplings discarded, and new ones made. And yet, no one could keep her from singing really. Someone always asked her to, always pushed her toward the front and begged for a song, paying her in peaches or shiny apples.

It was during this season of Delilah and her ongoing dirges that their conversations picked up again. Noah would see her at one of these outings and sit down next to her as if they were old friends and he'd ask her about the social life of the moon and stars, as if he were inquiring about the health and well-being of distant kin.

Serah looked forward to these exchanges, no matter how brief they were, no matter how silly they seemed to Patience or anyone else. And over time, a strange web of language emerged underneath, like it was possible to talk about nearly anything under the veil of the moon's mercurial nature or the sun's ruthless glare. If it had been a particularly rotten set of days, she might answer his question by talking about the dead moon and how dark everything seemed without it. "I wouldn't blame it if it didn't come back at all . . ."

These discussions made her even more curious about the women he danced with, the possessive one in yellow whose name she since learned was Clara, and others, too. And until the night he taught her to whistle, she began to think he never would dance with her. Maybe she wasn't a woman he could dance with. Maybe she wasn't the sort to be courted or sweethearted.

That night, she had been telling him about how Nan only pulls a plant out of the ground based on what the moon says.

"If the right face ain't up there, she lets it be."

He responded with a long low whistle. "The sun must be jealous as a clam."

"Do it again. That sound."

He whistled again, now adding another note to it, going one octave lower, in the key of one of Delilah's dirges.

For a moment, it snapped her home somehow, back to standing at the reef beside her twin brother, with him whistling at the fish in hopes of drawing them toward the net.

"I never could do that," she said.

"Sure you can." He showed her how to hold her mouth, how

to relax her face, but she couldn't get any sound to come out. "Watch me," he told her.

The permission to look at him up close felt unsettling, so different from the faraway glances she stole most times. The thick eyebrows and smooth skin, the dimple-like scar on his cheek.

"Give me your hand," he said. She allowed him to put her fingers close to his mouth, so she could feel the shape he was making. "See. Not so forced, easy."

She could feel his breath on her fingers, the warm grip of his hand holding hers, and a strange sensation flooded her body. She stilled herself, trying to follow it, this unfamiliar feeling.

He felt her stiffen and dropped her hand, turned his face away from hers, toward a clattering sound, where Delilah stood, readying her song again.

The strange sensation subsided. A cloud swept in, blocking the moon.

She blew out a spurt of air, then another, without any hint of a whistle at all. "Show me again."

He grinned. He whistled a few notes toward her, the same song as before.

"No," she said. "Show me again." She touched his hand.

And there was that feeling again, a strange tingling wave that spread from her fingers all the way up to her shoulders as he guided her hand to his lips. For the first time, she met his gaze directly.

After that, he didn't leave her side the rest of the evening. Even when Clara came by, he didn't waver, only introduced the two women in an easy manner, and went back to teaching Serah the different notes she could make, depending on the shape she made with her tongue.

FROM THEN ON, SERAH saw Noah regularly. If not weekly, then nearly every other. If there wasn't a frolic or a prayer meeting, he came over on passes with a husband going to see his wife on another neighboring farm. Noah never came to Serah's directly, because the Lucys had denied every request from neighboring men wanting to visit. Said they didn't want strange niggers on their property, as who only knew what those men might be capable of. A stance Mr. Lucy would feel vindicated in after the Manigault murder some months later.

The two often met at the creek on those Saturday nights. She'd slip off not long after the evening meal, groaning about how Nan needed her help with some arduous task. She'd then creep to the loom, where she could see the bank of trees just above the creek and wait for Noah's tall lean figure to appear. Over time, she told him things she had never told the women. Things that only multiplied in the gaps between seeing each other when weather or circumstance doubled or tripled the periods between visits. And it wasn't long before their meetings took on a certain ritualized order. Often, the confessions were first. Not necessarily weighty things, just the things each had been holding in to tell the other, only touching after they had talked themselves out.

When she tried to parse out the particular magic of it, it got even harder to pin down. She couldn't explain why he felt safe, why from the moment he sat down next to her, talking as if they were lifelong friends, she never felt the impulse to run away, why with him she remained more curious than afraid. And she never expected to like the sex. She figured it was something that might happen, because it was a thing that happened, regardless of how she felt about it. She assumed at some point its likeliness after realizing what a glutton she was for being touched by him. What was most surprising to her about the act was that it didn't come over her like the weight of the ocean, didn't pass through her like the bow of a steamship. That when it happened, it seemed like the horizon line meeting the earth, the most natural adhering of two things always coming back together. Whereas all sex before felt like a splintering, what she felt with him was the opposite, a deep and sweet mending. Her body became a map of all the places he had touched, and what lingered afterward in the soft soreness of her muscles seemed to her like a delicious telepathy between them in the silence that followed.

—⟞

WE WERE KIND AND held our tongues, and often pretended to be asleep when she crept back in after a visit. We didn't poke holes at her secret and weren't surprised when she couldn't keep it to herself. When she let it slip from her mouth, in that dazed way of beloveds, what he had said last time they had seen each other, how he could make an instrument out of anything, how he had given her a ring, a razor-thin band fashioned from a button.

It reminded us how young she was, how that first rush of love could take you like a strong tide. And who were we to deny her that fleeting joy? We knew some women went their whole lives and never tasted it or had it for what felt like seconds, as searing and haunting as a dream, before it left them and they convinced themselves that they had never known it at all, because that loss stacked among the others seemed the easiest to deny. Because even if you found it, how long before a white man raised his hand and put a body of water in between?

And maybe this was the small hiccup in our generosity.

"It won't last," we said.

"Young people hearts fickle as the moon."

"You know how many sweethearts I had way back when?"

"Mmhmm, could count mine on both hands."

What we were really saying, though, is don't get attached to anybody, if you can help it. If it ain't your kindred, ain't your blood, don't carry anybody's heart into your belly. Men are weak, ever hungry, flighty. Some nights, we'd laugh and tell her stories about men we had taken up with, men who courted us slow and heavy as molasses, only to find out later they had wives and children on a neighboring farm. We'd warn her about the temperature of a man's heart, how quickly it could turn to frost, the same way a northeaster could surprise the plants and freeze them quick-quick.

Serah would just laugh and shake her head. The folly of old bitter women, she must have thought. If she had been willing to listen, she might have heard the steady murmur of something else. The haunting of the disappeared, the husband swallowed up by sea or sky without warning. Sky took him, water took him, earth took him. Easier than saying he was beaten to death after running away, or his master died and he was given to an uncle in another state. Facts weren't friends. They could be fickle as paint. Hard to come by and easily changed.

But we didn't blame her for wanting. We crossed our fingers, made offerings to the saints on her behalf, in hopes they would let her have this one thing she desperately wanted. All week long, she waited to see him, and if he had been sent off on a cattle job, it could mean two or three. And so, when the occasion demanded, we braided her hair special, helped her dye a skirt red or indigo, and made her perfume necklaces of flowers stolen from Miss Lizzie's garden, in hopes she could enjoy this bright thing unsullied for as long as it lasted.

CHAPTER ELEVEN

Dorcas had lost track of just how many days she had been with the Harlows and how long it would be until she could return home. Her sleep was leaden and thick, and every morning, when she was yanked from it, either by the infant's high-pitched wailing or the angry shadow of its mother shoving the child toward her face, she spent the first few minutes lost and disoriented.

She slept on the floor next to the manger, as she was supposed to anticipate the child's waking, to hear it grunting or squirming before it began wailing, but she never did. The briny blackness of wherever she had gone in her sleep never gave up its hold so easily. She could still feel that heaviness upon her when she took baby Carol into her arms and the child burrowed its face onto her breast. She'd lift her blouse and the infant would latch on, the how, who, where, and why seeping back into her brain.

Carol was solely her charge, from the moment the infant woke up until the second it went to sleep. The child was to be within arm's length of her at all times, and what was worse, the child seemed to know it. The first few days, the hungry infant clung to her with a fierceness that she thought would dissipate in the days that followed, but it never did. It was as if the child decided the key to ending its deprivation was to fix itself to Dorcas permanently. Even once fed, Carol would not allow herself to be put down. If she woke up from sleep and found herself in the manger, she howled until she saw Dorcas was near, until the woman picked her up and held her.

This was disturbing enough, but what Dorcas found even more troubling was the child's ravenous appetite. How it only grew and grew, the babe fattening and lengthening, with swollen cheeks and wide watchful eyes. Not to mention, the growing strength of the child. How it held up its neck to peer around or spread its fingers to grasp at her collarbone, how its small pink mouth began to pull more and more milk from her with graceless ease.

As the milk seeped out of Dorcas, she felt something go with it. Something she couldn't name. She didn't fight the child, not consciously, but some part of her body tensed up, trying to hold something back. But the more she held back, the more the child seemed to want. She felt other things seeping out of her now, her memories and self-made things. A river flowed out of her. She couldn't explain what was floating out on that river, what was leaving her that she could no longer retrieve, or the gray widening blur it left in its wake. Not that there was anyone to explain it to. No one spoke to her, not really. As long as Carol was in her arms, there was no need.

Even Nan, the peevish cook, who came and went and tidied, who set down food and water for her sometimes, always seemed to be looking past her, always seemed to regard her with exasperation. Dorcas had an inkling of why that might be. It was because she refused to take up any task that had nothing to do with the child. If the child was sleeping, she stood by and waited for it to wake up. She would not rinse a cup or a dish or scrub the child's laundry. If that seemed wrong to the cook, she did not care. The house regarded her as a two-legged heifer, and so she would do no more than wait to be milked. That is what they rented her for. They would get nothing more. She said as much the first day and had barely said a word to anyone since.

But the truth was, they took more from her all the time. The child was a thief, and it stole more from her every passing day. She felt weaker, the child heavy and fat in her arms, weighing her down in the chair. Her vision grew soft, and all sound seemed to be coming through a long, winding tunnel. She'd think, *Next time I go down to the privy and relieve myself, I won't return.* But, once she was outside, the weakness always flared up. She couldn't tell one fuzzy tree from another, if she should follow the sun or go in the opposite direction. The one time she wandered way past the privy, the peevish cook spotted her near the loom and assumed she got turned around.

"Lost, huh?" Nan said. "Follow me. I'll take you back." The woman began leading her toward the house.

Don't take me back there, Dorcas wanted to say, but she held her tongue. She didn't know Nan, didn't know what thoughts the woman could be trusted with.

The truth was only her left eye was any good to begin with. The right eye had a cloud in it, ever since she was a child. The left eye compensated and did all the work, so it sometimes grew tired. But never this tired. It never gave up altogether, the way it seemed to now in this house, with this child at her breast. If she didn't give the child any more milk, or rationed it somehow, would some of her sight return on its own accord? Were all her memories and things now buried in the pale jiggly flesh of this squirming baby? What could she break the flesh with? What could she use to pierce the fat thigh or moonlike belly?

Maybe the loss of vision was a blessing and she was being spared from seeing anything more. On particularly hazy days, the soft blur of her vision turned the child into a faint, affable presence. The sucking sound became a lapping body of water, and a pleasant warmth washed over her. She felt faraway then, on the other side of that long tunnel, from where she could see the Harlows milling about, just pale streaks on a distant stage.

Other times, the whole house seemed monstrous to her. A faceless changeling fixed itself to her day and night, her nose was assaulted by a heady mix of curdled milk and soiled diapers, the warping floor planks creaked underneath her feet, and the room was full of ghosts and swirling smoke, while outside, swarms of iridescent blackbirds veered and circled the house, cawing and shrieking all the while.

A sudden cold spell sent the grackles farther south. Gone were their teeming circles in the sky, their shrieking chatter, or their strange presence lined up and at the ready. She felt their absence acutely, the company they provided, the questions they raised inside her.

Without them, the house narrowed, the husband and wife fighting all the time now. About food, about money, about her. "We should just take her back," he'd say. "Get a refund left on the contract before it's too late."

The wife always said no. "Until I see milk oozing out of your teat, I ain't talking about it no more."

And on it went, sometimes growing haggard and nasty between them, with blows flying in all directions. Dorcas did not look. She did not turn her head to see who swung and where such blows landed. She positioned her seat so it faced the window more than the room, and she kept her good eye focused outside.

White people didn't like the help to see them in low moments. They never wanted to be reminded that what stood in the rear of the room, feeding the child, or waving the flyswatter, or refilling the glasses with water, could see and hear their moments of folly and shame.

Soon, Dorcas found she could no longer mount the tunnel of distance she had been able to before. Now, the quarreling couple felt close at her back. The hungry babe lay on her chest, pawing and sucking and taking. She felt weak and light-headed.

And for the first time since her arrival, she produced less milk. There was a growing pain in her left breast, so she let Carol feed from the right and hoped that would be enough to send the child to sleep. It wasn't. Carol squirmed and howled and kicked.

"Try the other one," said Lizzie.

Dorcas shook her head. "I can't. It hurts."

"Sure you can. It's going to hurt sometimes. That's no reason for Carol to go hungry."

"She's had plenty."

"Well, she wants more."

Dorcas leaned over the manger and began to put the kicking child down.

"Don't you put her down when she's screaming like that!"

Dorcas pulled the child back into her lap. She put the child on her left breast and winced when Carol latched on, but as she predicted, nothing came out, and Carol began howling again.

"See?" Dorcas said. *I told you.*

"You're not even trying. Probably just a clog. You have to press out the milk, then. Like this," Lizzie said. She reached toward Dorcas's breast.

Dorcas winced and blocked the woman's hand, her grip loosening on Carol, just as the child wrenched backward. Carol fell to the floor with a loud thud. She lay still in a heap, not making a sound. Dorcas felt something crack inside her, the cloud in her eye seemed to break and seep outward at the sight of the stilled baby.

Lizzie kneeled down and began looking Carol over. The girl opened her mouth and screamed. Lizzie took the baby in her arms. "There, there," she murmured. "Go get Nan," she said, turning to Dorcas.

But Dorcas couldn't move, the seeping cloud made it all gray, hard to determine the boundaries of all the objects surrounding her, the origin of voices speaking. While Carol cried, another baby laughed. Another baby was gurgling, was giggling.

"I'm sorry," Dorcas said to the room, to the gurgling baby.

Lizzie sighed. "You should be. Now hold her. Carefully." Lizzie motioned for Dorcas to sit back in the chair, where she put the howling child back in Dorcas's arms.

Carol grabbed hold of Dorcas's shoulder with her tiny fist, the pitch of her howl lowering then petering out.

"You're lucky she likes you so much," said Lizzie, walking out of the front door, leaving it open behind her. Dust swirled inside the sunlight, now filling the room.

"I'm so sorry," Dorcas said to the child in her arms. In this new amber light, she could see her son's face so clearly. Adam. His small heart beating, a thick gurgling sound coming from his throat. There was his small body, no bigger than a head of cabbage. A bona fide caul baby. With her, then gone, and now back again. Old women always said it was bad luck to go naming a child before their ninth day of life. She couldn't help it, though. She named him early, when he was still just a melon inside her.

The suckling child they pushed into her arms two days after the burial was not Adam. And the pale mewling child searching for her nipple now wasn't either. Somehow, they had swallowed him whole, and she couldn't locate him. The chasm between this world and the one her son lived in felt fixed and vast. No matter what she did, she couldn't cross it. And somewhere stuck between the two worlds lies her grief, a swelling balloon she couldn't reach. It remained a blur, a threatening specter outside her periphery, a piece of hard flint pressing upon the unseeing eye. Until now. Until the sight of the small, stilled body punctured the balloon and its contents broke over her, in one unforgiving wave.

She shut her eyes tight and sucked in big gasps of thick, humid air. She jammed her breast in the child's mouth. She called on the warm solid blankness to come over her, to restore the soft, gray nothing she felt before. *C'mon, child, suck down this grief. Take it all back.*

CHAPTER TWELVE

Lizzie never told her husband about the baby's fall. Carol was fine, more stunned than hurt. There was a small bruise on her leg, but easy enough to keep hidden from him, as he never gave the baby any more than a passing glance. Until the children were old enough to talk, Charles had little interest in them.

She knew if she told him, it would be the final straw in his campaign to get rid of Dorcas. Ever since he and Sutton couldn't agree on a fair price for that swatch of land Charles wanted to sell him, her husband's fussing had taken on a heightened frenzied air. He complained all the time now that they could no longer afford Dorcas. She was just another mouth to feed, and they could barely feed what they had. "Let's take her back," he'd say, nearly every morning before the first cup of coffee. "You know every day that passes, the less money they'll give us on the contract."

"And what am I supposed to feed Carol? Animal milk?"

He'd shake his head. "You fed the other children just fine. Why should Carol be treated special?"

She started to dig in again, explaining the trials and tribulations of nursing, but she stopped herself. Why bother? He didn't listen, nor could he understand why her body wouldn't behave the way he thought it should. So, now, she no longer said anything. She no longer had the energy to explain, to curse, or to argue with him. She was full up with the incessant chatter and shrieking of cranky children, the thunderous screaming of a colicky infant, the noxious smell of sour milk, vomit, and soiled diapers in Texas heat. The rooms were too small, always full up with too many people. Not to mention having to watch another woman nurse her baby. How at first it felt freeing, to not have the infant fixed to her all the time like a new appendage. But as time went on, it felt damning. How dependent she was on this feeble-minded slave who mumbled to herself and stared out the window, as if searching for a sighting of the Lord himself.

Not to mention her foolish, luckless husband. How just the sound of him traipsing through the house could send her into a singular rage. The only thing that checked her anger these days was a small bottle of laudanum she kept hidden in the pocket of her dress. One or two swigs dulled every complaint and worry in her head.

It was only two days after Carol's fall, when she rose to find the bottle empty. It was morning and already Charles was fussing about the wet nurse, about his dwindling line of credit at the shop in town, and how any day now, the shopkeeper would cut him off unless he paid some portion of the debt or handed over some form of collateral.

"He won't cut us off now. He knows the falling cotton prices couldn't be helped," she said as she got dressed.

"Yeah, but everybody else singing that same song, too. Maybe I could give him Patience or Lulu for the season?"

She nodded. "That's a right idea." But she wasn't really listening. She had just slipped her hand into the pocket of the dress she wore last night and found the bottle slick and wet, the cloth soggy. She pulled the dark bottle out, only to find it was empty, nothing but air inside. She must not have corked it tightly.

"But not Dorcas, huh? You would cripple the whole farm to hold on to that teat," he said.

Lizzie's sight went blurry for a second, blood beat at her temples. She licked her wet hand, was tempted to lick the whole bottle, but he was right behind her, glaring at her now.

"Imagine that. No wonder you paid three times what that gal out there is worth. Bet you didn't even ask around. Bet you didn't even nail down proper terms," he sneered.

"'Course I did!" she said, spinning around to face him. "It was my money. And I'll pay as much as I like, since it's been my money keeping this catastrophe afloat ever since I let you drag me to this hellscape!"

He slapped her then, right across the mouth with the back of his hand, the way he often did the female slaves. And even with her face throbbing, the full insult of this action wasn't lost on her.

He stormed off and she sat on the bed, feeling her bottom lip tingle and swell. She opened the bottle and put her lips to it. It was dry as hot sand. She pulled last night's dress down from the hook and found the damp pocket, soaked and pungent with laudanum. She folded the material over so the pocket was exposed and put her lips to the wet cloth. It hurt her mouth to pucker her lips, but she ignored the pain and sucked what she could from the fabric. She drifted off to sleep across the bed, sucking the cloth like Carol sucking her thumb.

LIZZIE AWOKE SOMETIME LATER to the sound of Carol's wailing. She rose from the bed and walked into the front room, where Nan sat, rocking the child.

There was no sign of Dorcas.

"Did she go down to the privy? I told her not to go that far," Lizzie said, storming over to the door and opening it.

Nan shook her head and continued trying to soothe the crying child.

A fly buzzed past Lizzie's face and into the house. There was no sign of Charles in the yard, no sign of the wagon either.

"He take her?" Lizzie asked, but she already knew the answer.

Nan didn't say anything, just held the squirming child out toward Lizzie. "Here. I need to get dinner started."

Lizzie stared at Nan for a long moment, before taking the child in her arms. "Did Louisa and Ollie go, too?"

"No, they down at the creek," Nan said as she walked away.

Baby Carol looked directly into Lizzie's face and screamed. She couldn't remember the last time she had seen a look of such unadulterated disappointment. She didn't want to be left alone with Carol, but she couldn't demand Nan stay if she wanted dinner on the table soon.

"Stop it, Carol. Stop it!" she yelled fruitlessly as the child kicked and flailed. They were stuck together now. An angry baby and its angrier mother. Only Carol wouldn't be assuaged. She let out one high-pitched wail after another.

Alcohol. Maybe just a little whiskey or corn liquor on the child's gums would put her to sleep. Lizzie dashed around the house, looking for a bottle. In the trunk. Under the bed. Where did Charles keep the liquor these days? He was always moving it, from one hiding place to another. Swearing that she or the servants were stealing it from him.

She stepped outside, with Carol on her hip. Maybe he hid

it in one of the outbuildings. The barn or the smokehouse. She swayed in the sun, hoping the movement would calm Carol a bit. Carol grew silent, craning her neck, as if she was looking for Dorcas.

In the yard, Lizzie spotted Serah hanging the family's laundry on the line. The gal had watched William on occasion. She could leave Carol with her for two minutes while she tracked down the liquor.

Lizzie watched as Serah snapped wrinkles out of one of Charles's shirts and hoisted it up over the clothesline. The whole time, the girl seemed to be chewing something, a big unwieldy ball poking out of her left cheek, an activity that she stopped the moment she saw Lizzie draw near.

Charles was right, Lizzie thought with a sigh. *Anything that ain't nailed down.* A good portion of this evening's dinner was probably halfway down this girl's gullet. "Don't you move," Lizzie said, staring at Serah's mouth, her throat.

The girl paused, having clipped the back of the shirt to the line, the sleeves still hanging low. "Ma'am?"

"Don't you dare swallow it. Whatever you're chewing," Lizzie said, lunging toward her. She balanced Carol on one hip and held her palm out in front of Serah's lips. "Spit it out. Now."

Carol began to cry softly, but Lizzie ignored her. The girl spit a dark wet mass into her hand.

It wasn't recognizable but had a pungent earthy smell. "That's it? Open your mouth."

Serah did as she was told and Lizzie peered inside. Still, nothing recognizable. No bits of corn or green leafy bits clinging to her teeth. Instead, what was there was a chalky yellow substance, speckling her teeth and tongue.

"You stealing from me, girl? What'd you take?"

The girl pointed to the ground, to some yellowish rocks at

the far end of the yard. "Just dirt, ma'am. I like the taste. Makes me feel not hungry."

Lizzie dumped the wet lump on the ground and wiped her hand on her apron. "That's disgusting and I don't want to see it again. Now, get these clothes up on the line and go rinse out your mouth."

Carol was crying now. "Hush!" Lizzie snapped at her and swung the child around. She padded over to the smokehouse, but the lock kept sticking. She tried to put Carol down, but Carol began screaming louder. *I bear all things. I bear all things.* She swung Carol to her other hip and marched back toward the house. *Willful children. A foolish husband. Feeble-minded servants. I bear all things through Him that strengthens me.*

She stuck her head in the doorway of the cookhouse and asked Nan to make the child a gruel, but sticky sweet this time. No, she didn't care if it required using the last of the sugar. She wouldn't care if it required every jar of food in the pantry if it won her a couple hours of quiet.

———⤝———

When Junie was summoned to the Lucys' house after work, she wasn't sure why. Mail wasn't likely. She had seen Harlow leave and he hadn't come back yet. If there was news from home, it wouldn't be until he returned from town or wherever he went.

Junie sighed and scarfed down the last of her scant dinner. She grabbed some needlework and brought it along, as it wasn't good to appear idle in the Lucys' house. But that's not the real reason she brought it. She brought it because it gave her cover, gave her eye somewhere to land, somewhere for her jaw to point its tensions.

She entered the house, where Nan was playing referee be-

tween the Lucys' two older children. Nan just nodded and
pointed her toward the bedroom. Junie entered to find a strange
sight. Carol in the crib, asleep, her body slumped at an odd angle. Lizzie frazzled and wild-eyed, a stack of old letters spread
out over the bed. She was reading aloud. "'The ice thawed faster
than we expected, almost too fast. Little Phillip will start school
this year. It's a shame that he has yet to meet his aunt or his
cousins. We have to get them together before they're too old.'"

Lizzie looked up at Junie standing there, as if she'd been
speaking to her the entire time. "Little Phillip must be nearly
done with school now. Tell me. Did you think we'd be out here
this long?"

A rhetorical question. Junie sat down, pulled her needlepoint from her apron, and unraveled it in her lap. She sewed and
listened while Lizzie went on reading. Details of a wedding of
some distant cousins Junie had never heard of. Junie didn't care
to hear about the cake, the feast, or the dress. Or how the fabric
came from London, and the house they were going to live in was
designed by some lousy Frenchman. Junie only listened out for
the gifts, to hear specifically if anyone she knew might be gifted
to the new bride and groom.

Her children were owned by Lizzie's brother, Mason, and
her mother had fallen to one of Lizzie's aunts, so technically, her
kin were "still in the family."

"They'll stay that way," Lizzie often told her, but Junie found
no peace of mind in that. For mentions about them in the letters
to Lizzie became fewer and fewer. Most of the time, they weren't
mentioned at all.

Her children, Hannah and Patrick, would be about ten and
thirteen, respectively. And she imagined them tall for their ages,
gangly like she was, but Patrick, she decided, would be awkward
but fast, like his daddy. The tiny bowlegs she remembered having

grown more pronounced as he grew older, just like her husband's. Nelson was a proud man everyone called Ox, who tipped around awkwardly in real time, but in a race could outrun anyone. That combination of speed, agility, and clumsiness made him special in Junie's eyes. And there was a whole alternate universe where her husband and son were known by all in their neighborhood by this shared trait. Big Ox and Little Ox, they'd be called by kith and kin alike.

That sounded pretty in her mind, but what worried her now was that she couldn't picture the children anymore. How time must have changed the small faces she remembered, the ones she'd fed and swaddled and washed with a damp cloth. In the letters from home, they were phantoms, implied in general up-dates about illnesses and crop yields. "Fever laid low most of the hands the last few weeks, but most are recovering well. All except Gibson, whose cough hasn't improved." And only when she pressed Lizzie to ask about them directly did she get con-firmation that they were still on Mason's farm, only a few miles from where they all were born. But even then, the information was scant and thin. "Hannah is a fine hand and suits us well in the house."

After a long passage about the wedding procession, Lizzie stopped reading. "I want to go home."

Junie continued sewing.

"You hear me? I want to go home."

A homesick tantrum was coming on. They surfaced a few times a year. So Junie did what she always did. She got up and stuck her head out of the door, summoned Ollie, and sent him to Nan with a request for tea. She then sat back down, with her needlepoint in hand, and buckled in. These fits usually didn't last longer than an hour. They started slow, and ended high, with Lizzie weepy and needing a nap. And if Lizzie had gotten ahold of some laudanum, that could shorten the whole ordeal to about fifteen minutes.

Her job was to listen and nod fervently. Technically, it was probably the easiest thing she would do that day. She had spent the morning helping patch a fence. The posts were heavy and strained her back, and her hand still hurt from where a splinter broke off and lodged itself under the skin of her palm. All through Lizzie's chatter, she pressed on it, trying to coax it out, but she couldn't see it, could only feel it there. The more Lizzie talked, the more it stung.

Lizzie grew weepy, reminiscing about home the way a lush might. "Do you remember . . ." she'd begin. And she'd rattle off this list: a hiding place under the porch, the grand parades where Lizzie's father and brother would don spiffy uniforms and march with their muskets, the card games with her cousins, and the dances she'd go to with her brother. And the food, the peach pie Junie's mother made Lizzie's family after every harvest or the lemon cake she made special for Lizzie's birthday.

"That was my favorite," Lizzie said, a gleam in her eye. "Nan is a fine cook, but she's not nearly as good as Roberta."

Junie felt a sudden urge to pluck out that eye. How many seconds would it take to retrieve it? To yank it from the woman's silly head. The muscles in her hand jerked and the needle slipped from her fingers, onto the floor.

She hated hearing the woman say her mother's name. Hated hearing the woman flaunt the spoils. The special things Roberta made Lizzie and her family, special things Junie and her siblings weren't allowed and had never tasted.

It was Junie and her siblings who collected those peaches, peeled them and boiled them down, making the sweet jelly-like filling. And if Roberta tried to set anything aside for her children, the smallest portion of jelly after the pies had been set in the hearth, it was Lizzie's mother who'd find it and spit in it, as it was her habit to spit in all the pots after Roberta plated the food for the white family.

Lizzie's mother, Madeline, counted out every cup of sugar, every gill of flour, every cup of butter or cream, with exacting fortitude. She marked every sack, every container, kept copious notes, and wore the key to the pantry around her neck day and night. She didn't take it off to sleep nor to bathe, as Madeline was sure that the only thing that kept the help from eating her family out of house and home and into the red was her grip on that small metal key.

"I always thought we'd be like two peas in a pod our whole lives, just like our mothers were," Lizzie said. "Girls together, then wives and mothers. But I've had more children than you now." Her voice was glum, her weepy affection slipping into something else.

"Peas in a pod" was not how Junie thought of it, but of course, she understood the implication. She was supposed to be a mini-Roberta moving in lockstep with every season of Lizzie's life. She was to have children at the same rate, within months of Lizzie's own, so she could wean her own babies quickly, in order to nurse Lizzie's offspring fully and as long as they needed.

"Trial after trial. Cross after cross," Lizzie went on, waving her arms around. "The soil is cursed. Our wenches barren. All our seeds seem to go unflowered. Got so much debt we can barely see straight. When shall we reap? Huh? When, Junie, when?"

At the sound of her name, the room snapped back into focus. "In His time," Junie said. "Not ours."

Lizzie's glassy eyes focused on hers. "You're right. Absolutely right."

"And that stockman . . . you know God wasn't gon' bless that."

"Charles was desperate."

"Don't sound much like faith to me," Junie said quietly. The splinter in her hand was throbbing. She felt it pushing her to the edge.

Lizzie gave her a pointed look but didn't say anything.

"A fruitful marriage is blessed by God, made of people who choose each other." Junie's word hung there in the air between them, a rare moment of stillness in the house.

Lizzie avoided Junie's gaze, turning back to the letters. She brought them to her nose and inhaled deeply. "Still smells like home. We should go. Just for a visit. It's been ages," Lizzie continued. "I hear the steamboats aren't bad. They used to explode a lot, but they're safer now, I hear. We'd have to get Houston, but from there . . ."

Junie picked up the needle and pushed it through the fabric.

"I know I say this all the time, but I'm serious. A break from all this would be most welcome. And we'd get to see Papa and Mason and Annie. And I bet I could get Mason to bring Patrick and Hannah over. It would be a grand time."

"Patrick and Hannah?" asked Junie. During these tantrums, her children were never mentioned by name. Neither were steamboats or any of the logistics of actual travel. Before, the wish had always seemed desultory, thrown about and abandoned, its appeal dissolving the moment it reached open air.

Junie put the needle down in her lap. She couldn't trust it under her fingers. She needed to get out of that room. It had been years since one of these "letters from home" sessions affected her so. Usually, she felt them like pricks under the skin. She nodded and occasionally chimed in with the spate of required responses. "Oh yes, that sounds real nice." And sure, there were days when Lizzie wanted more than an obligatory nod or parroted response. She wanted Junie to grin and laugh, to participate in the fiction that they were just a pair of close friends, while they sewed or snapped beans. Usually, those days were the hardest, but even then, her family never entered into it.

Junie stood up. "Where is that tea?" she said. "I'll go get it." She stepped out of the bedroom and into the darkness of the hall. It felt thick, a palpable darkness. She pushed herself past the squabbling children. Ollie had grabbed a chunk of Louisa's hair and was pulling for dear life. She did not intervene, only stepped past them and rushed out the front door.

CHAPTER THIRTEEN

When Serah and Noah had been together for almost three seasons, she found herself wanting things the neighboring women had. Some had cabins they shared only with their husbands and children. Others had husbands that came to see them twice a week, both on Wednesdays and on Saturdays, when they stayed over until Sunday mornings.

Serah also began to worry about the flirtatious nature of those parties. Although she believed what Noah told her, that his relationship with Clara was just a dalliance, she couldn't help remembering what the women said about the changing nature of men's hearts. She wondered if asking the Lucys for permission to marry him would ease that fear inside her. Though she feared what she'd be inviting in, once the Lucys knew about him.

One muggy night in July, she tried to broach the subject with Noah. He was quieter than usual, sitting on the ground with his hands underneath his thighs. "You ever see a calf being born?" he asked after a while.

"No, don't think so," she said. "What made you think about that?"

He shrugged, not looking at her.

She gently touched his face and turned it toward hers. "Tell me."

"Helped one be born the other day. Haven't been able to stop thinking about it," he said, a look of awe in his eyes. "The mother died. I had it feed it and everything."

There was a fresh bruise on the left side of his face, an angry purple bulge under his eye.

"The calf do that?" she said, grazing the bruise with her finger.

He flinched, inching backward. "Run-in with the patrollers."

He caught the look of worry crossing her face and draped an arm around her shoulders. "Ah, don't you start fretting," he said, with a playful grin. "You know buckra can't catch me." He kissed her forehead.

But they did? She started to say but held her tongue. Perhaps being married might help alleviate this problem, but how could she broach the subject? Maybe she couldn't ask him about the two of them getting married directly, but she could ask if the abroad husbands he knew had ever been denied passes from Sutton. And then slowly tease out what he thought of the practice in general.

"Hmm, don't know if it suits me," Noah began. "Besides, Uncle Ned told me I should look to marry a free woman, so my children be free . . ."

His words gave her a sudden headache, a dull throbbing at the base of her skull. She waited a few minutes, tuning him out, to see if the throbbing would pass. It didn't.

She disentangled herself from his arms and stood up, holding her head. "I feel sick."

She began walking. "I need to go home."

"What's wrong?"

She just shook her head and sped up, climbing up the bank of the creek, with him scrambling after her. She hurried across the Harlows' property line, where she knew he wouldn't follow.

She avoided him for a while after that, not going to the creek or loom on Saturdays. If there was a frolic, she wouldn't go. She'd stay behind with Nan, quilting or knitting. And when Lulu and the others returned, she'd pester them with questions about Noah, if they had seen him and whether or not he had asked about her.

Lulu was not moved by these pleas. "Talk or don't talk but leave me be. I ain't your go-between."

The next Saturday, finally ready to talk, she went out there to the loom and waited, but he never appeared.

─╼

DAYS LATER, WE GOT word of a murder at the Suttons' place, the big one to the west, where Noah lived with more than fifty people. We heard it first from Nan one morning, who fidgeted nervously while setting down the midmorning meal. She lingered about, scouring the yard for a sign of the Lucys while she shakily poured out tins of bitter coffee. She whispered what she had heard on a midwifing job the day before. "A white man dead. They say Phillis's husband slit the overseer's throat with a bowie knife."

Lulu let out a low whistle. Junie shot her a look.

"They catch him?" Patience asked.

"Naw, that's how I know. I was in the middle of a birth when the search party came on through. Y'all be careful. If they don't catch him soon, they'll be through here after while."

We nodded, scarfing down the rest of our food, and rushing off to the fields before there was any sighting of the Lucys.

About a day later, Junie confirmed it. She had been summoned to sit with Carol for a few hours one evening. She had gotten the child clean and fed and was finally getting the baby to sleep in a back corner of the house. With Carol was so quiet, they must have forgotten she was there in that dim, smoky room.

Mr. Lucy trudged in, after riding for hours with the search party. He removed his hat and sat it on the table.

"Y'all get him?" Ollie asked, bouncing around excitedly.

"Yeah, got them both."

"Both?"

"The nigger and his wife," Harlow said, sitting down and pulling off his boots. "The two were in cahoots. Teamed up to kill that poor Mr. Manigault. Poisoned him first, then stabbed him. They both gon' burn."

"Can I go next time? Please?" Ollie asked.

"We'll see," Harlow said, petting the boy's head. Harlow began unbuttoning his shirt and walked down the hallway and into the bedroom.

Junie was frozen and remained that way until Ollie followed his father into the next room.

To our faces, though, the Lucys insisted the whole episode was nothing more than a nasty rumor. Sutton's overseer was fine. He was just fired for incompetence and sent away. The Lucys maintained this lie even as they instituted new rules and practices, locking us up into the cabin nightly and then coming by at daybreak to remove the lock from the door.

By the following Sunday, we could tell just how far things had tightened. There was no longer a procession of abroad husbands returning from weekend visits with their families. We didn't hear word of any frolics or even rumors of the kind. There weren't even any invitations to sanctioned quiltings or candy stews.

We saw Harlow less during the day as Nan told us he was off riding with the patrol most nights. And after delivering a baby on the Davidson farm, the drayman who brought Nan back told her how even the Tejanos working cattle on his farm had been run off the land for fear they might collude with our kind.

The Lucys only conceded that the Manigault incident happened when the white folks in the county decided on a public hanging of the couple and brought all the people they owned to witness it.

We won't recount that horrible day in August. Not here or elsewhere. We won't recount what slipped into the eye despite squeezing them shut. Most of us no longer itched to speak for a while. We held each other aloft and while we might have gathered together at a funeral; that, too, was denied us. The white folks kept the remains and did unspeakable things to them. We weren't allowed to wash their bodies nor consecrate them for the hereafter. Without such rites, we worried they'd be forever lost, unable to rest or return home, stuck wandering about the hell of Texas for all eternity.

WHEN ONE PARTNER GOES to glory, its mate soon follows. Patience remembered an old friend telling her that once. How some birds followed their mates even in death. It bothered her now, that she couldn't remember what kind of bird was being spoken of, or how these creatures even made it happen. If the bird's small heart simply stopped beating some hours later, or if the grieving wretch just willed itself to crash into the earth at the first opportunity. Sure, it wasn't akin to what happened to the husband and wife hanged for the murder of John Manigault, but in the weeks since that awful day, those two things became inextricably linked in her mind.

She didn't know the couple, had maybe crossed paths with the wife at a quilting party once or twice. The pair, Phillis and Aaron, were two people who while alive she had never considered, which made it strange that she thought of them all the time now. Of them dying together that way, before a crowd, at the base of a tree, the branches a cross between them. She had kept her eyes shut most of the time, but still it haunted her. More feeling than image. Not one singular sound, but the cacophony, and the weight of the quiet that followed.

It seemed as close to the crucifixion of Christ that she'd ever get to in this life. A strange and holy sacrifice. But for what, she couldn't figure.

"You said you were going to braid my hair, but you just steady sitting there," Lulu said, interrupting her thoughts.

"I'm waiting on you," said Patience. Around her, the women were rushing about, readying themselves for a frolic that, in her mind, no one should risk going to. She didn't try to dissuade them, though. She understood what they were hungry for and some weren't going to be alright until they got it.

Lulu plopped down on the floor in front of her and handed her a comb. Patience carefully took down Lulu's hair, sectioned it off, and began plaiting. No matter the task these days, Patience's mind drifted back to the couple. She knew others were feeling it, too. The rest of the women seemed itching for noise, chatter, or music, to drown out whatever swirled about the moment one grew still. Some may have just felt the need to verify they were alive and couldn't do so without an open-throated laugh bared to the moon, a lazy two-step with someone nice to look at, or a frenzied ring-shout amidst the trees.

"You sure you don't want to come?" Lulu asked.

"Too tired. Maybe next time."

Soon as the lie was out of her mouth, she regretted it but was too tired to tell the truth. The holiness of what she'd witnessed gnawed at her. She came away from it, resolving to give up alcohol, to give up frolics, to be more exacting in the rites of her faith. She'd follow the narrowest road, to feel some bit of comfort around what continued to rub raw in her mind.

"You scared?" Lulu pressed.

She tried to form the words, but she couldn't figure out a way to say it that would make sense to anyone else. That the kind of joy they were seeking that night she saw no point in anymore. She'd wait until they left to begin the calming staid rituals of the liturgy. She found no joy in that either, but there was something comforting about that.

"No, now be still so I can finish," she said. Once she was done with Lulu's hair, she allowed Serah to borrow a skirt, and was glad to see them all go. A new hollow sound filled the small cabin and she met it gladly.

She began her evening prayers with the Act of Contrition. "I hate my sins because they offend thee . . ." Of course, there were moments in that hollow where she grew sleepy, where her mind wandered. How a sudden memory of Jacob could easily up and derail her focus.

How strange of the two of them to survive separately this way, as if they never made a child, never shared a heart. How strange of her to still be alive, with Silas gone. Perhaps Jacob followed him. She couldn't know for sure. But wasn't it stranger still that she hadn't?

Saint Aaron. Saint Phillis. She couldn't help thinking of the couple that way now. The Catholics had so many saints and she never knew what qualified each one as such. Christoph and Francis and countless others. She didn't need a priest or a pope to verify what she had witnessed. The creation of saints.

CHAPTER FOURTEEN

Several months had passed when talk of a secret memorial for the executed couple spread to all the farms. The night of the event kept changing, now that the weather had cooled and the possibility of high howling wind might offer enough cover.

When the night was finally settled upon, it was very short notice, and yet, we all had it in our minds to go. It was a Tuesday, a day when the patrols were typically a bit laxer and more cursory. And we had few worries about getting off the farm, as we knew how to get out of the locked cabin by then. Not to mention, the Lucys had become so nervous about sprees of "murderous Negroes" that come nightfall, they carefully locked their own cabin after bolting down ours.

Late that evening, we pushed the table under the window hatch and hoisted Serah through it. Once on the other side, she grabbed a stool from the loom and placed it down underneath the opening for those of us not so light on our feet.

The walk was long, through a dark, tangled brush, and the strange map someone had drawn on a piece of cloth was blurry and hard to decipher. We bumbled around for a while, until we saw a lookout, a large man posted at the edge of a wide valley who looked us over for a long moment before waving us in. "Watch your step," he said, pointing to a string of grapevine strung low between several tree trunks. We stepped over it and joined the procession of ashen faces, circling two leg-length mounds of dirt. Whitewashed crosses stuck up out of the earth. Several pots were turned upside down to trap the sound of a fading dirge. Every so often, we heard whistling, pairs of lookouts signaling to each other, confirming no danger was near.

The song rose up again. People seemed to come and go, a throng thinning and thickening. And we were unsure if people were leaving, or just trying to lessen the feeling. By then, we were fastened at the elbow, our arms linked, as if the song might unmoor us. A man was preaching, in a low voice, and we all leaned forward to catch the prayer.

We didn't notice Noah behind us until he slipped closer to Serah. We allowed him entry into our line, where he slid in next to Serah, his arm encircling her waist. Her body leaned into his, and he bent down and kissed her forehead.

We let them be, fixating instead on the preacher's voice, the low wheezy tone of it as he spoke about redemption and the riches awaiting us in heaven. He barely spoke about the couple at all and didn't assuage our worries about the ability of the two souls to get back home.

A sharp whistle cut through the dirge. One short piercing blow, followed by two others.

"Patrollers!" someone shouted. The lookout motioned for us all to run west, hopping over the grapevine and leading everyone away from the galloping horses and drunken men hurtling toward us.

One by one, the patrollers hit the strung grapevine at top speed, the horses and riders thrown to the ground. The men yelped and groaned and cursed.

We laughed and laughed as we ran. Pealing bouts of laughter that slowed us down, but we didn't stop running, as we didn't know how long they'd be down for and how many might come after. In the commotion, the large throng split into smaller groups, scattering into different parts of the forest. We slowed down once we got close to Harlow's property line, and it was only then we realized Serah wasn't trailing behind us.

—⚡—

SERAH FOLLOWED NOAH TO a large hulking oak tree with a hollow inside, large enough to hide in. They hurried down into it, crouching along the walls of it, on opposite sides of the opening. They could hardly see, and the longer they sat there waiting, their legs cramping underneath them, the harder it got to tell how long they'd have to remain there. The forest grew louder. The buzzing crickets and whippoorwills, the screeching owls and howling wolves.

The longer they sat, Serah felt as if she was stuck in some strange and timeless void. Unable to see or speak, her feet asleep, tingling and heavy, as if they had grown roots and were now a part of the large tree. Inside her were both queasy cold fear and boiling rage. She could hear him breathing and was surprised that even with all that was happening outside, she had the sudden urge to kick him hard. In the leg or the chest even. *Marry a free woman.* The gall.

"I'm sorry," he whispered after a long while.

"Shhh . . ."

"I didn't mean it."

"Yeah, you did," she whispered back.

An owl screeched nearby. She tried to shift her feet, moving the left one first then the right, but they were both so numb she had to push at her ankles to get them to move. "Where you going to find these free women? Maybe they got free brothers."

They both knew the law didn't work that way. The condition always followed the mother, but the words still stung the way she wanted them to. She heard him suck in a breath, heard him moving now, blocking the small opening where she could see a small crack of the outside world. She saw the jagged crack fill then clear, and for a moment, she didn't know if he was inside or out.

"Noah?"

No answer.

He made a noise as he ducked back inside the tree and sat down near the opening. "It's probably safe now but let's wait a bit longer. You hungry?"

He unwrapped a bundle of cloth.

"What is it?"

"Corn cake."

She ate a few pieces and then folded the cloth back over the rest.

"Been thinking a lot about Mexico," he said. "We could go there."

"Yeah? Where's that?

"Way south. I met a man from there when we was moving the cattle, and he sketched it out. He said to follow the river as far as you can and then you keep going some days more after that. He said it's a long way, and the farther you go, there's hardly any water at all, but it's possible to cross."

"Why would you take me? I ain't your wife," she said. She knew she was being silly, but the wound inside her was still itching and angry and she just couldn't leave it be.

He groaned. "What is it going to take for you to know that I'm serious? If you need me to get permission, to get Sutton to marry us, I'll do it, but why you need their word on things, I'll never know. Their word ain't worth a bucket of spit, far as I'm concerned."

She knew he was right, and she tried to pin down what it was about the whole thing she wanted. It wasn't the sham ceremony with the cast-off dress and the bored white man raising his Bible in the air. Was it the witnesses she wanted—the cluster of friends and neighbors who would hold them to this public declaration? Or was it the step itself and what it signified?

"I got it," he said. "Bind us together."

"What?"

"Don't play dumb. You probably been working roots on me since we met."

"I have not! Whatever you're feeling and doing is all your own self . . ."

"Then bind us together now, husband and wife."

"I can't do it now. I don't have the right things."

"You sure that's it? See," he said, "it's you who's not serious."

She moved closer to the opening and stuck her head out. "Let me look." She crawled out of the tree and stood up, feeling off-kilter and stiff-legged. She foraged together a makeshift kit. Some damp earth, some long reedy blades of bear grass, a splinter off the tree's bark facing the moonlight, and what little she saw of the molted skin of an insect.

"Come out," she told him. "I need the moon. And some of your hair."

He crawled out and sat down opposite her, where she had

laid out all the things she collected. He pulled a skinning knife out of his pocket and unwrapped it from a piece of cowhide. Slowly, he began cutting off a small chunk of curly hair from behind his right ear. She took the hair, rolled it between her fingers, making one long twist. From her own head, she untucked her plaits, fixed neatly at the base of her skull, and from the end of one braid, she pulled loose a few strands of hair until she got a few pieces that were long enough. Then she approximated a ritual where she braided the bear grass and weaved in hair from both their heads.

She had never done a task like it, had always been cautioned against it, in fact, but conjuring elders who warned of the consequences did so because often they were done without the consent of the other party. They were usually employed by jilted lovers, folks desperately seeking people who didn't want to be sought. That wasn't the case here, but she didn't know of any case like hers. And where normally she'd take that as a sign to stop and ask around, she felt as if the void of the tree had opened something, a space that might no longer be available to her in the days to come.

With more hair from both of them, she made three braids in all, whispering a prayer as she worked, placing the corn cake down as an offering.

"You ready?" she said.

"I am. Are you?" She knew he didn't believe much in Conjure, but like most folks had a healthy nervous respect for it, believing in its possibility to hurt him but not to sway his mind to do things he didn't want to do.

She tied one of the braids around his wrist. "I take you, Noah, to be my husband from this day on until death parts us. So help me God, ancestors, and saints."

The words felt strange in her mouth. The silly grin fell from his face.

"You do?" he said.

"Yeah," she said, with a shy smile.

He leaned over and kissed her.

"Your turn now."

He took the second braid and tied it around her wrist. "I take you, Serah, to be my wife from this day on until death parts us."

They kissed again.

She then dug a small hole in the ground and dropped the last braid in. He helped her fill it back up with dirt.

"That all?"

She shrugged. "I don't know. I never married anybody in the woods before."

They both laughed.

"Come here, then, wife," he said, leading her back inside the hollowed tree, where they willed their bodies to merge until light broke in some hours later.

───⤝───

As the sun rose higher, Serah's happiness lasted only until she reached the farm's property line. She considered hiding out in the woods another day to try and blunt the wrath she knew was coming, but she wasn't sure if that would make it worse. She went around to the well first, drank until she was full, then crept to the fields. And though she wanted nothing more than to go to the cabin so she could wash herself and change clothes, she thought she might fare better if she went straight to work. Maybe Mr. Lucy had gotten a late start and hadn't noticed she wasn't out there. He was mercurial in his management of the day's work, sometimes stopping by at particular intervals, and other times, just at the day's beginning or end. Only around harvesttime did he remain out there the entire day.

She made her way to the row, without stopping by the main yard to grab a pickaxe or a hoe. Instead, she began weeding with her fingers one row over, as if she had been out there all morning. A few hours passed that way, the sun growing hotter as her stomach growled. She ambled over to Patience to ask if she had brought any food.

Patience put a finger to her lips. *Quiet.* She ducked her head, peering backward over her shoulder. She then fished out a piece of corn bread wrapped in cloth and gave it to Serah. "Lucy knows," she mumbled, before drifting away.

—⟵

WHEN IT WAS TIME for our lunch break, we approached the yard as if it were quicksand. We grabbed some water from the bucket while we waited for Nan to emerge from the cookhouse with a tray of corn bread or ashcake. The door of the small building was closed, which gave us pause. No one could cook in there with the door closed, the hearth produced too much smoke. We shouldn't have been surprised when the door opened and the Lucys came out. He, with a thick bundle of weeds in one hand and a snake whip in the other, and she, with a tray of food.

One by one, they called us up and made us choose between our hunger or the whip, dividing us in two lines. He called every name but Serah's, leaving her to wait and watch. Junie and Nan chose hunger and stood opposite Patience and Lulu, who both said they'd take the whip.

The Lucys exchanged glances. Of glee, or surprise, we couldn't tell.

Harlow then raised the whip, cracking it high in the air. It's an ugly stupid sound.

He struck both Patience and Lulu each ten times, without

stripping them down to the skin. Afterward, Patience was in so much pain, she couldn't eat, while Lulu pushed through and ate so much she made herself sick.

We weren't surprised that Serah's punishment was a combination of the two. No food, surely, and like Patience and Lulu, ten lashes while clothed.

But we weren't dismissed yet. We were still there when they pulled Serah from her knees and made her stand. Lizzie had to hold her up, while Harlow slid the iron harness over her head, the same one he used years ago. It rang and rang as they secured it in place. "Won't be no more sneaking off now," Lizzie said.

"Now get on, the beans aching to be cut," Harlow added, dispersing us back to the fields.

The harness seemed heavier than before, the bell louder somehow than the last time. Serah complained that it cut through every thought, made her teeth ache. We sent her to work on the opposite end, many rows over, where we hoped wind and distance would dull the sound. When we returned from the fields, we hung around the yard longer than usual, hoping Lucy would appear and remove it, but he didn't.

In the cabin, we took up her sewing and made her sit or lie still so we could all have some peace. Serah had brought in some mud to slather up there, but we warned her not to tamper with it, for fear Harlow would burst in if he didn't hear the clanging sound every now and again.

⟜

Serah, who couldn't find a comfortable way to lie down in the harness, tried to sleep sitting up, the upper part of her back propped against a pillow she wedged in between her and the cabin wall. She'd drift off, then shift in a way that sent the bell clanging, jolting her awake. She had stuffed a rag inside it and loosely fixed it with twine, so she could rip it down if Harlow appeared suddenly. The rag helped to blunt the sound, but even then, she still couldn't sleep. Even with the medicine Nan had given her, the pain in her back and legs kept waking her up.

She stared into the pitch-dark of the cabin, where the only light depended on the brightness of the moon and its ability to leak through the holes in the roof. This night, there was no leakage and she imagined herself back in the warm cozy cocoon of the tree she and Noah hid in. She did her best to keep her mind there, like a pin fixing a hem it mustn't let fall. Any worries about whether he, too, had been punished or when they'd see each other again were best left elsewhere, somewhere far from the hollowed tree and the wooded area that surrounded it.

CHAPTER FIFTEEN

TIRED AND SLOW, NAN MOVED through the woods in search of a welcoming tree. A nippy edge in the morning air pushed her to move a bit faster as she pulled her jacket tighter around her midsection.

She swam through it with her walking stick, ducking spindly branches and tangled roots jutting out of the ground. She had been working almost nonstop for the last two days, guiding the arduous labor of Ada, a panicked house girl on the Davidson farm.

This was her fourth job this year, now that the Lucys realized that hiring her out to catch babies could bring in a handsome profit. Farmers paid the Lucys nearly three dollars per successful birth, and she knew she was way cheaper and right more dependable than the young white male doctors entering the trade by the dozens.

After a long delivery, Nan tended to the mother and baby.

She boiled the soiled sheets and bedclothes, got some soup down into the mother, and the child successfully latched on to the woman's breast. She even smoked the clothing and bedding, so the small room would be clear of ill spirits and energies during the child's most vulnerable hours. Technically, the smoking should be done in two days' time, but she knew it was unlikely she'd be able to make it back over so soon.

And now, she was finally onto the last of her tasks, burying the afterbirth in the woods during the long walk home. She just needed a willing tree.

Hardly any seemed pliant. She spoke to two elms and a cedar and nothing. They didn't seem to want any part of it. She wasn't sure of their reasons exactly. The more tired she was, the harder it was to hear them. A wishy-washy oak seemed persuadable. She squatted down at the base of it and put down the two light sacks she was carrying. One contained her midwife tools—a soiled apron, pieces of cord, strips of cloth, scissors, small pouches of pestled sassafras, jimsonweed, and fever grass—and in the other smaller sack, a tangled ball of rags wrapped around the mother's placenta.

Nan started to burn it hours ago, but Ada howled so and plucked it from the hearth with such speed, it surprised Nan. The woman begged her to bury it proper, out in the Texas soil, in hopes that the child would be protected by whatever gods had dominion over this portion of the earth. Nan tried to dissuade her, but the woman wouldn't listen, clearly frightened that something dangerous was already after the child.

Nan prayed with her, but she could tell Ada wasn't soothed by fervent appeals to Jesus. And the more she sat with the woman, she found she couldn't say no. After all, she was the first to hold the woman's son in her hands, the first to watch him draw breath, to stir him to crying and then soothe that cry, the first to wash the boy's tiny head and face and feel the sharp bird-like bones of his back. How could she spend the last two days preparing and making the way for his birth only to deny him this one last thing?

Plus, Nan didn't believe in ignoring the woman's fear. Even though she was a Christian, she hadn't let go of all the old ways either. She knew there were plenty of neighboring Christians who felt like she was straddling, that the Christian path allowed for no other sources of knowledge or help, but that never made sense to her. Why, there were all kinds of things Jesus was perfectly suited for, but there were others, practical immediate things, where He was less so. It seemed foolish to deny oneself all the help that was possible.

She poked at the dead grass with her walking stick. Underneath, it was hard as a rock. Without her small pick, she'd have to use the scissors. She pulled them out and plunged them into the ground, twisting and opening the blades in the dry, packed soil. It hadn't rained for weeks and the dirt was hard and slow to give. She kept digging with the dull scissors until the hole got larger and deeper, but it was still barely deeper than her index finger. Exhausted, she leaned her back against the tree and let her eyes close for a minute.

The minute multiplied and spun. A bird's urgent cry startled her. Her eyes snapped open, and the black lid of sleep slid away. The sky was darker now, the sun having shifted behind the clouds.

Something rustled behind her. She turned to see a possum eating greedily, a couple feet away. Its white pointy mouth stained with a pink wet substance, its furry black body lying among the tangle of rags and bits of bloody raw matter.

"Get," Nan yelled, backing away. The possum didn't move, only opened its mouth and bared a row of spiky teeth at her. "Get," she yelled again, chucking a few rocks at the animal.

The possum raised up on its hind legs and hissed.

She lobbed her scissors at the creature. Hit, the possum screeched and darted off, leaving the tangled mess behind.

A terrible feeling washed over her. What should she tell the new mother now? Ada would think the child doomed. When she had left her, the woman was already stringing together two sets of names for the boy. A shadow name she'd use to derail the evil already stalking her son and the boy's true name, the name that would only be known by a select few. She warned the new mother not to name the babe so soon. It was bad luck to name a child before the ninth day. Before then, the child was merely visiting, the portal between this world and the one he came from still open. He could just as easily turn back toward it. But Ada ignored the warning, pleading instead for Nan to get the after-birth buried quickly, before the moon showed its face.

Nan assured her she would and left. What else could she do?

Maybe it was best to never mention the possum to the woman, Nan thought. She retrieved what matter was left and stuck it in the hole, but it wasn't much. A heavy feeling settled in her chest. That was the thing about baby catching. The responsibility didn't end once the baby came out, or once the mother was back on her feet. A baby catcher was always tethered to those she had delivered. She understood this earlier than most, when she was just an apprentice, helping out her own mother as a girl.

Back then, she'd hoped to be a seamstress, not a midwife like her mother or a healer like her grandmother. And it seemed strange that she had ended up so much like them, after all this time, when it had been nearly a lifetime since she'd seen either of them.

As a girl, she declared she'd never be woken up at all hours by those sick with fever and boils, that she would never make her own children sit bedside over ailing patients, fanning away fever 'til morning. She'd never have people showing up at her door, day and night, telling her to drop whatever task she was in the midst of and come here, get in this wagon or walk these many miles because so-and-so's fixing to have her baby soon.

Not that sewing and laundering for white folks was trouble free, but it seemed a heap better than cleaning up the deluge of vomit and excrement that flowed so freely from the sick and ailing. But that was ages ago, back in Maryland, when tobacco was still king, and she thought the rest of her life would be spent at the nexus of the Chesapeake.

She'd see the watermen fishing, the Black men who worked the huge nets for the canneries, catching shad and herring. One even taught her how to read the water, how the colors were a code of sorts. How they could tell its depth and what fish may lie underneath by the hue of the water, be it brown, green, or blue.

She was sure she'd marry a waterman one day and have all the fish she and her mother wanted. And she'd learn how to sail, too, how to steer and navigate the tiny boats down the winding rivers with ease.

But cotton intervened. The big churning maw of industry geared up and sucked her and millions of others farther south, toward the Carolinas and Georgia and Alabama, and farther still. And by the time she reached Texas, still then part of Mexico, in an outpost colony riddled with yellow fever and delusion, she convinced herself that her earlier selfishness in regard to the sick was partly to blame.

The sun was shifting again, hotter now. She covered up the hole and retrieved her belongings, trying to think of some way to mitigate what had gone wrong with the afterbirth. It would plague her, she knew.

The path grew denser with brush and moss and she moved slower, watching her steps. In the yellow grass, the scaly green head of a box turtle stretched toward her. That might do just fine, she thought.

She set her walking stick down on top of the turtle's shell and pulled out her scissors. She reached down and grabbed hold of it, the tiny head and legs retracting inside the shell.

"Not gon' hurt you, fella."

With the blade of the scissors, she scraped three symbols into the shell. Two crosses and a cosmogram, a request for protection for the new babe. She turned to the west, holding the turtle so it faced the direction where the sun would set, and she let it go. It remained still, in its shell. She went on farther and when she looked back, the turtle was gone. With the dirt so hard and the river dry, she wondered if the turtle would get very far, but it seemed her best hope for reaching the boy's ancestors. It would be up to them to do what the tree couldn't.

Once she returned to the cookhouse, she fell asleep in the back room without removing her shoes or repacking her sack. But after a few decent hours of sleep, she found the boy's fate still haunted her. She wasn't sure why. She had delivered many babes that grew up to live horrible, stunted lives, no matter how much spirit work she did. And there was little way of knowing if those efforts might be in vain or if they had actually shepherded a soul through a gauntlet of tribulation. It was the reason she got in the habit of keeping a few souls back, returning them to the other-world, so they could choose again—a different time and place, a different mother in better circumstances. It seemed a way to balance the scales a bit.

But she worried now that maybe she hadn't managed to balance anything at all. Evil was always hungry, and maybe more so now. And that perhaps she had only succeeded in starving it, making it so ravenous and torrential in the lives of a few, instead of sporadic and peripheral in the lives of many. Maybe now, it couldn't spread out, all it could do was devour whole the few souls still coming.

Before the week was over, she'd add more animals to the boy's protective army. Another turtle to carry messages to the boy's dead people, and by Christmas two dead chickens. She didn't kill the chickens herself, but instead gave six sweet potatoes to Mariah, a new root worker located on the other side of the creek, to wring their necks and bury them at opposite ends of the new mother's yard, where they would stand sentinel in the spirit world over both the babe and his mother.

CHAPTER SIXTEEN

Even with the harness removed, Serah was fading. Her skin paled to a strange gray. And by the time we were all standing around in the hot sun, watching her marry, she was nearly invisible. Or maybe it was just the heat making everything waver, that made it seem as if she was disappearing.

If the sun was paying us any mind from up there, we must have looked a gay affair, all crowded together and dressed as if for Sunday service. We were all there and the neighbor folk, too, stiff and carefully arranged.

At the fore of the crowd were the Lucys. Mr. Lucy waving a sweaty Bible in the air, and Mrs. Lucy, off to the side, fanning herself, in a light blue dress. Serah and Patience stood closest to them, both stock-still, their faces damp with sweat, pale swishy fabric hanging from their shoulders. Serah's dress was a dingy yellow, Patience's a faded gray, both refashioned from Mrs. Lizzie's old nightgowns.

Mr. Lucy cracked open the Bible and began reading from a turned-down page. "The Good Book tells us 'Two are better than one, for if they fall, the one will lift up his fellow; but woe to him that is alone when he falleth.'"

Serah stared at something low on the ground, a dark seeping oil stain in the dirt. Her arms were folded across her stomach, her fingers fidgeting with what looked like a soiled piece of twine tied around her wrist.

"'If two lie together, then they have heat. But how can *one* be warm *alone*?'" said Mr. Lucy, closing the Bible with a dramatic flourish.

"Amen," said Lizzie enthusiastically.

It was hard to tell if Serah was listening at all, to the white man officiating the ceremony or the man standing next to her, nodding and murmuring along in agreement.

"We are gathered here today," Mr. Lucy went on, "to join Serah and Monroe, Patience and Isaac in holy matrimony."

❧

THE TWO MEN, MONROE and Isaac, came some months ago, shortly after the New Year. They arrived half-starved and ashen, bought cheap off a planter fleeing the malaria of Houston's river bottoms. The first few days, the two men were dizzy and light-headed, barely mumbling a word, while they readily attacked trays of corn cake and drained buckets of water without measure.

Of the two, one was older and broad-shouldered, with a thick beard. The other was lanky, bare-faced, and full-cheeked, like a giant child. We learned later the older one was called Monroe, the other Isaac.

But we didn't care to learn their names. We only wanted to know what purpose they were brought to serve. Were they breeding niggers like Zeke? Or were they just men, who would pull the plow, fell trees, and load the drays, so we no longer had to?

We avoided them best we could, took to eating our meals earlier, and since Mr. Lucy soon employed them in one building project or another, we got our way for a while. They slept in the barn and we retained the cabin and, for once, didn't mind being locked up together inside it.

They built a storehouse and an additional room onto the Lucys' house, and the couple took this as a sure sign that their luck was turning around. A stretch of good weather followed, leading to a good early showing, where we produced the most bales we ever had in a single harvest. Twenty-four bales, almost double what we made most years.

After that, the two men were set against each other in a grand race to build two cabins identical to ours. One on either side of the one where we lived. And it was then that we had to consider them. Look at them, hear them, smell them. They thought us rude and haughty, spoke about us in a dialect we couldn't decipher, and we debated among ourselves whether it was better to be recipients of their love or their hate.

We paid little attention to the race itself, or the chest thumping it brought out between the two. How they enjoyed riling themselves up and putting on a show, and though we were sure this was for our amusement, we didn't give them the satisfaction of laughing. Softening toward them seemed dangerous, and we still hadn't figured out all the contours of this particular danger.

We pretended not to notice their different approaches to the competition. While Monroe concerned himself with speed and the progress of his competitor, pushing himself to get a shoddy shell of the structure up in a day, Isaac moved at his own pace, only seeming to care about the soundness of the logs he chose, the rightness of the pegs, the alignment of his corners. So it was little surprise that Monroe finished first.

The night he finished, Mr. Lucy showed up at our dinner full of praise, the two men following behind him. He broke out a barrel of cider and gave everyone a round, and with a toothy grin, revealed what the reward was.

"I told you I had women, didn't I? Now, Monroe, for your reward, you get first pick for a wife."

Monroe gave a sheepish look at first, then pointed at Serah.

Mr. Lucy clapped him on the back and laughed, the kind of low chest laugh often shared between men. "Good choice. And I expect many portly children, you hear?"

Monroe nodded at him, then at Serah. She turned her face away, shutting her eyes tight.

"Isaac, your turn?" Harlow said.

Isaac shook his head. "Got a wife I like back home, sir. Don't have need for another."

Mr. Lucy laughed and clapped Monroe on the back again. "Tell him he can choose, or I'll choose for him," he said, his voice light and without edge. He turned to Isaac. "Or would some hickory oil make all this go down easier?"

Hickory oil. Another euphemism for a whipping of some kind.

Isaac took a long look at him and at us, while we each prayed to be unseen, invisible, ugly.

And when Isaac didn't answer, Mr. Lucy clapped him on the back, too. He handed him another cup of cider. "Don't ruin a good time, I say." Harlow squinted at us, closing his left eye. We all looked elsewhere, avoiding the roving eye and where it might settle once it landed. "Patience. Yep, she's the one, alright," he said finally. "Now that that's all settled. Monroe, you and your wife will live in the cabin you built. And Isaac, you and Patience will live in the one you built. Isn't that a treat?"

We had all stopped eating by now, the food sour in our mouths. Patience's eyes darkened, a sudden redness around the rim, her fists balled up at her sides. Serah, on the other hand, was surprisingly calm, as if she had heard nothing. The only thing that gave her away was a slight twitching in her face she kept trying to hide with her hand.

THE NEXT DAY, SERAH and Monroe moved into one cabin, Patience and Isaac in the other. That first night, when the sun descended and dark filled the sky and the door of the cabin closed shut, Serah felt as if she had been locked in a small airless tomb. Monroe was there, fiddling with a stubby candle that wouldn't stay lit.

"Why mice love to eat these things, I'll never know." He chuckled. "You not afraid of the dark, is you?"

Serah felt the panic inside her grow louder. All day it had been a low-grade hum, but now it was an incessant clanging, like the bell of the harness.

"Try a pine knot," she said, her voice shaky.

He shook his head. "It's getting late and I rest better in the dark." She could only see the shape of him now, on the opposite side of the room. She was sitting at a small table he had made, carding, even though she couldn't see much. She laid the thick tuft of flax over the metal teeth and pulled and pulled, until the crackly sound of it grew louder.

She heard him lie down on the bed strung up on the left side of the cabin, the cable holding the mattress creaking in response.

For a moment, she felt her own tired body, her aching back and clenched shoulders, and wanted nothing more than to lie down, too. But there was only one bed in the room. A singular bed they were expected to share.

She pushed her work aside and laid her head down on the rickety table and closed her eyes. Within minutes, his loud snoring filled the room. Serah awoke with a jolt and stood up. Carefully, she pulled the front door open and slipped outside. She scoured the area for the Lucys or any trap they might have set. Earlier, Harlow had made a big production out of not having enough supplies to lock down all three cabins, as he had already had the men's leg irons made into other tools. And she worried his whole performance was a ruse to see if she would try and sneak off the farm to see Noah.

She hadn't seen him since the night of the funeral. She had heard from the neighboring folk that he had been laid low with the cat-o'-nine-tails for some weeks, and afterward was sent up to Sutton's ranch to work the cows, but where that was, she didn't know.

She crept outside and pushed open the door into the middle cabin, where only Junie and Lulu lived now. Junie stirred and raised her head. When she saw it was Serah, she shifted over on the edge of her pallet. "Don't let them find you here in the morning."

Serah closed the door and lay down next to Junie. She pulled the covers up to her chin, even though it wasn't particularly cold. She stared at the sky, through the holes in the roof. A distant star winked at her. She gazed back at it but could no longer find joy in it or the lazy stars around it. Instead, the star was a speck of some kind, a strange indifferent witness to Noah and their union, and it seemed cruel somehow to be left with a witness so useless as this one.

⤙

IN THE WEEKS THAT followed, Serah never got a full night's sleep. She moved from the fields to the loom to the new cabin in a daze, her hands a moving blur, a glazed fatigue in her eyes. At dusk, she made food for both her and Monroe, grinding enough corn for their dinner, before making ashcakes or corn pone along with a strip of herring.

Whereas the women had always taken a communal approach to dinner, rotating who cooked each night so the rest of the group could get started on that evening's sewing, the presence of the men in the quarters quickly terminated this agreement. When the men first arrived, they stayed in the barn, only steps away from the cookhouse, so Nan was responsible for feeding them. Now that they were in the quarters, that duty fell to the women. And as Lulu and Junie immediately refused to cook for someone else's "rusty husband," the task soon fell to the "wives" alone.

Serah made Monroe a plate and sat down to eat quickly before picking up her sewing for the night. He talked a river while they ate, no matter what happened that day. And she'd nod and make the expected affirmative sounds as required, all the while waiting for him to pass out on the bed and leave her be. Most of the time, his chatter was filled with the same talk. He'd tell her stories about home, about Virginia and tobacco, about working rice in Georgia, about his first wife and firstborn. These stories would run into one another, the links between them porous as rain. She only half listened, unsure if he was talking to her or himself. And only later did she realize that there were things he wanted her to know. He didn't have the women to trade with the way she did, to give things to hold when they got too heavy. But the truth was, she didn't want his things, not his memories or the rough-hewn objects he had begun making her. And she was too young to know that was the worst kind of rejection there was.

Her aim was to keep only the hands visible, as if the constant cooking, washing, darning, and sweeping would keep the man from climbing on top of her one night. She tried, though. She made herself a pallet to sleep on the floor in one corner of the room, where her few belongings lay—some changes of clothes, a lock of hair from her mother, a small cluster of blue beads. Among these belongings, she hid a small treasure of pointed rocks, even carrying one in her apron pocket as she moved about the day. She fed her saints daily and drew lines of protection around the pallet, powdery lines of salt and grave dirt that kept Monroe constantly complaining about the floors and her inability to keep them clean. Sometimes, she'd return from grinding corn and see him sweeping the lines away, fussing all the while. "Where this white stuff coming from? Am I dying? You dying?"

She just shrugged and waited until he fell asleep, before putting down a fresh line, fainter than the one the day before. In the morning, she'd wake up before him, not long before the cow horn blew, and if he stirred during the night, she awoke then, also. This is the bargain she made with the exhausted parts of herself now always threatening mutiny, always threatening unconsciousness at the slightest stillness. The only bit of relief seemed to be in the effect that lack of sleep had on her mind. It razed time somehow, made it so only the smallest square of the present seemed accessible to her. Everything else—be it missing Noah or the other women—felt as if it was lost, somewhere trapped behind a heavy impermeable curtain.

⚓

AFTER A WHILE, SERAH could no longer live on such little sleep. Her fitful naps transformed into heavy dense slumbers she found hard to wake from.

It was then, one Wednesday night, when Monroe crept

beside her, positioning himself on the edge of her pallet. He pressed himself against her and she wasn't sure how long he had been there, when she woke up in alarm, thrashing and slapping. Her hand hit his back with a loud crack that echoed throughout the room.

"Stop it," he said, grabbing her arms.

But she continued to flail, now thinking of her pointed rocks, trying to grab ahold of one.

"Quit it and I'll let you go."

She paused her thrashing. And he shifted over a bit, releasing one arm while still holding the other lightly. But he was still too close to her, his breath on her neck, his bare thigh touching hers.

"I've been patient, haven't I? Even let you work your little roots until you got comfortable. But my High John the Conqueror ain't never failed me," he said, chuckling softly. It had occurred to her that he might be working roots of his own against her, but when she last swept out the cabin, taking extra care to poke around his few belongings, she hadn't come across anything that appeared to be a charm or a mojo bag.

She kept still as she could, still searching for a pointed rock with her free hand, but there wasn't anything there, just dirt and dust.

"I found your little rocks, if that's what you looking for," he said slowly.

She took in a sharp breath. The room was dark, and she still wasn't used to it, still felt disoriented in the new cabin, the way the chimney was on the opposite wall, the sparse furniture, taller and arranged at odd angles. She wondered how fast she could get to the poker leaning near the firebox. There were sticks there, too. Kindling and such.

"I'm a good man, can be a good husband to you, if you let

me. I can be real sweet to you. Now, we been getting along real good and I say it's about time we start acting like husband and wife." He kept his hand on her arm, his thumb now grazing the frayed bracelet on her wrist.

Serah snatched her arm away and in one deft motion, slid aside, placing her back against the wall and drawing her knees up to her chest. "But we not married. Lucy just put us together like he does the cows," she said. Her mind spun back to the conversation the women had been having the first few days after the two men arrived, if it was better to inspire their hate or their love. In the close walls of the dark room, she instantly knew the latter was her best chance.

"You know a gal needs some things," she continued, "before she can take a man on as her husband. You can't just mount her like a horse and expect her to care for you. You ain't never court me proper or do none of the things I was told a good man does before you can call him your husband. And just 'cause you say you're a good man don't make it true. I need to see for myself. Give me some time to know for myself."

He didn't say anything for a long while. She worried then that he could see the futility of her plea, that there wasn't anything he could ever do that would turn her heart toward him or make her regard his presence with anything more favorable than benign indifference. She would never choose him because she never had a choice in the matter. And the choice was the thing.

"Alright, missy, I'll give you that. Long as you stop with the roots and things. We gots to meet in the middle, don't we?" he said, with another low chuckle.

"We do, yes," she said, though she had no intention of stopping any of her efforts. Already, she was trying to figure out what she could use that might overpower his High John, while she waited for him to get up and move back to the bed on the opposite side of the room.

But he didn't move. He just lay there, his limbs now spread out over the pallet, a loud snore erupting from his throat.

———

NAN HAD LONG SUSPECTED Monroe's tolerance with Serah would soon wear thin, so she wasn't surprised when Serah came to the cookhouse, asking about poisonous herbs. At the time, Nan had her hands full with Carol, so she told Serah she would think on it but hadn't given the request another thought until she saw Monroe slinking around the Lucys' house a week or so later.

She had just stepped outside with a sack of the Lucys' dirty laundry, when she saw him and Lizzie talking a few feet from the house.

Monroe stopped talking when he saw her, but Lizzie, her back to Nan, waved him on, shifting Carol from one hip to the other.

"Spit it out. What exactly is the problem?"

"She's still . . . cold. Mean. Never kind to me. No matter what I do for her," he said, lowering his voice.

"Mmhmm," Lizzie said. "And?"

"Ma'am, I'm not a savage. I'm not the sort to thrash a woman for it. I've been nice. Understanding."

"You want me to whip her?"

"No, that'll just make it worse. She'll probably stop speaking to me then."

"What do you care whether she's hot or cold at all? Long as she does as she's told." Carol started to cry and Lizzie turned back toward the house. Seeing Nan, she pushed the baby toward her. Nan dropped the sack and came forward, taking the child in her arms.

"Ma'am?" Monroe said, not having moved from his spot.

Lizzie turned and glared at him.

"She say," Monroe began tentatively, "we not real husband and wife, maybe 'cause we never got married proper, you know, like with a Bible and a meeting of some kind."

"Does she now?" Lizzie said.

Nan pinched Carol's leg, causing the child to cry louder.

"Alright, I'll see to it," Lizzie said, waving him away. She turned back to Carol. "What now, little girl?"

Later, Nan worried she caused the conversation to end too early, but she wanted to distract Lizzie before she committed to any real action. Carol kept the woman's mind full, easily diverted from one moment to the next. It seemed likely that if Carol's wailing kept up for the next several hours, the whole conversation might easily slip from Lizzie's mind.

CHAPTER SEVENTEEN

"To HONOR AND OBEY, UNTIL death or distance do you part," Mr. Lucy said loudly, slapping the Bible for emphasis. There was an uproar of clapping and cheering. Mrs. Lucy laughed and twirled. The crowd surrounding the couples stirred to life and rushed forward to greet them.

Only the couples themselves seemed out of time. Isaac whispered something to Patience, and she released her grip on the sides of her dress. Unlike Monroe and Serah, the two were of the same mind about the whole thing. They both had spouses elsewhere and were content to live as siblings under the same roof for now. They'd have to deal with the Lucys and their expectations at some point, but until that time came, they'd manage.

Monroe took a hard look at Serah, searching her face to see if this whole affair had changed anything inside her. Would she hug him? Touch his arm? Or even meet his gaze with a warm smile? He waited a long moment for some signal from her, before reaching out to draw her near. But within seconds, she was already gone, moving through the throng of people to a tall young man standing in the back. The man wore a low hat and an ill-fitting jacket, but he could see the man's eyes were fixated on Serah, and when she reached him, she collapsed against him and buried her face in his chest. The man wrapped his arms around her, whispered something in her ear, and only loosened his grip when he looked up and saw Monroe's eyes narrowing in on him. The two men exchanged looks, a whole conversation of some kind, each accusing the other of being the true interloper.

Monroe started toward them, unsure of what he'd say when he got there. So, this was the reason, was it? All this time, her rejection felt impersonal, more like a skittish deer trying to settle its nerves, but now, seeing the young man, it felt different, more pointed, more offensive. Though in some ways the act of winning her over wasn't personal to him either. He wasn't even sure he liked her. She wasn't kind like his first wife, or a good cook like his second. When she washed his clothes, she left yellow clay streaks that dried and caked in the sun. Not to mention that smelly herb she insisted on wearing, saying it helped with her sinuses, but he had never heard her complain of sinus trouble, never seen her with so much as a runny nose. If he wanted her at all, it was only because she was there. Because he liked the softness of women, how they made the most horrible things feel better. How even when they cussed you, it sounded sweet. And it didn't seem like too much to ask in this godforsaken place to look at one person and have them look back at him with something like kindness in their eyes, even if it was temporary.

That she had already had someone made sense, and seemed like something that shouldn't rub him wrong, but it did. Maybe because she never said as much, or he had never noticed it on her.

Or maybe just seeing them together in that way reminded him of home and what he'd lost. Hating whatever separated him from his family made him feel stupid and impotent at the size of it all, but hating them, this young man in a stupid hat, he was easy to hate. As was she. Easy to make the reason for all that was going wrong now.

Harlow stepped in Monroe's path, put a hand on his shoulder, and grinned a mischievous grin. "This was a mighty expensive affair, but I don't mind 'cause I know you're good for it."

Monroe nodded.

"Let's drink to all the children you'll have," Harlow said, leading Monroe to a spread of food and drink that rivaled any Christmas feast he had ever known. Harlow poured him a shot of whiskey and signaled for the fiddle player to start up. "To a blessed and fruitful union!" he said to Monroe, clinking his cup. "Now, where's Isaac?" Harlow looked around at all the people, milling about, eating and drinking. "Why the Mrs. had to invite all these swill-bellies I'll never know!" Harlow then looked at him and laughed. "Drink up," he said. "I know you'll do me proud, won't you?"

Monroe drained the cup, the liquid burning a line of fire down his throat and into his stomach.

"Whooo. That's good, ain't it, boy? You want more?"

Monroe nodded, his eyes roving the throng for another glimpse of the two lovers. Without seeing them, he imagined them clearly, in the throes of another embrace, rubbing against each other as lovers are wont to do, and laughing at him, at his cast-off faded jacket a size too small, his tattered trousers, his gifts of whittled spoons and furniture, and he had a sudden urge to pummel them both.

—≺

PEOPLE ATE, WHILE SERAH and Noah lingered about in opposite directions. She stood at the end of a long table, nibbling a bit of sweet potato, while he hung around the fiddler. And it wasn't long before they both vanished from the party, meeting at the creek the way they had all those times before.

A strange and heady feeling washed over her, being in his arms now. He was talking fast, a stream of chatter to dislodge the disorientation of being so close to one another after so many months apart.

"We tried it your way, but we got to do something else now," he said.

"But the patrols are worse than when Manigault got knocked over."

"It's the only way."

A firefly swam past Serah, moving toward the flat gray water.

"What about Sutton? He's got money to burn."

"No, Mexico is the only way."

Something about the finality of his words made them both quiet for a long while. Serah stared at the lowering sun.

"I should talk to him. Today," said Noah, speaking about Monroe. "You know, make it clear."

"Don't do that. You start peacocking and it'll be worse."

"Worse how?"

"Just worse."

"Fine, Bird. What then?"

She tightened her arms around him. "Still got that knife?" It flashed across her mind. The curved skinning blade he carried with him that last night in the woods.

Noah's eyes widened. "Not on me. But I can get it. You think it'll come to that?"

She wasn't sure. If Monroe had a truly ugly side, he hadn't shown it to her yet. What did Nan tell her he said to Lizzie that day? That he wasn't a savage sort. But could she trust that? Should she trust that?

She could see now the worry in Noah's face. She shook her head. Maybe she was assuming the worst. "No. I can reason with him."

Noah didn't look convinced, but she didn't bother trying to convince him further.

She kissed his face. "C'mon. We should head back. I'm sure someone's looking for us by now."

Noah groaned. They rose to their feet and headed back to the farm, only letting go of each other once they reached the flat area of the yard, where the party was still in full swing.

—❧—

"CAN I HAVE SOME?" Lulu asked Monroe, pointing at the cup of liquid in his hands. He gave her a curious look and handed it to her. She sat down next to him and brought the tin to her lips. She took a long sip but didn't relinquish the cup. She felt him looking at her but pretended she wasn't aware, instead looking at the crowd of people eating and drinking. Someone she couldn't see was playing a fiddle and people were dancing to it. A couple of women had moved into the center and were now doing the buzzard lope. She had never learned how.

"You not going to give it back?" he said.

"No," she said, flashing a wide grin at him. "It's mine now."

A look of confusion fell over his face. He opened his mouth to speak and immediately closed it. She wasn't sure what spurred her on—his confusion, the strong heady liquor traveling down her chest, or the sway of the two women dancing. "So, why you pick her, anyway?" Lulu said, turning to him.

"Huh?"

"Serah? I say what made you pick her?" she said, smiling up at him again.

"I don't know . . ." he said, the tension in his arms growing slack. "What do you care?"

"I don't. Was just curious is all . . ."

"You don't have other things to be curious about?"

"Oh, tons," she said, giving him a lingering glance.

He was softening now; she could feel it. "She's young. Figured she'd be easy to deal with. That's all."

Lulu laughed. "Oh, you figured she'd mind you? Do whatever you say?"

He gave her a sheepish grin.

"Well, it's not too late to change," she said, resting a hand on his arm.

"It's not?" he asked.

"What Lucy care for? Where the babies come from don't make him no never mind. Long as they coming."

"I suppose it don't," he said, staring at her curiously. "And you'd like that? Me telling Harlow that I want you instead?"

She stared at him for a long moment, not saying anything. His words came easy, just as she thought they might, but when they washed her over, she felt nothing. Sure, there was a slight rush of triumph, but not the warm feeling she'd hoped for. She closed her eyes for a second, searching around, but no, it wasn't there. All she could feel was his anxious sticky gloom.

"Lulu, that what you want?" he said.

She shook her head, drained the cup, and handed it back to him. "No. I was just saying."

His face changed, his mouth now open in surprise.

"Oh, look, there's the lovely bride now. I should go give her my well-wishes," Lulu said, nodding her head in the direction of the property line, where two figures were standing. From here, it was hard to see them clearly, but that yellow flimsy dress was a dead giveaway. It puffed up with air like a balloon. Serah was wrestling with it, walking toward the party, with Noah trailing behind her.

Lulu turned to see Monroe's face change again, from surprise to anger. She stood up and moved away from him, slipping back among the revelers, and was there in the middle by a table of dessert, in time to offer Serah a slice of gooseberry pie. The girl took the plate and Lulu looked back to see Monroe watching the two of them, a red pall over him.

The sight of him alone and angry confirmed why the warmth wasn't there. It's strange she didn't recognize it before. How alone he was. No one wanted him, not Serah, not any of the women, or neighbors even. Maybe the former wives he sometimes spoke about, but it's likely they were just more pliable than Serah. Women stuck with him who were better at hiding their disdain. Any interest in him, ignited by that initial pang of jealousy she felt when he first chose Serah, was completely gone. She had cured it.

❧

THE HORRIBLE EVENT OVER, Serah hovered at the edge of the yard. She had already helped the others clear and wash all the dishes. Things Nan said could wait until tomorrow, she took up also. She swept the debris in the yard, in slow, weightless strokes, as she sensed a storm brewing in Monroe's small cabin.

She thought about the land, what was on the other sides of the surrounding farms. How far could she walk, in one direction or another? Could she outrun the dogs? The gangs of white men with guns? Should she trade the certainty of one angry man for the possibility of half a dozen?

She looked for something else to do, something to delay the moment when she'd step into the mouth of the cabin, where she knew he was likely waiting. There hadn't been more than two words between them since the ceremony, but she knew he was angry. She had kept her distance from him most of the day, and yet he seemed always about, a fixed eye glaring at her. It was frustrating. She, who had become very good at going unnoticed, at being softly invisible, could no longer be so. Maybe it was the stupid dress, the flouncy flimsy nature of it, the way it caught light and swam in the wind. Or just that her desire to be invisible was so strong it gave off a smell. The kind that couldn't help catching people's attention, the kind so naked and raw it drew some near or turned others away in disgust.

And since she had little idea what was waiting for her inside those four walls, it seemed the best option was not to return to them. She wished she was more prepared, that she had put together a trick bag by now, with some illness in it to lay him low, some legion of tiny reptiles to take up residence in his leg. That, or some way to pry the High John from his grip, but she still hadn't learned where he kept it.

The moon was hidden by the clouds, which made it even darker. A pocket so black she could barely see her hand, now that they had extinguished the torches and lanterns placed around the yard. One by one, they went out, like a sequence of notes, a low bass falling to the bottom. She thought about Noah, how he felt like a dream evaporating. How long could she lace hope around it? How long could she let the hope of it make her reckless in thought and deed?

She picked up a stick and carried it low, scraping a trail in the dirt. A circle, a pointed arrow, a series of linked curlicues. She was pointing souls now. A whole army of them to nest inside the four walls. And she hoped by the time she got there, a war would be happening between her saints and his. She crossed herself and spun, left then right, as if she was trying to reach some hinge in the air, unlatching some hidden thing where all the otherworldly help could pour out of.

She was so tired. Of the day itself and all that happened and what awaited her next. Tired of the whole mess of it, this strange life that seemed stuck in one place, on one note, like a fiddle with only one string. She was tired of the man's dumb anger, how solid it was, like a large deep rock, and how he kept shoving that rock toward her, as if it was hers to climb.

She pushed open the door of the cabin, one piece of dark opening into another. He wasn't snoring like usual, the only sound the scratching of mice in the corners. She waited for teeth to seize her throat, like a panther or a bear swooping in with lightning speed. And when a wooden post slammed into the back of her head, sending a throbbing blackness over her entire body, she felt a surge of relief, as she waited to see God's face and hear Gabriel's horn.

HE TOOK HER ON the floor, then, with blood in her eye. He took it less because it was the wedding prize he felt owed him, but more because the presence of the other man dared him to do so. He wanted her to know what happened when he wasn't kind or patient. And more so, what happened when one didn't respect the grace they were being offered, when one spat on it plainly, turned their back on it clean. Now that he had literally "put the fear of God in her," he would have no need to be ugly again unless she made him, he told her. It was up to her, he said. She could live in heaven, or she could live in hell. It was her choice.

⤙

WE BEGGED SERAH THEN to come and stay with us. Lock-ins were few now, but that night had changed her. Noah kept sending her messages, and each time she refused them, telling his little boy messengers not to come back. They kept on coming, one with a handwritten letter she had to get Junie to read to her. "Bird, if you don't love me no more, tell me and I won't bother you again."

From then on, Serah and Monroe's cabin became a battlefield. Each trying to best the other, wound the other, conjure the other. She left mojo bags under the steps, laced his food with sedatives. He'd wake up half-blind and zombified. She set aflame his High John the Conqueror and any other protective work she didn't recognize. Afraid to even touch it, she swept it all into the fire, along with his clothes and shoes. She started working on his senses then. Hearing, taste, and sight. His tongue numb, his foot lame. Each changing with the weather, rotating with the sun.

We dragged her out some nights, but she'd go back, shutting the door on us. And as darkness settled over the yard, a bell went off inside them both. Some nights neither would start up, they'd stay in their protective corners watching each other. Other days, it was bound up in the air and there'd be no stopping it. He'd throw a plate at her, and she'd charge him with a poker, stabbing him in the arm with its sharp end. We didn't know she was that spry, that wily, and it seemed a surprise to herself, that she could wound and hurt this mountain of a man. And then there was no ending it until she drew blood. She was collecting it then— his skin, his blood, his hair, his semen. And she kept pushing to get it. Her pain tolerance growing higher, dulled by sharp blows of her own. This fighting of theirs grew into something we couldn't understand. The way they scratched, slapped, and kicked each other. Sometimes, wrestling on the floor until they both were bruised and sore. How somehow it seemed some dark and twisted catharsis, this bloodletting of rage they unleashed on one other. And how sometimes at the end of it, tired and smarting, she'd mount him, the weight of her hand heavy across his nose or throat, until he was gasping for air. If any sex happened between them, she controlled it, brought order to it, refused to be surprised by it ever again. And slowly he grew thinner and more sickly. So sick, he lay up in their cabin, wheezing like a man twice his age. It was then that he begged her for forgiveness. That if she healed him, he'd do right, he'd do whatever she wanted. And we're not sure we ever saw her happier than she was then, when she had Monroe's whole life in her slim brown hand.

—⚔

SERAH KEPT NOAH'S LETTER under her clothes at all times, tied around her torso with a piece of thread. Sometimes, it scratched and crackled as she moved about. When she was alone, she'd take it out and trace the funny slanted characters with her index finger. She had memorized it by now, had made Junie read it so many times the paper was soft and stained with grease. And though she worried it might slip out one day, that someone might find it, she couldn't bring herself to get rid of it.

The truth was she couldn't say whether she still loved him. The parts of her that loved him, that lay with him beneath moon and sky, were somewhere else now, inaccessible and unknowable. What she remembered felt like something on the underside of the sea. A glimmering country somewhere far off, much like that Freedom-place neighboring kin whispered about, some place unmapped and ephemeral, its coordinates unknown.

What she had now, in place of her love, was rage. It woke her up in the morning and kept the hoe alive in her hand. Part of her wanted to kill Monroe and the other part wanted him to live a long wretched life, one where she could wreak all kinds of hurt and havoc as long as she wanted.

—◁

MONROE'S ILLNESS BROUGHT A reprieve. Sickness made him quiet, made him fearful, and thus calm. The Lucys couldn't diagnose what felled him, and fearing contagion, they sent Serah back to the cabin of women. She nodded dutifully, covering a grin with her hand.

Among us, she said little. She was mercurial, at turns joyful and distraught, but still primarily silent. When we asked her what trick she had used to lay down Monroe, what pestilence she had loosened inside his body, she only shook her head and gave a sly close-mouthed smile. Nan dosed the man with calomel and castor oil but didn't press Serah to tell her anything more.

If there was a frolic or a candy stew, she declined going, but wouldn't share with us what she'd rather do instead. And we'd return to find her gone, only to hear her slipping inside the cabin hours later, filthy and wet.

And so we shouldn't have been surprised to discover that she had taken up with Noah again. Though, gone was the girlish giddiness of before—the flowery talk and the silly sweet grin so hard to contain we'd tease her by holding her chin. Maybe she was reassembling herself somehow. Putting herself back in a moment before Monroe and Isaac ever came.

CHAPTER EIGHTEEN

"Tell me about Silas," Isaac asked Patience one night, some weeks later. She found herself stunned by the question. It's not that she and Isaac didn't speak; they did. Quite easily at times about their children, "former" spouses, and such. But most days they were too tired to talk and they both liked silence, didn't feel the need to fill it, the way their neighbors did. Compared to Monroe and Serah, their cohabitation had been largely uneventful. Isaac was a considerate and kind housemate, whose calm temperament often matched hers. Most evenings after they ate, he often helped her with her carding or sewing, and before sleeping, they both spent a good deal of time praying. Separately, of course, as their traditions were different, but he never mocked her the way the others sometimes did. Thinking she was haughty now or putting on airs for not wanting to go out into the woods with them like she used to. He let her be.

And when he was tending to his own spirit ways, he sometimes allowed her to watch. It reminded her of her father. The bowls of water, the symbols and figures he drew in the dirt floor of the cabin.

When she made the mistake of mentioning it to the lone other Louisiana Catholic among the neighboring folk, the woman told her she should report his bedevilment to the Lucys. That if she wasn't going to work to convert him, she should do everything in her power to get out of that house. Patience nodded to get the woman to shut up, but she knew she had no interest in either of those things. She would never report him to the Lucys, and she wasn't sure she wanted to go back to the cabin with Junie and Lulu.

It startled her now, this question of his. So much so, her fingers faltered, and she had to yank out the last two stitches that she had sewn and do them over again. "Why you want to hear about him?"

"'Cause I want you to see something," he said. He sat on the floor, weaving the base of a basket, plaiting thick strands of fever grass.

Patience tried to speak, but she couldn't. The lump in her chest moved up into her throat. She sucked in air and blew it back out. "I can't."

"Close your eyes and try."

Patience put down her sewing and shut her eyes. She sat there a moment, just trying to breathe. In and out, in and out, then a deeper breath, in and out. The dark expanded, the room growing wide around her. She could feel a breeze now, hot rays of sun heating up her skin. A warm concentrated weight in the middle of her back. The boy's breath on her neck, babbling just beneath her ear. She was in that old Louisiana widow's yard, hanging wet clothes on the line. Silas hitched to her spine by a piece of cloth tied around her chest.

In an instant, he was older, now in the Lucys' yard. She was hanging clothes again and she let him put his feet atop hers, and cling to her legs as she moved down the line. He'd laugh and hang on, then fall off, begging to do it again. "C'mon, Ma, again."

"Just one more time and then you got to help. Alright?" she heard herself say.

"Yes, Ma."

He climbed on again, and she could feel him there, his small hands clutching her legs, his head thrown back and laughing. A glorious song.

"You act like he's gone gone. He still here," Isaac said, his voice breaking through the reverie. "Our dead don't leave us."

When she finally opened her eyes a good while later, the room was dark and still. She stood up slowly. "Isaac," she whispered.

"I'm here," he said. He relit the fire in the hearth. "You alright?"

"Believe so."

"Good. Go to sleep. If you have questions, they can wait 'til sunup."

She did have questions, but she was too tired to argue. She felt barely awake, barely alive even, as if she were conducting this conversation from somewhere else entirely. She lay down on her pallet and pulled her covers over her head, her mind already drifting. Her limbs felt heavy, but everything else inside her was so light, it seemed likely to float away.

Isaac tried to explain it to her the next day, but most of it was lost in translation. He knew of no equivalent in English, so he told her in Fula. She didn't understand the words, but some sense of it became clear.

"A door was opened" was all she really understood, but she

wasn't sure how or why. When Sunday rolled around, she set out to make a treat for Silas. She traded a neighboring woman a gill of oats and a thin slice of bacon for two thimblefuls of freshly tapped maple syrup and a small tin of flour.

Back at the cabin, she got a fire going in the hearth, then proceeded to make real biscuits. She combined the flour, salt, and water into a stiff mixture. There was only enough batter for about four biscuits, but that would be fine, she figured, as she set them all in the hearth to bake.

Once done, she set out two bowls and put a hot biscuit in each one. The other two, she wrapped up in a cloth and set them aside for Isaac. A pang of guilt stabbed her in the side as Jacob's face flashed quickly across her mind. No. The act of setting food aside was as sisterly as it was wifely. Nothing more.

She shook off the bad feeling and returned to the two bowls, steam rising from the flaky brown bread. She cut both biscuits open and drizzled each with syrup.

Placing one bowl at the end of the table, she sat down at the opposite end, placing the second bowl in front of her. "If only I got some butter, huh, Silas?" she said. "But I know you won't be able to resist either way." She laughed and closed her eyes until she could feel him there, faint but warm.

"We thank the Good Lord for this food. And this company."

She picked up her biscuit and bit into it. A delightful sweetness flooded her mouth, her chest. She savored each bite, chewing slowly. She sat there, longer still, 'til the warmth of Silas's presence faded.

She rose slowly. She cleaned her dishes and utensils, while leaving Silas's plate undisturbed a little while longer. She'd have to ask Isaac to teach her more about his spirit ways. This small bit he had shared with her had already loosened something inside her.

How full she felt now. So different from when she performed those rites and rituals she'd brought from Louisiana. How pressed down they had always made her feel. Emptied. Hollowed out. That was fine before, but she wanted something else now. Something fuller and sweeter.

CHAPTER NINETEEN

WHEN SERAH SNUCK OUT TO see Noah late one night, she didn't know it would be the last time. She walked the path slowly through the cool air. She couldn't remember ever traveling the path at such a snail's pace. She was always excited before, always in a hurry, but the last few weeks, she could barely muster anything more than mild interest.

Initially, she just thought it was dread, a perpetual worry that whatever she unleashed on Monroe would soon come spiraling back toward her. Even with him gone, that feeling hadn't subsided. He had been away for weeks now, as Harlow had rented out both Isaac and Monroe for the harvest as soon as the ailing man could stand. It should have alleviated her anxiety to know he was miles away, but that only amplified it.

At the bank of the creek, Noah was there already, sitting in the grass, facing the dry riverbed. She tiptoed up behind him, until she was about an arm's length away. She slipped her dress over her head, along with the slip underneath it, and stepped out of her knickers. That first chill of the season crept over her.

She softly called his name. He turned, a grin spreading across his face once he saw her. She remained still while he looked at her in the moonlight, ignoring the crisp edge in the air, and the mosquito landing on her lower back, its sharp beak piercing her skin. She didn't move until Noah gathered her in his arms.

"You sure?" he whispered in her ear.

"Mmhmm."

Ever since the wedding night with Monroe, she wouldn't allow Noah to touch her. Something as simple as his fingers grazing her leg would set her on edge. This was a new body, with new scars, new bruises. A different territory than the one he knew before, and she didn't want him trying to remap it.

He laid her down on the grass and she took him between her thighs. Even with the moon behind him, his face in shadow, she could feel his gaze, watching her, as if he, too, was trying to determine had she only given him her body, because he no longer had her heart.

She didn't know. She wanted to believe she could go back, be the person she was before, doing the things she had done before, but it was becoming apparent now with every moment that passed that she couldn't.

The light of it was gone now. That didn't mean that being with him was without pleasure, without sweetness, but it was different now, as she was different now. She held on to him, wondering if she could be content with that difference. Wasn't that marriage—to weather any shift in altitude, longitude, latitude?

Afterward, he laid his head on her stomach and began droning on about Mexico. His fever for the place was full-blown and he spoke of little else.

"That old vaquero told me so. If we can't get to the Trinity River, we can try Old Bahia Road. That'll take us south, too. We just need to go soon."

She stroked his back. "It's too late now. Cold weather be here soon."

"Then when?"

"After winter."

"That's too late." He didn't say anything for a long while. "You can just say you don't want to go."

"I do want to go." She did surely. She just didn't trust that they could. She knew trouble would find them on the road and she'd be at the mercy of whatever they found, just like she was here. Weren't the two devils she knew better than the dozens of devils they'd cross out there?

"Do you?" He raised his head and looked at her. "'Cause I won't be mad if you don't. But I will be mad if you make me miss my chance . . ."

She nodded. But that wasn't what she was doing. She was saving him from peril, not just keeping him close, but also keeping him alive. Out there was nothing but death and torture—cropped ears, sliced heel strings, and burned flesh. Even if she didn't love him like she used to, she loved him enough to save him from that.

CHAPTER TWENTY

NOAH WAS GONE. SERAH KNEW this before anyone said so. Two weeks went by with no sign of him. On Sunday afternoon, she lingered near the property line, by the split-rail fence, watching the procession of neighboring men heading home after visiting their wives on other farms. Of the two she knew from Sutton's farm, none had recalled seeing Noah, but they reassured her halfheartedly that, though they had not seen him, he was likely fine and there was little to be concerned about.

She thanked them both and didn't hold either up any longer than was necessary. Just a few awkward moments longer than normal, long enough for the men's bodies to betray their words, for their eyebrows to shift suddenly when they averted her gaze, or their fingers to fidget and widen the holes in their tattered pants. She understood the lie and was grateful for it, their attempt to dissuade and temper her worry until the inevitable moment when it couldn't be avoided any longer.

But the lie was still a lie and it left her looking for confirmation elsewhere. She was left trying to read the sky, the filmy surface of creek water, the unwieldy ripple of high grass along its banks. She dissected the cries of birds, the differences in tenor and pitch between owls, grackles, and sparrows, while watching the horizon for the sure descent of crows.

Anything could be a sign. There was no comfort in that, though, just a steady crazy-making. The more she scratched, the less she found. She grew obsessive about rites. About dipping twine in turpentine and stringing it around her navel. About leaving salt and fresh water out for her saints daily. She went tarrying alone and came back with nothing but a rash of fresh insect bites, dotting her arms and legs. There seemed to be no presence she could find that would signal anything to her or lessen the disorientation that missing him created.

⟶

WE WEREN'T SURPRISED WHEN Levi Sutton showed up looking for Noah one evening in November. Men on Noah's farm told of his relationship with Serah, and Mr. Lucy promptly led him to our door. The rest of us were asked to leave while the two questioned her. We stood outside, watching through the doorway as the two men pelted her with questions about when she last saw him and if he had been talking crazy, with wild ideas about stealing himself and running off somewhere.

She dulled her face. "No, sir, no, sir." She knew nothing of the kind, hadn't seen him in a long, long time, as she was a married woman and her husband didn't approve of her jawing with other men, she told them.

The two men exchanged looks as she rambled.

"Go on outside and wait with the others."

"You believe her?" Sutton said as she came down the steps.

"Hardly. Lying is her second tongue," Harlow said.

From the doorway, we all watched as they searched our room. They rifled through drinking tins, chipped bowls, jars of dried leaves and old coffee grounds. They emptied our pallets of ticking and moss, feeling around for God knows what. They dug their clammy hands into every hidey-hole and crevice, pocketing any silver money we had, dumping caches of our keepsakes onto the floor—colored beads and buttons, rusted coins with crosses etched into them, locks of hair and bits of cloth from lost kin—all into one mounting pile. They grumbled about cleanliness and godliness, about our seeming idolatry of petty objects, our obsession with trifles and trash, while they fingered our dresses and underthings and shuddered at rags stained with menstrual blood.

"You allow 'em to live like this? Just nesting in their own filth?" Sutton asked, shaking his head at Mr. Lucy. "My wife is down at the quarters every week, with a bucket of lime, making sure every cabin is square from top to bottom. And our folks are hardly ever sick. Healthier than the horses, I tell you."

We watched them come down the steps and move into the next cabin, where a newly returned Monroe was inside, whittling.

The two men barged in and we inched up the lane behind them to see what they would do next. First, they ejected Monroe, who rushed down the steps and came over to us.

"What they looking for?" he said.

We shrugged and shifted a bit closer, where we watched them through the open door, a new pile already forming on the ground. Since there was nothing under the bed, they groped the few pieces of clothing hanging along the wall. They shook shoes, emptied more ticking and moss from the mattress, ripped the lining out of quilts and stuck their hands deep inside. They pushed the table around, looking for holes in the dirt floor. A rusty lid glinted. Harlow tried to kick it aside, but it did not move. He bent over and lifted the lid. It covered a hole about three inches in diameter.

"What's in there?" asked Sutton.

"I don't know. I'm not sticking my hand in there."

"You big baby, do I have to everything myself?" Sutton grabbed a poker and stuck it down the hole. He then leaned in close and yanked its contents out. On the ground, he placed what looked like a few small pouches, a rolled piece of cloth that crackled like a leaf, and a bundle of knotty cotton root stems.

——⚓

SERAH WAS FLUSHED WITH shame, seeing the two men paw her things and rip them open, adding them to a growing heap in the center. On the heap were a string of blue beads, the first mojo bag she had ever made, and a piece of cloth from Noah's shirt, with a snippet of the letter he had written her sewn inside it. She was grateful now, she hadn't kept the entire letter, but only one piece of it, the words on it faint, having been touched too many times. Even so, it still worried her. It felt wild and reckless, this keepsake, and she wondered about the smell of it. If his scent on the cloth lingered, she almost wondered aloud about Sutton coming by without his hounds. Only then did she notice the women glaring at her, how Patience was muttering something under her breath, how Junie was cutting her eyes in her direction, and Lulu was still as a stone.

Patience then leaned forward, her chin jutting over Serah's shoulder as she spoke directly into Serah's ear. "You left them inside there? With him?"

The two men exited the cabin and came down the steps. In Harlow's hand was the bundle of cotton root stems. He motioned to Monroe. "You stealing from me? Going to make a go of it with a crop of your own?"

"They ain't mine, sir. You know I wasn't even here during picking time."

"Don't lie. You know I can't stand a liar—"

"They got to be hers," Monroe said, pointing at Serah.

Harlow looked over at Serah, his face hardening. He motioned her toward him, but she didn't move.

Serah watched Sutton instead, a smirk forming as he watched Harlow closely. She looked to see if his interest in the matter grew or flickered out. That would likely determine the length and brunt of this drama.

A pair of hands shoved Serah toward him. She could feel the women at her back, their persistent hot glare on her neck. She had to smooth this over.

Something pulled at her insides. She was afraid of the two white men standing in front of her, but the women spawned a feeling in her not dissimilar. A different shade of fear that was hard to describe.

"It's mine," she said. "But I'm not stealing from you or trying to make my own crop. I use it to make teas when I'm ailing. When my head hurts or my blood comes down. That's all." She tried to look contrite and small and not worth the fight. "I won't do it again," she mumbled.

Harlow's mouth grew thin. He reared back and slapped her, a loud stinging smack, that hurt her pride more than her body. But she fell to her knees under the surprise of it, a loud gasp escaping her lips, her hand rising up to her face.

"What you go and do that for?" Sutton said, offering his hand to help her up. "Don't you know cruelty only hardens them?"

"Says the man whose favorite cowman has gone fugitive."

"That can't always be helped when you own as many as I do. Some are going to run no matter what you do, but most just want to be guided with a decent and firm hand. Isn't that right?" He looked toward Serah for agreement.

She looked at Harlow and then back at Sutton. There was no right answer.

"Answer the man. He talking to you, ain't he?" said Harlow.

Serah nodded, her face still stinging. Harlow's jaw tightened even more.

"Sorry to say every man isn't built for it," Sutton said, wiping his hands on his pants. "The clock is ticking. What about that last one?" He pointed to Isaac and Patience's cabin.

The door was open, and it was plain to see no one was inside. The two men waltzed in, did a cursory kicking of clothing and objects, before turning around and coming back out.

"I must go. You alert me if you see any sign of him," Sutton said to Harlow as they came down the steps and walked away.

For a long moment, everyone was quiet, if not watching, then listening as the two men headed to the north part of the farm. Serah strained to hear and inched a bit closer in the direction of the men, listening for more information about Noah and their pursuit of him. Behind her, unnoticed, a group had formed. Three pairs of eyes had collected at her back. Within seconds, she was gently seized, ushered toward Junie and Lulu's cabin, and led up the steps, the door summarily shut behind them. Reeling, she was, but she knew better than to speak.

Inside, the hands turned her loose. She stood on one side of the room, the others all gathered opposite her, awaiting an explanation. If there was to be some formal council on the matter, deep in the woods under night sky, where Nan would step in and guide all their feverish and disparate temperaments into one cohesive and patient voice, it wouldn't be now. Instead, a low whisper formed in the room growing to a soft cacophony, everyone speaking at once. There were too many faces, too many voices, too much anger and feeling in the room to sift through.

"What the hell, Bird?"

"You left them *there* of all places?"

"How you even have that many left?"

"Told y'all to hide them under the house, not *in* the house."

"They were under the house!" Serah shot back, but she was drowned out.

"I keep mine in the garden now."

"Yep, I bury mine in between the plots."

"How simple!"

"How stupid can you be!"

"I'mma beat some sense into her."

"Me? Didn't know nothing 'bout it, sir. I'm just a simple Catholic who don't consort with them root-wearing daughters of Satan," Patience said, with an exaggerated flourish, eliciting laughs from Lulu and Junie. There was a break in the tension then, as if the whole cabin had taken a breath.

Serah stared at the women and they glared back, but her resolve was collapsing, a tough shell slowly cracking like an egg. Her eyes slid up to the ceiling, where she looked at the holes in the roof. She blinked at the clouds as Junie moved close to her. But when she saw Junie's face blocking her vision, she stepped back, so her body was against the wall, her eyes again drifting to the roof, because Junie's face was too much to take in.

"Didn't mean to leave it there so long. I thought Monroe might have hexed it to get back at me, so I couldn't move it."

"Does he know what it was for?"

"No," Serah said, shaking her head. "I'll fix it. Just tell me what to do."

Junie squeezed her shoulder. "Wipe your face."

"I don't care 'bout them tears. I'm still whipping her ass," Lulu shouted.

"Then you gon' have to beat mine, too," Patience said. "Leave her be."

"Fine. How you want it?"

Patience met Lulu's eyes with a hard glare.

"Lulu, go somewhere," said Junie, with an exasperated sigh.

"Y'all better deal with her," Lulu said as she turned and left, slamming the door behind her.

"What do we do now?" Serah said.

"Wait and see—" Junie said.

"Have a baby," Patience said.

Serah made a face. Patience laughed. "I knew you weren't serious."

"You're joking?"

"Not really."

"Don't scare the girl," Junie said.

"I'm not scaring her. I'm just telling her the truth. It's only a matter of time before they come sniffing around again. They threw a big wedding with a bunch of vittles. They expect a litter in return."

"We didn't ask for—"

"Don't matter. That's what they want."

"Then why don't you have one?"

"Because I didn't mess up. They didn't find the remedy in my place, did they?"

"Pay, stop it. Let's not start that again. If one comes through, they be pairing the rest of us up with Monroe in no time. Or worse, buying new niggers to put us with."

Patience let out a slow breath.

"We just have to wait and see," Junie went on. "And keep our eyes open."

"You say so," said Patience.

They both turned and looked at Serah, who seemed frozen, a glassy look in her eyes.

"It's water under the bridge now," Junie said. "We got to look toward what's coming."

CHAPTER TWENTY-ONE

ONLY WHEN THE STEAMBOAT TICKETS came, did Junie start to believe the trip to Georgia might be real. She had been summoned to the house that evening to help out while Nan was off midwifing, but once she arrived, Lizzie ushered her past the two squabbling children in the front room and into the bedroom, quickly shutting the door.

The sound of Lizzie forcing the door shut stirred Carol from sleep and she began crying. Lizzie picked her up and stuck a strong-smelling cloth into the child's mouth. She then sat down on the bed and leaned against the headboard. "My eyes hurt. Read to me," she said, pointing to a stack of letters on the dresser.

Not since they were girls, back when Lizzie taught her the alphabet, had Junie been asked to read aloud to Lizzie, instead of the other way around. And for a moment, she wondered if it was a trick of some sort. "Please," Lizzie said.

Junie could see Lizzie's face was flushed and teary, and

maybe a bit swollen on the left side. She started to offer to grab a compress but thought better of it. Every minute in this room was a potential tinderbox. It was best to just do as she was told.

She sat down on a chair and began reading. "'I say Valencia is a fool to marry a man with nothing to offer her but himself. She'll find out the hard way, I suppose. Like you did. But I fear she won't listen to me. Write her and tell her yourself,'" wrote Beatrice, Lizzie's cousin. "'Yes, it was rash for Charles to take your wet nurse, but you should have spoken to him first. He has to lead you as Christ leads the Church.'" And between gossip about this person or that, there were details of the bad blood growing between the Lucys, typically over money and mismanagement of the farm. Junie tried to keep the surprise out of her face and read the words in a flat monotone. She knew the Lucys had been fighting a lot recently, but she was amazed to see it laid out so plainly.

"'It's important that you all remain united,'" cousin Beatrice went on. "'Especially in these times.'" Lizzie began blowing her nose loudly. Junie paused and skimmed the next paragraph.

"'We too have had a panic recently. Some plots of insurrection among the slaves in different counties have come to light. I dare say all of the South must watch out for Northerners in sheep's clothing . . .'"

As Lizzie wiped her nose, Junie carefully switched to the letter underneath, and resumed reading aloud the moment the sniffling stopped. "'Dearest sister, I agree,'" wrote Lizzie's brother, Mason. "'A visit from you is long overdue. Please find enclosed five tickets from the Blackwell Ferry company, from Houston to Savannah. The man promised me these are exchangeable . . .'"

She heard the words as they came out of her mouth, heard them swirling in the stale air of the bedroom, but until Lizzie pulled out the tickets from between the pages of a beat-up Bible, it didn't dawn on her fully.

For a moment, she found herself stunned by the array of tickets Lizzie laid on the bed, the bold stark type on the small slips of white paper. She touched one, tracing the lettering with her fingers. March 10th, 1860. It wasn't a trick. It said just what Mason said it did, just what Lizzie said it would.

"When is that?" Junie asked. Her sense of time was fuzzy. Had always been. If the Lucys had calendars, they were never in plain sight. She could track events and seasons, but not the names of the months or years connected to them.

Lizzie sighed. "Not soon enough."

Before today, the Visit was a thing over there, but now it was real. She felt it, a transference of some kind. Even after Lizzie pulled the tickets away from her and slipped them back inside the Bible, she still felt the figures under her fingers.

From then on, the trip became a thing inside her. That night, she dreamed of those tickets and who she hoped awaited her on the other side of that long journey. The next day, she pinched herself whenever the thought arose, but the hope kept rising in her chest. There seemed to be no way to stop it. It was sneaky and clever, seeping into moments both busy and quiet, alike. The thrumming of the loom didn't drown it. Even the work songs she hated didn't crowd it out.

Little upset her then, because she was already gone. A phantom self was moving around doing what needed to be done on the farm, while the rest of her was in Georgia, sitting with her children in front of the fire, telling them stories. They would be too big to sit in her lap now, but she imagined them that way anyhow, nestled in her arms, her cheek against their hair.

She just needed to get the rest of her body there. Over that big swath of land and that big body of water.

IT WAS A DAY for churching, but there wouldn't be any churching, covert or otherwise. Noah's disappearance had white folks on edge, had them watching everyone as if through a looking glass.

Already, rumors were circulating, and it was easy to guess which ones were started up by Sutton or the Lucys or the Davidson family. The fugitive has been captured, they'd say, each spouting a different horrid demise. He'd been eaten by panthers, sundered by ghosts. He'd been flayed and hanged by voracious thieves and ne'er-do-wells en route to California. Or the soul dealers got him and cut his heel strings, before taking him to work sugarcane in the bowels of Louisiana.

Serah was unsure of what to believe. Each possibility awful and haunting. For a time, she believed each new rumor, held it under her tongue, barely breathing until the next one came. And only then did she give up the former. It wasn't long before she didn't believe anything, because of how often they shifted, how widely they differed. She even heard that he had been transferred to Sutton's ranching property permanently. The most benign rumor of them all, but she didn't believe it, because Sutton still seemed to be looking for him.

She felt buoyed by the possibility that Noah remained out of their reach. The only thing that punctured that buoyancy was the fraying bracelet around her wrist. Would her binding be his undoing, somehow snapping him back into the vicinity the moment he stepped too far out of range?

She figured the best person to consult might be the root worker, Mariah. And that Sunday, when she saw Harlow's wagon pull away from the farm, with Monroe and Isaac in tow, she figured it might be the most opportune time to go and visit.

Mariah didn't live very far away, only about a mile or two north of the creek, tucked away behind a thicket of black willow trees. Serah knew the way, having tagged along with Lulu once, but she'd never had the nerve to try and consult the woman herself.

Even second time around, the sight of Mariah's place still stunned her. It was a clapboard whitewashed house, with true glass windows covered with bright busy curtains. It had a real sitting porch and a large front yard that was swept and raked daily, its clean furrows still visible.

The front door was closed, and a few people were sitting in the yard, awaiting their turn to speak to Mariah. Serah typically didn't mind waiting, especially if she could overhear a bit of their conversation, but she knew she couldn't wait long. She had only a couple of hours before someone would realize she was gone.

Another person came and left, and now there was just one woman in line in front of her. A handsome young man was now pacing the yard, holding a glass bottle out in front of him. Inside the glass, a large spider inched along to the right a few paces. The young man followed the direction of the spider, flattening the distinct lines in the dirt.

"Hey, Elias." The woman in front of Serah waved and grinned at the man.

He paused and waved back.

"A damn shame," the woman said to herself, chuckling.

"What is?" Serah asked.

"All that man wasted." The woman shook her head. She then turned to face Serah. "You know I'm joshing, right?"

"Of course."

"'Cause I would never go after anything or anybody belonging to Mariah."

"Of course." Serah nodded.

Serah had never seen Elias in the flesh until now, but he was the subject of much talk among the neighboring folk. He was Mariah's husband, and besides him being a handsome, strapping figure, he was also a good ten or fifteen years Mariah's junior. And while Mariah was known all over the region for her ability to win over stubborn hearts for the unrequited or dissolve once ironclad marital unions, a good deal of women put their stock in her solely because of her hold on young Elias. He was never rumored to have a sweetheart or two on a distant farm the way other men were, nor had anyone ever seen him at a frolic hugged up with anyone other than his wife.

The door flung open wide, and a man staggered out, a dazed expression on his face.

"What you want now, Amy?" a voice said from inside. The woman in front of Serah scurried up the steps and into the house. "Harry try to quit you again?" the voice continued, the door shutting firmly.

If the neighboring women were swayed to believe in Mariah's powers by her hold on the young husband, the men among the neighboring folk believed in her for different reasons. For them, it was the house, the swath of land it sat upon, and the seemingly hands-off arrangement she had with the man who retained the deeds to both her and the land.

On paper, she and the land were said to be owned by Martin Robison, a senile planter who split his time between Navarro and San Antonio. And it was rumored to be a strictly contractual agreement, for to be a free woman in Texas created new quandaries, as little could be done without a white man's signature. And so it was a shell game. Robison left her alone and she paid him a small fee annually to cover the taxes of owning her. The land and her mobility were said to be a gift or a payment, depending on who was telling the story, for removing a generational curse from his lineage.

The door flung open again, this time Amy coming out and waving Serah inside.

Mariah stood in the front room and motioned for Serah to sit down at a small table, ornately carved with figures of swimming turtles and slithering snakes. "What brings you, dear?"

To some, Mariah's appearance was the most beguiling thing about her. She didn't look like anybody anyone would assume to be powerful. She had soft worn brown skin and sleepy eyes, and she wore her graying hair into two neat plaits on either side of her head. She looked like any regular old granny. A fact that was remarkable, seeing as most two-headed persons and Conjurers were known by their difference. The presence of the gift was usually visible. A shriveled hand or lame foot, shocking blue gums or catlike eyes. Others were fluid beings—shape-shifting and gender variant, like *omasenge kimbandas* in the old tradition.

Not to mention, she always dressed as if she were on her way to the grandest frolic no one had bothered telling you about. Her blouse was dyed a deep red and her skirt, an intricate weaving of stripes and checkered cloth. A brilliant multicolored blue-and-orange sash was tied around her torso. And if anyone asked her about the mix of color and pattern, if there was a secret to the wondrous ways she put together what would be cacophonous on another body, she'd laugh and say, "Evil follows a straight line. I don't give it a place to land."

Serah traced the figures on the surface of the table. One frog in particular captured her eye.

"I said what brings you," Mariah said, a hint of impatience in her voice.

"How hard is it to break a binding?"

"Depends. On who's bound and what they been bound with."

Serah showed her the bracelet and told her its origin story.

"You only used hair, right? No blood?"

"That's all."

"It's not very strong, then. Don't take much to bust a few strands of hair."

"Oh . . . that's good," said Serah glumly. A weak binding shouldn't impede him getting farther away, but hearing that only upset her. She couldn't help seeing an endless ocean materialize before her.

Mariah's eyes widened. "Honey, you want to make it stronger? If you got something of his, it's not hard to do."

"You can?"

"Yeah, it wouldn't take much. I could web it. That's the cheapest option. For a little more, I could build a dam . . ." Mariah ran down her list of possibilities, each ritual more elaborate than the one before it. "And then it wouldn't take much to call him back to you."

It was tempting, Serah had to admit. "And he'd be unharmed?"

"Can't promise you that."

"What can you promise?"

"Can't promise nothing. The work ain't certain. It's just a strong hand guiding things in a favorable direction."

"Hmph." She was torn. The carved frog on the table seemed to be waiting. Judging. Just how selfish could she be?

"Do you want it or not?" Mariah peered past Serah toward the window. "'Cause it's getting late."

Serah could see the sun setting, a fiery orange spilling into the windows.

"No. He can't come back here. Not now anyway."

Mariah shrugged and tapped the frog on the table. "He'll take your offering." She stood up and opened the door.

Serah placed a blue bead on the frog's mouth and was surprised when the grooves in the table kept it from rolling away.

"If you change your mind, you know where I am," Mariah said, waving goodbye. Serah left the house and hurried back through the woods, the way she had come.

CHAPTER TWENTY-TWO

1

Dear Bird,

The light keeps changing. Not just the brightness or the length of it, but the when and how of it pouring through the trees. I make these letters knowing they'll never reach you. Without ink or paper, the wind and clouds will have to carry these words. And while it's likely they won't do my bidding, I'll keep talking anyway 'cause I know on the other side of this, there will be a reckoning. If and when we gather again, you will have questions. I'll do my best to answer them as I go.

You were right about the strangeness of weather this time of year. The heat has burned off and there's a regular threat of rain. But at least the day is shorter, leaving more hours to travel.

Milly, the old mule, is with me. She's slow, but she's all I could get. And at least there's plenty of corn left on the stalks to eat. We need to get as far south as we can before that changes.

Noah

2

BIRD,

We go as far as we can that first night and spend the morning hiding in the woods. We must be on the edge of a farm though, 'cause I can hear a horn blaring every few hours.

It spooks me. I get on Milly and we ride until she's too tired to go on, but where she stops, there's nothing but prairies. Fields and fields of yellow grass as far as I can see. I kick her a few times to get her moving again. Even the last drop of water doesn't make her budge.

You know how I feel about the plains. I suppose they shouldn't bother me much after so long on Sutton's ranch, but they still give me an eerie feeling now and then. The flat emptiness. How the sounds carry. How the common screech of a barn owl now strikes me as a child screaming.

Last time I ran away, it was the plains that did me in. The smoke from my small fire was visible from miles away and I woke up to a shotgun pressed to my forehead. I like to think I'm wiser now. Can let my stomach go empty longer. A pouch of pecans and a few ears of corn will have to keep me until the land changes again. That is one thing I do know about this place. It will change again. Forest, swamp, desert, or plain. It's all here.

N.

3

Bird,

I was a fool to give Milly the last of my water in a place as stingy as this. We reach the Trinity and it's nothing but rocks, a dried-up suggestion. The banks are empty though, so we lay out and rest for a moment, camouflaged by a hill of large stones.

I kneel down and poke a finger in the dry, light-colored soil hoping to find dampness. All I find is angry-looking beetles with clenched fists. One pierces my hand, drawing blood. I yell out. The blackbirds upriver squawk in response. They circle and swoop, as if trying to determine if we are of any use to them. I wave them away, worried they'll draw attention to us.

I pack up and try to lead Milly away. She's too weak to ride and I pull her behind me. But again, she's stubborn, stamping her feet, and pulling back on the reins. A small sack of dried corn strung over her back falls to the ground and spills. I salvage what I can, losing most of it to the blackbirds.

N.

4

Where the river and the road meet should be a holy place. Especially, when the river is dried up, and the two cross each other like siblings in a shared bed. Won't surprise you it's the opposite. It's rife with soul dealers and smugglers.

Just this morning, I saw a caravan. I was lying in the bushes some feet away from the road, trying to gauge its safety. I had laid there some hours, until I had gotten cold and stiff. Little had passed by. Only an old oxcart hauling some timber. But something told me not to move just yet. And that's when I heard them, the whisper of a hymn floating in the air, the slow clopping of horses.

Three wagons inched by. Behind them a ragged band of men, women, and children hobbling along. I shut my eyes to it. My stomach grew queasy. Their limp hymn poured down into my ears. "Nearer my God to thee," they sang. "Nearer to thee."

You never really forget the coffle, do you? No matter what comes after. The nauseating weight of it. The clinging smell of rust and blood. How confused your limbs get when affixed to someone else's. A man beside you lurches forward and you're yanked along with him. A man behind you passes out and you have to drag his weight along for a mile or more, before he's unhooked.

If I managed to get away with more than a dull Bowie knife, maybe I could be useful to them. José said to make the road proper I'd need firepower, a gun worth a damn and a horse worth more. I have neither, but I couldn't wait any longer.

Whatever they say about me back on Sutton's place ain't true. Not in substance or in deed. Survival looks different after a man has tried to eat you alive with his fingers. When he's tried to lick the bone while you're still inside the bag of skin. No matter how you stare down the wolf, he comes back, with new fangs, new claws.

I hope you understand.

N.

5

BIRD,

Beware of what they call a road here. It's more of an idea than anything else. It peters out and returns, rises up again more solid than before.

Last night, the road took Milly. It was dark, another black night with a dim moon. We were moving slow, as the trail was hard to follow and we didn't want to be led away from it over the plain.

Suddenly, the ground began thrumming, as if it were alive. I couldn't see where it was coming from. It seemed to be all around us. Louder and harder, it grew. Milly was spooked now and I held her bridle tight in my fist. I rubbed her head with the other hand, trying to calm her down, but she only grew more frantic, kicking and rearing back.

Too late, did I see the wave coming, thick plumes of dust billowing up in the air. The first beast sprang through the cloud, a wild-eyed mustang. Behind him, a sea of buffalo, cattle, and horses, all speeding directly toward us. I couldn't see where it ended. Only heard men whistling and shouting somewhere in the distance, in a language I couldn't parse.

Milly reared back again and the reins slipped from my hand. Off she ran. I ran after her, but at the nearest tree, I stopped and flung myself up, grabbing hold of the highest sturdy branch I could reach, and climbed as far I could.

The roar became deafening and Milly got swept up in the stampede. She was carried along for a moment, before she disappeared into a pileup, where I imagine she was soon trampled. I waited for the stampede to clear, the dust to settle, so I could climb down and see, but there were men all about now. Cherokees, I think, from the look of them. Some rode by slowly, sitting high on their horses, their bodies streaked with sweat. Two younger men followed on foot, guiding a team of horses. I feared one of them saw me. He swept the area with his eyes, scanning the trees.

I tried to sense if they would be a help to me, but there was no way of knowing. They could just as easily sell me back or help me make my passage. It wasn't worth the risk.

I remained still. Closed my eyes. Waited for them to move on. I must have dozed off, 'cause the next thing I remember is falling through the air, landing on my arm. The pain was blinding, but I could see it was first light. I lay there for a moment, getting my bearings, before I pushed myself up to see about Milly.

I walked up the road but strangely there was no sign of her. There were a few carcasses. Two buffalo and one horse. A vulture circled and landed. I kept walking, expecting to come across her, but I never did.

Bird, this only confirms to me that this place is more dangerous than we know, and we must leave it. It eats whole so many things, and with such greed and sureness, there's nothing left to mark them by.

N.

6

DEAR BIRD,

Another narrow escape in territory familiar. You know this geography. Crooked plow lines and snaking rows of crops. Some corn, peas, oats, cotton. And the hunch proves right.

I find the lane where the quarters are. A jangle of clotheslines, among them a five-star quilt drying. I see a similar pattern tacked across a window hatch. "A flock of geese" pattern. Could it be a sign?

I knock on the door and an old woman answers. I show her my arm. Ask if there's a healer among them.

She sizes me up for a moment. And I must have looked a sight. Ragged and dirty, weeds and grass in my hair, holding my arm to my chest like a broken wing.

"You running, boy?"

"Yes, ma'am."

She nods and lets me in. She gives me water and lets me drink 'til I am full. Then she rubs a salve on my arm, wraps it tight with a piece of muslin.

And when she makes me a plate, I could cry. Corn bread and salt pork.

"When you done eating, you got to go. Children

be through here soon and you know they tongues too
loose."

"Yes, ma'am. I thank you. You done plenty."

She pats my back. "Hurry up now."

I scarf down the rest of the pork and save the corn
bread for later. I thank the woman again and leave. At
the edge of the lane, there are some men returning from
the fields. They give me a curious look but I don't stop. I
just keep walking, as if I didn't see them. One calls out
to me, but I keep on, moving a little faster now.

But the man is insistent. He catches up to me, gets
in my face.

"You hear me talking to you."

"I didn't. Hard time hearing, you know."

"What you doing over here?"

"Visiting."

"Visiting who?"

"My aunt."

The man sniffed. "You don't look like no visitor to
me. Look like a fugitive. One who's going to do what I
tell him, if he don't want me turning him in to my white
folks."

I stopped. "What you want?"

"You got any money? You fugitives always got a little
something on you. A shilling or a five-pence?"

"No, all I got is this corn bread and some pecans."

"You won't mind if I see for myself," the man said,
reaching for the sack strung across my good shoulder.

"Don't put your hands on me," I tell him, reaching
for my knife. I brandish it with my good arm, though
I doubt I could make a good wound with it in my left
hand. He backs away and I take off running.

I hear him behind me, calling somebody for help. Lucky for me, they're slow in heeding.

N.

7

BIRD,

Whatever mojo I got is fading. Animals no longer skitter past, but stop and stare at me, full-sighted. Even the prairie chicken teases me, as if I'm no threat, which I'm not with one lame arm and no gun, but still. Its yellow jaws swell up full and round, like an omen.

The plains are no place for a man by his lonesome. It's full of secrets. Ditches, graves, and pimple mounds. All the plants have teeth. The tall grasses hide snakes. Berries tempt me, red and sweet, only to sour in the belly, and put me on my knees for hours.

Maybe it's best I don't make these letters anymore. Maybe each day is best left to itself and what's inside of it shut up and left there. The band you tied around my wrist is fraying. Maybe it's the reason I've been circling the same ground.

N.

8

What I thought of as darkness before seems a world apart from this. Sometimes I think I've gone up yonder, all the way round, now on the underside of that cosmogram. The world underneath the world. That would explain the sounds and what I've seen. Or maybe it's the way the mind works on its own after a while.

In the pines near Bastrop, I find others heading south. Among them, a man called Aaron who had already made a life down in Mexico. He married a Seminole woman, had children even, but a white man kidnapped him and dragged him back across the border. He was sold upcountry nearly a year ago and is just now making his way back.

This man, Aaron, warns me about the desert, the strip of land between here and Mexico proper. He gives us options, but none are good. We can go straight down, he says, through brush country, until we reach the river. Or we can go west, also through dry country, toward Eagle Pass, where a band of Seminoles and fugitives have a town there on the borderline. I ask him which is shorter, he can't say. "Which is easier?"

He can't answer that either, but I'm glad for the company and the assistance. Maybe Aaron will prove a better navigator than me.

N.

9

We should've never left the pines, but we grew so hungry after several days. Too hungry to catch anything really. Not even a possum or a squirrel. All our traps failed, and Aaron didn't want to use his last ball of ammunition. There were maybe five of us total, a band of bruised freezing runaways. Three men and two women. All too tired to agree or make much sense anymore.

"We should go toward town," one woman said. "One of the missions will feed us."

"No, we should rest, set new traps. Wait 'til nightfall and then pass on by," Aaron said.

They didn't lie about the missions. There were several in old Goliad. Ghostly white buildings ruined by the war between Texas and Mexico. But they looked unchurched to me, so I didn't trust them. I hung back while the others knocked on the door. A white priest welcomed them inside. I stayed out there in the lane for a while, just watching, thinking maybe I was wrong. That I had cheated myself out of a warm drink and some hearty vittles. And just when my stomach got the best of me and I approached the door, a young Mexican shooed me away from it. He shook his head. "*Mentirosa . . . malvado . . . a cheat . . .*"

I was still unsure what he meant, but I followed the man down the street, where he led me to a small house, where he and his sister fed me and let me trade them a piece of silver for a Mackinaw blanket.

I was still eating at their table, when I heard a commotion outside. They told me not to go out and I watched through the bottom portion of their covered window as Aaron and the rest got hauled away. I could hear the white men doing the hauling arguing about what to do with them.

"The bastard shot a priest. Who's going to buy him when the devil's got a hold on him so?"

N.

10

Bird,

Just wanted to let you know I reached brush country.
New terrain. Mesquite, shrubs, prickly pear. But it rains a
lot. I make a tent by hanging the blanket between a few
shrubs until it passes. When darkness falls and the wind
howls, specters loosen from their hiding places and roam
free. It's best not to look at them directly. They dance,
they sing, they loom large like cornstalks. I don't protest,
though they scare me.

When the rain stops, they follow me. More haints
come out, some with monstrous blue heads, some with
wings and scaly backs. A grand parade following me all
the way to the Rio Grande.

N.

11

Oh, what joy to reach the river, but what a surprise it
was. It was shallow with white rocks all around it and
a few pecan trees along the banks. I walk upstream and
barely find enough to cover my knees. I step in anyway,
wash myself in the clear blue water, and am thankful to
find my net, still tucked away, deep in my sack. I catch as
many fish as I can, though I got my tinder wet and had
no way to start a fire.

I leave there, thankful and relieved, with a full net of
small redfish and bass, convinced the hardest part of my
journey is over.

Some hours later, I follow a drift of smoke to a small campsite of vaqueros. One says he'd let me fry up my fish, if I was willing to share. We cook it up and eat well.

And I'm lying there in the dirt, too full to move, when the vaquero breaks the horrible news to me. "Oh, *mi amigo*, that wasn't the Rio Grande. That little gulp of water was the Nueces. You've still got miles and miles to go."

For the second time in days, I could've cried.

N.

12

The strip of land between the Nueces River and the Rio Grande is a hellish one. The men at the campsite told me so. They were heading north, outrunning something else—debt higher than the Sierra Madre.

"Keep every eye open," they warned me. As the strip was full of desperate men—grifters, deserters, and bounty hunters. I did as they said and still, a white man caught me foraging for food and roped me with barely two words between us. "Oh, lucky day. You gone be my ticket, boy." I told him I wasn't running, that I was allowed to hire myself out when I could, but he didn't believe me. Instead, he wrapped himself up in my blanket and dragged me to a blacksmith, where he tried to bargain for a set of irons.

While there, he goaded two or three white men sitting around, each waiting for their turn. "Oh, I'm going to get top dollar for this fugitive. They'll give me at least two hundred. Maybe three!" He directed his comments to a scruffy man swinging a pair of horseshoes. "Barnes, you should come in on this. Let me use your horse and I'll give you a percentage."

Barnes snorted and spat on the ground. "I wouldn't give you a tin of my piss."

The blacksmith refused to front the man a set of leg irons and we had barely gotten more than a few paces away, when Barnes appeared, trying to rob the man of his hot ticket. The two quarreled. Each firing upon the other. I took off, not waiting to see who won. I saw a horse tied to a post and ran toward it. I yanked the tie loose and hopped on. I took off, dipping around the blacksmith's yard and out past the edge of town, going as far as I could.

N.

13

When I reach the Rio Grande, I can see why it's called a great river. It's so beautiful I wish I could gather it up and bring it to you. A mighty winding, careless thing, it is, in the way water can be.

Aaron warned me it's not easy to cross. It's deceiving that way. The current is stronger than it looks. It makes one think he can just walk or swim across it, but the bottom is unsure and the banks aren't safe. Soldiers and Texas Rangers roam up and down the perimeter seeking runaways.

But never mind those no-account bastards, the river says, for it is the true divider of persons. If you manage to look on the surface and baptize yourself in its waters, it likely means a gauntlet lay at your back. Miles of thirst and hunger, wolves and soul dealers of all stripes are somewhere behind you. And now, just one lowly unassuming river.

Like all devils, it seduces. It shimmers in the sunlight and it feels like all I need to do is hoist myself upon it, paddle lightly, and soon I'll reach the opposite side. When it takes me under, I'm surprised for only a moment, but one moment is all it needs.

N.

14

Bird,

Remember the traveling preacher's talk about heaven. Pearly gates, tables full of food, grinning faces of kith and kin. I still don't believe him. But the Negro colony down here is probably the closest I'll see in this life. I nearly drowned, but the Mexicans who fished me out of the river knew exactly where I was going. And I arrived in Nacimiento de los Negros half-dead on the back of a dray, but I made it all the same.

The town is small and growing every day. Some folks have been down here a full generation or more. But most are like us, running from Texas or Louisiana, or Oklahoma. A few Seminoles from Florida are thrown in, but I suspect they were exiled from the Seminoles' town not too far away.

The folks here got small farms, work their crops, and sell them at the market. It's not perfect. Capture is a steady threat, with the Rangers and other soul dealers charging across the border to kidnap folks, but we're far enough south that it happens less now, or so they tell me.

I wish you could see it because I can't describe it proper. The land is rocky so the crops don't yield much. Most men do some cattle work also, and the songs they sing are both familiar and new, now full of Spanish words.

Listen, this might be my last letter for a while but don't be cross with me. Let me get well. Get a plot of my own to farm and some chickens, too. Let me build you a small clapboard house with a real floor and a real bed.

N.

CHAPTER TWENTY-THREE

By THE TIME OF THE first frost of the season, Serah had already begun to suspect what she was feeling in her body was something more than a flu. Her stomach was jumpy, always upset, always threatening to empty itself. It was tiring, made her sore, in throat and abdomen. Made others upset at her for wasting food. Got so others reclaimed her breakfast, her lunch. And she was too weak from vomiting to fight anyone to keep it.

Every winter, Nan complained about the drop in temperature, however mild. How cold could settle under her joints and in her fingers. Serah thought maybe that was happening to her, too. Winter had finally come for her body but instead of her joints, it attacked the flesh. Made her back ache, her breasts tender, her stomach a queasy, roiling sea.

She went to Nan, to ask if she had something that might help with the nausea or the soreness. Maybe she could diagnose this particular strain of winter illness.

"You ain't catch cold, you caught," Nan said flatly.

"What you mean?"

It was hog-killing time and Nan's hands were lodged deep in the guts of a pig, the shiny loose liver, the translucent slick spleen. The sight usually didn't bother Serah. But this time, the bloody gore of it, the foul smell of it—both sent her reeling. She backed into the wall, clamping a hand over her mouth.

"I mean caught. With child. Now, get out of here before you mess all over my floor," Nan told her.

Serah stumbled outside to retch in the yard. Her head hurt; her stomach ached.

OVER THE NEXT FEW days, Serah spun between two distant poles, wanting it and not wanting it. She spent days thinking of nothing but trying to kill it. She'd chewed cotton root for hours, until her teeth were yellow and chalky, and her jaw tired. And she cursed herself for how sporadic she had been before, only chewing it when she felt like it and stopping anytime she grew tired or bored or hungry.

She had taken to speaking to the spirit directly, willing it to loosen itself from her. She asked her saints to help it along, send it back to the otherworld so it could choose again. Often, she thought of what Junie said that day the cotton roots were found. If she had one, it'd be the stockman all over again, with Monroe put to them all, one after the other, and back again. She had already betrayed the women once. They'd never forgive her this.

But there were days when she couldn't help imagining a family in a white clapboard house, just like Mariah's. Noah would be sitting on its porch, a sweet brown babe asleep in his lap. He'd look up and grin at her, easy as the breeze. And it was then, she got to thinking about generations and lineages, and what if they did kill him, he was gone from this earth as if he was never here. This soul lodged inside her may be the only thing of him that remained. And on those days, she did nothing at all—no cotton root, no camphor, no rue. She followed the women to the fields and back, spun yarn until her sight blurred, and then took her hunger and nausea to bed, as the sun had long set, and nothing but cold dark was to be had anyway.

She was capricious that season. Avoiding the women and then wanting nothing more than the sound of them, the joy of their raucous laughter, the sharpness of their wit. She hated the cold that flooded her body but wanted the feeling of frozenness, of long-standing numbness.

Sharp cold beget a howling colder wind, heavy nausea followed by a black fatigue. There was little she could manage after a day of breaking up the ground or spinning thread all day.

And that didn't change until Harlow showed up one evening and walked her over to Monroe's cabin. Monroe hadn't been back long from his last job, barely a week had gone by. And in that time, the two hadn't said much to each other.

Monroe was sitting by the hearth, warming himself, when Harlow appeared in the doorway.

"Since you're here, thought it was time you got your gal back," Harlow said, pushing Serah inside the room.

Monroe stifled a groan. "Thank you, sir."

"Did you not want her back? You want another?" Harlow asked him.

Serah watched as Monroe's face grew puzzled. Monroe looked at her. Was that all it would have taken for them to be separated? Or was it a trick?

Harlow hadn't closed the door and she looked outside at the blackening sky. She inched toward the door. Maybe she could hide out in the woods a few days, but she'd be on her own. None of the women would bring her any food. They might even blame her for whoever Monroe chose next, if he dared ask.

"Don't know, sir," Monroe began, trying to suss out the temperature in the white man's face. His eyes stopped at the man's waist, where a shiny new revolver sat on his hip. Serah followed Monroe's gaze and saw it, too.

"You can speak freely."

"Well, we alright, but a better match might be made with one of the others," Monroe said carefully.

"How come?"

Both were quiet for a long moment, unsure of how to answer, or what was being asked.

"What a disappointment," Harlow said, sniffing the air. "It's been over a year since I threw y'all that fancy wedding affair and you both promised me portly children." He narrowed his gaze at Monroe. "What good would it be matching you with another, if you can't make butter with the one I give you? You make good on your promise and maybe we can talk about another match."

Harlow turned toward Serah. "Go on, now. Get in." He shoved her toward the bed.

She sat down on it, next to Monroe.

"For God's sake, act like you're husband and wife. Do I have to get in there with you?"

She got underneath the blanket and Monroe did the same.

Harlow moved toward the door. "This time, I'll give you some privacy, but if I come back tomorrow, and y'all still acting like clergy folk, I won't be so kind."

━⤚

WHAT EMERGED THE NEXT few days between Serah and Monroe was a steely tension. The two sizing each other up, waiting for the first blow. They were both extra cautious about where they sat, where they stood, what they drank, what they ate. They wouldn't share water or food, each preparing their own meals, each securing their own water from the well, and keeping it covered and in sight at all times. They each donned their own protective work, in front of the other. Part ritual, part performance. Serah could tell he was still angry at her for making him sick the way she did that summer, and in truth, he had grown sicker than she expected. And she couldn't say for sure if it was because of the work she had done on him or something else. They all fell prey at one time or another to the mysterious ailments of this country—fevers of all kinds, boils, influenza, dropsy, pneumonia, pleurisy, malaria. Though she knew many who didn't believe in that possibility. If anything befell them, it was because of the malicious root work of their enemies.

His belief that it was her doing wasn't necessarily a bad thing, she figured. It made him cautious, tentative. Made him less of a bully, lording over her with his size and strength. And so, she didn't say much more to dissuade him of the notion. Instead, she narrowed her eyes at him and drew shapes in the air and on the ground. She put down salt around herself, prayed to her saints, whispering loudly enough for him to hear. Neither slept well the next few nights, dozing off and jolting awake, intermittently throughout the night.

One evening, during their nightly chores, she figured she'd at least try broaching the subject of a truce with him. She was sitting at the table, sewing, while he was trying to repair the chinking in one of the cabin's walls. She watched as he pulled moss and rags from the crevices and replaced them with mud.

"You think that'll hold?"

He shrugged. "We'll see."

When he was done, she handed him a cloth so he could wipe his hands.

"How 'bout we call it even?"

He gave her a funny look. "It ain't even. Won't ever be."

"A truce, then. At least until it's warm out. And if you still mad then, we can—"

"Don't care about then, I care about now."

"Fine. What then? You want to poison me. Maybe you already did. You see I can't keep my dinner down half the time. Ain't that enough?"

"Nope," he said firmly.

"When we even then? When I'm dead?"

"Sounds good to me," he said, grinning at her.

THE UNSEASONABLY COLD WINTER turned the cabin into a burial pit. A heavy snow collected on the roof one night, and hearing the wood creak under the weight signaled to Serah they were being buried alive together. The temperature inside the cabin grew so cold it became hard to continue the way they had been, seething and wary all the time. They worked together to finish sealing the cabin walls and fortified the blankets with more moss and hay. She knitted woolen socks for them both, while he helped card sheared wool so she could make more things with it.

And while her belly had grown a bit rounder and more taut, it wasn't much more than the usual bit of monthly bloat, which was easy to hide. Besides, she wore most of her clothes all the time now, two dresses layered on top of each other, a slip and a pair of woolen stockings underneath, and a woolen jacket. The hours of daylight were so short, she washed and dressed in the dark each morning and did the same at night.

They made up new rules. Attacks during sleep were off-limits, as was food, because there was so little of it, once Harlow had cut their rations. Whereas formerly they were each allotted one peck of corn per person weekly, now they were given one peck to share, along with the smallest sliver of bacon. More would be given, they were told, once they delivered portly children.

Soon, the performances stopped altogether. They saved the salt for other things. Whatever Monroe hunted from then on, he brought into the house—rabbit, squirrel, quail. From her garden plot, she added turnips, radishes, and onions. They managed a decent meal between the two of them, but she let him attribute her constant chewing of cotton root day and night to pica, a fruitless attempt to assuage her hunger.

The effort of getting sufficient food to eat was enough to make them almost friendly sometimes. But if any chummy feelings managed to develop, the Lucys quickly dashed them.

Harlow's nightly rounds were one thing. These had always happened intermittently, but these days, they were constant. At some point, nearly every evening, he made his way over to the quarters and pushed inside every house, making sure every person was present and there weren't any neighboring folks among them. In Junie and Lulu's cabin, he was usually only there a few minutes, but now, with the couples he lingered. With Monroe and Serah. With Patience and Isaac. He'd pose dirty questions, wanting updates on procreation.

And when he was tied up with duties for the new vigilance committee—all the men in the county had weekly shifts now—Lizzie filled in. On Saturday mornings, she'd barge into each cabin with a bucket of lime in a supposed fit of cleaning. When Lizzie entered Monroe and Serah's, Lizzie would take particular care to sniff the sheets and rifle through Serah's dirty laundry, looking for menstrual rags.

"Don't know why y'all insist on hiding them from me," she'd say, as she did a quick sweep over the floors, using the broom to parse through Serah's belongings, hidden behind a trunk or stacked in a corner.

Afterward, she'd hand Serah a rag and motion toward the bucket of lime. She'd watch as Serah scrubbed, pelting her with questions. "You taking care of all your wifely duties, aren't you?"

This curious behavior left no doubt about what agenda had risen to the top of the Lucys' list. They felt this most acutely on the coldest nights of the year. Long after midnight, Harlow'd show up drunk after riding with the patrol. He'd shove his way inside, and stumble toward them in bed, waving a lit pine knot with one hand, a gun in the other.

"Y'all do it, yet?" he'd say, shaking Monroe.

Say no, and he was just in time for the show.

Say yes, and he'd say, practice makes perfect. Go again.

———❦———

For once, Monroe and Serah were of the same mind. They whispered all the time about killing Harlow. They worried the walls might hear them, that even the rotting logs couldn't be trusted, but they couldn't help themselves. Some nights, it was just a salve, other nights it formed a steely net in their minds—how might they do it, would they need more help than just the two of them? The drunken whooping of the vigilance committee outside would pause this talk, but any sighting of an intoxicated Harlow would unravel it. They buried roots under the steps and scoured the clearings for dark, twisted twigs whose protective power they might harness. It was widely known the effects of Conjure on white people were so-so and fairly unpredictable. No one was sure why—maybe it was the lack of pigment in their skin, the straightness of their hair, or the European gods they brought to the country. But Monroe and Serah kept laying down new tricks anyway, even when the cold weather broke, and it was time for new corn to go into the ground.

—⌇

NOTHING WORKED. NOT ON Harlow and not on the stubborn soul burrowed inside her.

In a fervor, she doubled her efforts. Too much camphor, which made her jittery, rue broke her out in tiny rashes, and juniper had no effect at all. And the days when it seemed to work were the darkest of all.

But then a sign would appear. A strong smell set her gagging; a strange flutter sent a wave of motion over her stomach. And for a full hour or more, she found herself happy. How stubborn this child was, so unwilling to abandon her.

In truth, she had never understood the maternal thing and had seen all kinds on her last farm. Women so besotted with their offspring, loss made them suicidal, and other mothers who couldn't bear to look at what came out of them, let alone hold it or feed it. She wondered now which category her own mother fell into, but she had so few memories of the woman that she had no way of knowing for sure. Her mother had been sold off when she was barely knee-high, so what she had in place of a face or a voice was what little her father had told her and a lock of the woman's hair. Nothing she had, the stories nor the lone memento, could answer the questions that overwhelmed her now.

She feared she would be like those detached mothers, and only in those brief moments of happiness did she consider that she might be the opposite. Both possibilities terrified her. And she worried that the window of time she had to persuade the stubborn spirit was surely closing.

CHAPTER TWENTY-FOUR

RIDING WITH THE PATROL A few nights a week didn't ease Harlow's mind any. If anything, it reaffirmed just how close the edge was, if his labor force ceased to grow. He was stuck with the poorest questionable sort of men—landless louts, slaveless ones, too. Each unable to afford the dues the vigilance committee required to avoid spending half the night on patrol a good portion of the goddamn week.

One cold night, he was fed up. He pulled up to the quarters and slid off his horse. His legs and backside were sore, and there was a fresh gash on one side of his face from a run-in with a low-hanging branch. He wiped a trail of blood from his cheek, while he stood there staring at the three sad leaning cabins. Nearly everything he was worth in the world was asleep in those three dilapidated buildings.

He pulled out his flask and downed a swig of whiskey, but it did nothing to tamp down the watery fury lapping inside him.

There should be double, triple the number of buildings here by now. All with bodies inside them.

He fired up his pine knot torch and charged toward Isaac and Patience's door. He burst inside, gun in hand. "Up, up, everybody up."

The two jolted awake, sitting up on their pallets.

"Y'all know the routine. When was the last time y'all made connection?"

Harlow could see it in their faces, a ripe bound anger so strong it gave off a smell. Neither spoke. Patience looked at the gun, the floor, while Isaac's face was a mask, his entire body stilled. Harlow watched him carefully. The man appeared as if frozen. Harlow couldn't find the hitch in it—his chest didn't seem to rise, his eyes didn't seem to blink. It was strange.

"Cat got your tongues? No matter. Let's get on with it."

The two didn't move.

He cocked the gun in an exaggerated fashion. In the other cabin, that was all it took for the process to get underway, but these two didn't budge.

Finally, Patience said something to the man Harlow didn't catch, in a language he didn't understand. She pulled Isaac's arm and Isaac followed her lead.

She got down on all fours and raised her nightgown. Isaac mounted her and as he began, his eyes locked on Harlow's. He grunted and pushed against her, but kept looking at Harlow, with a look so intense, Harlow felt glued down by it.

Harlow's mouth went dry, the nerves under his skin all began firing at once. His heart sped up in his chest and his groin came alive. Don't look at me, boy, he started to say, but the words wouldn't come out, just a dry stirring in his throat.

He tried to step back, raise his gun with his right hand,

but his body disobeyed. It would do nothing. Only his member raised up and paid any attention.

Isaac kept on staring, kept looking at him, through him. Harlow pulled backward and fell against the door. He then turned and rushed down the steps.

Outside, in the crisp night air, his wits returned. He grabbed his gun and started to charge back inside, but the doorway stopped him. The rectangle shape seemed to be growing somehow, now stretching and towering over him like a huge mountain.

He turned and sprinted away. When he looked back over his shoulder, all he saw was the same tiny cabin amidst the two others. He smacked himself upside the head, in the face. "Get your wits about you," he mumbled to himself as he went on. He wasn't a superstitious man, didn't believe in tales about magical niggers.

Fatigue was making his mind soft. How was anyone supposed to work all day, ride half the night, and still be of sane mind and sound body?

At the house, he locked the front door and checked the windows. He threw another log on the fire and lay down. *Sleep it away*. He almost laughed to himself, but when morning came, the night lingered on his tongue like bile. Before he opened his eyes, the first image he saw was of Isaac, the man's dark eyes boring into his. A smirk appearing on the man's lips.

CHAPTER TWENTY-FIVE

SPRING WEATHER WOULD BE SERAH's downfall. One day, a sudden swing in temperature left her in sweaty wet clothes for hours. By the time she and the rest of the women got the first quarter of cotton into the ground, the heat had burned off, and she grew chilled to the bone. She made a beeline to her and Monroe's cabin, while Lulu and Junie argued about whose turn it was to grind that evening's corn.

She figured she had the room to herself for a good while, since Monroe often disappeared with Isaac to smoke and blow off a little steam before coming inside. She shut the cabin door and put down a piece of wood to bar it from opening. She got a fire going and then peeled off her damp clothing—the long dress and chemise. She had just stepped out of her knickers, when the door flew open and the wooden bar snapped in two.

She yanked the skirt up and held it in front of her, when Monroe stumbled into the room, a large scaly fish dangling from his hand. "Look what I got—" The words died out in his mouth.

He looked away at first, a reflex, then looked back at her, a slow recognition dawning on him.

"Get out!" she yelled, wrapping the skirt around her midsection.

He closed the door behind him and turned to face her. "That what I think it is?"

"No, now get out."

"The hell it ain't. Prove it."

"Leave," she said, stepping back away from the fire, hoping the dimness made it harder to see her.

"Naw."

The two stared at each other for a long moment. She softened her voice.

"Monroe, out . . ."

"I'll go. Show me your belly first."

Even so close to the fire, she was getting cold. Her feet, her legs. She couldn't stand there forever with the skirt wrapped around her and at the same time, she could think of no way to put it on without exposing herself.

The inevitable had arrived. She dropped the skirt and his eyes widened.

"Now get the hell out."

He shook his head and left.

She laid out her damp clothes in front of the fire. She put on a pair of dry knickers and pulled a shift over her head, and a flannel shirt. She would get dinner started and when he came back, she would talk to him plainly. But what if he was already up at Harlow's, telling the Lucys all about this recent discovery? He wasn't above it, especially if he believed they'd reward his telling with a gift of some kind.

She couldn't hold the spoon without shaking, couldn't stir the bland watery sauce she'd thrown together for the fish without spilling bits of it on the floor. She cut the turnips up, got them boiling, when Monroe came back through the door.

She was mad at herself. She should have been better prepared, she thought, but it didn't occur to her that all of her efforts against the stubborn spirit would be unsuccessful. That her body would betray her and give away the secret while there was still a secret to tell.

He moved to the table, with the fish cleaned and gutted, the stench entering the room before him. Without speaking to her, he fried it up and slammed it on the table, smoke rising up off the singed flesh. Scales glittered on his arms, his pants, his beard.

He sat down at the table and rested his arm between the pan and her. He wasn't sharing.

They sat there in silence. She ate her turnips, he his fish.

"How long you known?"

She shrugged.

"He's been a demon for months now and that would've ended it. You could've ended it," he said. "You must like it, being treated that way."

Serah shook her head. "I don't. But it ain't his business. Ain't yours neither."

"How you figure?"

"'Cause it ain't yours."

He laughed. A slow dark laugh. "And I'm supposed to believe a whore like you. You've been lying since I met you."

"Believe what you want. It ain't yours and it won't be sticking around here."

He ran a hand over his shaved scalp. "You really are touched in the head?"

"I'm sounder than I ever been."

"You harm that babe and I'll put you in the ground myself."

"So you say."

"I promise you that."

"A man of your word, huh?"

"I am."

Serah laughed. Under the tables, her knees were shaking, but she looked him in the eye. "Me and mine ain't got nothing to do with you. This spirit going home."

Monroe laughed. "And where's that, huh? Ain't no home for us niggers. No heaven or hell neither. You ain't figured that out yet?" A wild look came over his face. "Death may be better, but that still don't give you the right."

She laughed. "Why don't it? Didn't you just say you'd kill me yourself?"

"That's different. Ain't got no problem killing you to protect my kin."

"It ain't yours. I swear on my life," she said.

"But it could be."

"It ain't. I know it."

He examined her face for a long moment. "It's that no-account nigger from before? The one at the wedding?"

Serah didn't answer.

"And that man just allow you to run roughshod, huh? Allow you to kill his generations 'cause you say so?"

"He ain't here."

"So what? I ain't letting you do that."

"You don't care nothing about this baby. You just want more rations. You just want Harlow to leave us be."

"Shit, don't you?" He pushed back from the table and stood up. "Do what you want but I'm telling. Thanks to that nigger of yours, my part is done." He moved toward the door.

"Wait," she said, following behind him. She grabbed hold of his arm, but he pushed her aside easily and left.

Not long after, she set off, too, but only got as far as the loom before she heard the dogs howling. She went inside and prayed for a sign. Maybe she'd make it through the woods, protected, made invisible by the powers of her saints, but her faith was waning. She searched her mind for stories of the faithful, those who passed through a forest of demons, who swam through an ocean of sharks, but they seemed abstract, hard to hold on to. There was no tangible thing to pull from, no practice she could apply to what awaited her on either side of the Harlows' property line.

CHAPTER TWENTY-SIX

THE VISIT WAS NOW SET for the end of July. Originally, it had been March but now that there was an established school for Ollie to attend, Lizzie didn't want to rip him out of it before the term ended, she told Junie.

That was fine. Junie kept her hope contained. A manageable size, not too large that it suffocated her, but loose enough to puff up and make the days bearable. But she knew something was wrong when she was summoned early one Tuesday. When she was told to go to the house, they were sowing a second planting of corn and were only a third of the way through.

She walked past young Louisa playing on the porch and into the stuffy house. In the back bedroom, Carol was crying, and Lizzie was retching over a chamber pot, her face red and damp.

Lizzie wiped her mouth on her sleeve and looked at Junie. "It's happening again."

"What?"

Lizzie groaned. "I can't take another. Lord forgive me. Not right now. Not so soon." Lizzie shot a weary glance at Carol.

Junie wet a towel with water from a nearby pitcher and mopped Lizzie's face. She put the chamber pot near the door and ushered Lizzie into bed. "You sure that's the problem?"

"Sure as my hand. My monthly's late. It's almost always near the fourth, but May is nearly over and not a goddamn streak," Lizzie said.

Junie pulled the blanket up over Lizzie's shoulders and then pulled Carol into her lap.

"Finish feeding her," Lizzie said, motioning to a bowl of gruel near the manger.

Junie fed Carol a mouthful. "Mmm, that's good, ain't it?"

Carol bounced from side to side, as if she was trying to nod.

"You talk to her like she can understand you," Lizzie grumbled.

"I always talked to my babies when I fed them. We had some of the best talks then . . ." Junie trailed off, suddenly embarrassed for sharing that thought aloud.

But Lizzie wasn't listening. She was grumbling still, mainly to herself. "Stuck like a pig all over again. And I was so careful. I wrote all the way to New York and paid nearly ten dollars for those fancy pills they sell up there. Dr. Vinter's or something. Guaranteed to make sure your monthly arrives like clockwork! Pure hogwash."

"Aww, it won't be so bad," Junie said, a sinking feeling spreading out over her abdomen. "Fresh air will help. Besides, motion sick, baby sick, it's all the same. You just have to keep moving. The trip will be just the change you need."

"Optimism never was your strong suit," Lizzie said dryly. "She done?"

Carol seemed to be playing now, with the spoon, a bit of

grucl dribbling down her chest. Junie dabbed at the spill with a rag.

"I'll write Mason tomorrow," Lizzie said. "Hopefully, he'll be able to get a refund. And maybe we can go next year. Definitely next year."

The sinking feeling in Junie's abdomen tightened. Next year. There would be no next year or the year after that, she knew. Another infant would make sure of it.

Lizzie might as well have said next decade or century even. The years would stack, and Death would come close, tapping one forehead after another, and soon her children would fall to another member of Lizzie's rotten lineage or be sold at estate.

If Junie was in her right mind at that moment, she would have left, would have gone out into the morning and let her confusion and rage meet the sun, but she was glued to the chair, the gassy child gurgling on her knee.

Lizzie continued her grumbling. "I should sue those Dr. Vinter's quacks. Make them reimburse Mason."

"Can't the pig be unstuck?"

"Huh?"

"I said can't the pig be unstuck?" Junie said louder. "Dr. Vint's can't be the only way to fix your problem."

"What you saying, gal?"

"I'm just asking. Every year, when we kill the hogs, there are certain ways we go about the slaughter. The hog's got to be boiled so the hair can be removed. The hind legs got to be pinned, and the body hung high off the ground, so that first cut down the belly can be done clean. Now, we do it that way, but I'm sure every farmer round here got his own way of doing it, a way he swears is better than the man next to him."

"So?"

"So, are you a sow or a person? 'Cause when a sow is stuck

in the mud, she stuck, but a person has a mind, and all kinds of ability to unstick themselves in whatever mud trying to hold them back. Now maybe I'm speaking out of turn, but it seems like you acting more like a sow than a person these days and have been for a long while."

Lizzie's face turned red. "I should flay your hide, talking to me that way."

"Maybe so, but I'm just saying what cousin Beatrice would say if she were here."

Lizzie didn't answer. She turned her face to the pillow.

Carol began squirming. Junie pulled the baby into her arms and softly began singing a lullaby. A song she knew Lizzie would remember from back home, one they both heard Junie's mother sing many times. "Go to sleep, little baby. Mama went away and she told me to stay and take good care of this baby." She sang another verse and then stopped. The room grew silent and heavy. Junie could feel this one simple dream of hers moving past her, out toward the horizon, climbing farther and farther away in the sky.

"Sing it again," Lizzie said.

Junie sang the song again, the child now asleep. When she finished, Lizzie raised her head, her eyes watery. "I want to go home."

"I know you do."

"I don't want to be stuck," Lizzie whispered.

Junie grew still, barely moving, holding her breath.

"How do I unstick myself?" Lizzie continued.

Junie's mind raced, trying to remember who might have a stash of cotton root hidden somewhere. After the last raid, she burned most of hers. But she couldn't offer up the cotton root, could she?

Junie shrugged. "I'm not privy to those things but I can ask around."

"Would Nan know something I could use?" Lizzie asked.

"She may. I can ask her for you," Junie said.

"But you wouldn't say it was me asking, would you?"

"'Course not." Junie slowly stood up and eased Carol down in the manger. "Y'all rest." Her stomach was roiling. Her performance of indifference was two seconds from buckling. She tucked the blanket around the baby and slid out of the room.

She walked out the front door, a warm breeze hitting her in the face. It wasn't refreshing, but it felt steadying a bit. She realized then she was drenched with sweat. She walked on down farm, out of the sight of the small leaning house.

CHAPTER TWENTY-SEVEN

SERAH HAD TO DIG THE hole herself. A small hole, about a foot deep and a foot wide, just large enough for her belly to fit into. Afterward, she was forced to lie down on top of the hole and then lashed fifteen times with a black snake whip. This was considered light, as it wasn't the customary forty lashes. Here, she put the babe in the earth. Pressed it into the ground, the soil making one shield, her back another. It seemed like an omen.

According to the Lucys, she had finally pushed them to the breaking point. Weeks ago, after Monroe blabbed about the pregnancy and what she had said to him, the Lucys brought her into the house to be under their watch at all times. For them, this seemed a perfect solution to fill in the gap of cooking and housework needed when Nan was away catching babies. However, Serah couldn't abide it. The closeness of the walls, the constant yapping demands of the Lucys, the lack of any sliver of privacy. The proximity was suffocating, not to mention painful.

She knew the Lucys had horrible tempers, but being within arm's reach of them now meant a different level of vigilance. They were hitters—slappers, pinchers, projectile throwers. It didn't help that she was doing everything in her power to be sent back out to the quarters. She burned up meals, singed nearly every piece of ironing, let the wash dry streaky and marked with yellow clay soap. And to add insult to it all, she'd sometimes disappear for hours—going to the well for water and proceeding on past it, just to hide out in the loom for a few moments of peace. The last straw was a half-raw chicken, pink and still laden with feathers, that she served on a plate to a table full of guests.

Facedown in the earth, Serah wondered if what Monroe said was correct. Maybe she was touched. Half-crazy. Moon-sick. Heat-stroked. She had wanted the child in the earth and here it was.

⤙

Afterward, Nan greased her back with hog lard to ease off the strips of clothing stuck to the open wounds, then coated it with a cool salve. Serah felt dizzy from the pain and the sedative tea Nan gave her. It brought on a strange slippery blackness that came and went. She heard Nan talking, but she couldn't quite hold the thread of her speech.

"They used to tell us when we were little, these marks came from wolves. The long stripes were from the claws and that if we didn't mind, or stay close to home, the wolves would come get us and carry us off into the mountains."

"Did y'all believe them?"

"Sure, for a while. We'd hear the dogs howling at night. And Mama say, 'See, look, they hunting now.' It was a long time before I realized she didn't mean the ones on four legs." Nan chuckled. "Your people never told you that?"

"Nah, but I'd believed it, if they had. You tell your children that?" Serah asked.

"Sure, every living one."

Serah had never heard Nan speak of her children. She tried to raise her head to get a better look at Nan's face, but she couldn't.

"How many children you have, Nan?" Serah mumbled.

"Oh, I don't know. Dozens of children. A hundred grandchildren maybe." Nan raised up her walking stick and squinted at it, one side lined with tally marks.

"I don't mean how many babies did you catch? I mean your *own* children . . ."

"They all my children."

All? Before Serah could get her next question out, the heavy black sleep rose up and snatched her again.

CHAPTER TWENTY-EIGHT

ONE SUNDAY MORNING, JUNIE INVITED herself on one of Nan's medicine walks. She lied and told Nan she wasn't looking for anything in particular, just wanted the company. "Also, I figured you could use the help . . ." she said, letting her voice trail off, motioning to Nan's walking stick.

Junie had never lied to Nan before, but she would do so now because she knew the old woman would talk her out of what needed to be done. And she didn't need much from Nan, just a bit of guidance in the right direction. She knew there were things other than cotton root she could use. Had heard Serah speak about other remedies with middling results, but she didn't have time for middling. She needed something sure.

She watched Nan approach a cluster of tall spindly plants surrounding a cropping of bushes. Nan moved near them, touched them slowly, surveying the leaves and the underbrush, before pulling out her mattock. She gently dug up the plant, root and all, and wrapped it up in a rag.

"Pokeweed? I thought you stopped using that."

"Nah, I'm just more careful now. It's the best thing I can find for rheumatism."

"What else can you use it for?"

"I only use it for that," said Nan. "'Less I'm cooking up the leaves."

"What other folks use it for?"

"Don't know. You have to ask them."

Hmph, Junie thought. She'd have to try another tactic.

They moved deeper into the trees. Nan paused at a sassafras tree, the leaves sickly and drooping from the heat. Nan circled the tree and peered at it, before peeling a few pieces of bark from it. "Thank you," she whispered, tapping the trunk with her fingers.

Junie stood on the other side of the tree, pulling down a leaf, its shape like the cloven hoof of an animal. "Bird told me," she began flatly, "the cotton root didn't work for her no more. Wonder what else she could have tried."

"Heard she tried most everything." Nan shrugged. "Sometimes a spirit can't be turned back."

"What else she try?"

"A heap of things. As you can tell, none of them worked."

"Would any of them have worked? I mean if the spirit was willing."

"Maybe. But then, you don't need much, if the spirit is willing."

"What you need then?"

"Anything that'll bring down the blood probably fix it."

"Like snakeroot?"

Nan shook her head. "Tansy's better, but hard to find out this way." Nan pointed to a tall hairy stem with tiny leaves. "Like this pudge grass could work. But it can be poisonous, likely to kill somebody if it ain't picked at the right time."

Junie stared at the plant and moved closer to it. What were the odds? she wondered. There had to be other things.

"You hurting? You need something?" Nan asked.

Junie shook her head. "Just wondering."

"Never seen you wonder 'bout such things before? Don't tell me you're caught."

Junie laughed. "Me? Hell naw."

"'Cause the remedy you got is still the best thing. Don't let Bird screwing it up make you think different."

"I ain't caught."

"Alright."

"But what if ain't me?"

"Then tell whoever what I told you."

"What if it was a Lucy?"

"Then I'd let Gabriel and Lucifer sort it out among themselves."

"Even if it means another Lucy in this world," said Junie. "Another Lucy whose first breath will have them looking at us again." Junie picked up a leaf and began rolling it between her palms. "They may even bring that breeding nigger back. Bring him 'round and make us all lie with him again. Well, not all of us . . ."

Junie's words hung in the air. An accusation. A reminder to Nan that she had been spared. Junie hadn't planned on dredging all that up, but if it got her the aid she needed, then she would. She studied Nan's face, the old woman's mouth now drawn into a tight line. "He was awful, remember?"

"You laying that at my feet?" Nan said.

"Not the first time, maybe."

Nan sucked in a breath, as if she had been struck. She turned away from Junie and began walking.

Junie could have told her the truth. Children were one of the few things Nan rarely spoke about. And as such, she knew the old woman would understand the hunger inside her, but she couldn't say it. She couldn't even mention the trip aloud, not outside of Lizzie's bedroom. Outside of those four walls, it sounded like space travel, like some phantasmic dream she had made up. Nan would only unravel it.

Guilt was more reliable. Nan was one of those souls who took on too much responsibility for those around her. Every babe she delivered, every head she dotted with oil and washed, every lone body she healed with herbs and roots, she carried with her somehow. It was a thing Junie had always warned her about. All that webbing and tethering, tangling her up so.

Nan stopped and bent down in front of another tall weed, hairy like the last one. "When it sprouts, maybe. Just the leaves and flowers should do little harm. The oil is the real killer." She stood up slowly, massaging her hip, then raised her eyes to Junie, with a cold and squinted glare.

Junie felt like she had been pierced, but she didn't flinch. Instead, she met Nan's hard gaze with a stony one of her own.

"I'll bring it when it's ready," Nan said. "But after that, we square. Don't ask me again. For that, or nothing else. And if you poison her, don't look to me for help."

Nan began walking again and didn't say another word to Junie the whole way back. Junie followed behind her, her eyes stinging, the yellow sky a shifting blur. She would beg the old woman's forgiveness later, she vowed. After the trip.

After the trip, she'd take it all back.

Nan was true to her word. A few days later, she brought a bundle of clippings of the plant to Junie. Her manner was cold, but she told Junie how to prepare them and how often to administer them.

Junie soaked the leaves and purple flowers in water for hours, then boiled them down a few hours more, and then gave Lizzie the decoction. She made Lizzie this tea twice a day for almost a week, after which Lizzie began spotting. Not a full flow, but enough to signal that maybe the remedy was working. Maybe any day now, a full flow would course down the white woman's thighs, and their plans for the trip would be back on.

The spotting disappeared, but a full flow never followed. Junie went back to Nan to ask for more of the plant, but Nan didn't answer, didn't even acknowledge she heard Junie speaking to her. Instead, she went on chopping onions with renewed vigor.

Junie wandered out there herself, into the woods one morning, but she couldn't tell one leaf from another. So many things looked alike. She remembered the area but couldn't remember the exact plant. Not to mention, she didn't see the little purple flowers anywhere. Instead, she looked for a bare spot where Nan would have uprooted the plant and found a bare patch covered over with grass, but it was hard to tell if it was anything more than some animal's hiding place.

She kept walking until she found a spindly plant with leaves with tiny blue buds that looked similar. She tried whispering to it, asking it as she had seen Nan do, but before she could even get the question fully formed in her mind, she stopped. If it said no, would it change her mind? It wouldn't. Better not ask, then. And what about the possibility of it turning poisonous already? Nan didn't tell her anything more about the timing or how to handle the toxic parts of the plant.

It made her furious, not knowing. She was so close to the

goal. And it had been going better than she expected. Lizzie hadn't complained or fought about drinking the bitter decoction. She'd drink it all down. She'd hand back the cup to Junie and say, "It must be working now. I feel awful."

Junie dug up the plant and prayed for the best.

She was optimistic until she pestled the blue buds some hours later. It didn't smell the same, but she went on, soaked the leaves and flowers, and then set them to boiling. The smell was undeniably different but hard to describe. Less pungent and more woodsy. She tasted a spoonful, then another. It was bitter but not like she remembered.

She couldn't risk using it. She'd have to go back to Nan, and maybe she'd tell her the truth this time. She fretted about it all through the morning's hoeing. And when the women came in for their midmorning meal, Junie went looking for her, but Nan wasn't there.

Later, after work, when Junie came to the yard to grind her corn, Nan still wasn't there. She pushed her way into the cookhouse, where she found Serah scrubbing the pots.

"Where's Nan?"

Serah didn't say anything at first, balancing the pot on her large belly while she scrubbed at a stubborn spot with a wet rag. The room was dim and smoky as always, and she couldn't see the girl's face really, only her set, stubborn jaw. She wondered what Nan might have told her.

"What that old heifer say?"

Serah looked at her blankly. "She went to catch a baby on the Ryans' farm. Said she be there a few days, I think."

"Oh. That all?"

"Yeah. You alright? You look funny?"

Junie nodded. "The Ryans? Whereabouts?"

Serah shrugged. "New people, I hear. Friends of the Lucys

some ways from here. They came and got her. But I tell her you looking for her."

"Don't bother," Junie said, stumbling outside. Dusk was falling and the balmy weather was hot and sticky, like the inside of a closed mouth.

It had been a full day and a half since she had given Lizzie her last dose and she needed another. Now.

———

SERAH BEGAN TO WORRY the babe would never come out. Her big widening belly would just continue to expand, until it was able to touch the opposite wall of any room she found herself in. The child would continue to grow and grow inside her, choosing to remain there.

Things ached and swelled. Her back, her feet, her fingers. Her vision blurred; her breasts leaked. A full-scale mutiny from scalp to toenail. And sometimes, it seemed just as likely that it would be she who was expelled, instead of the other way around, the soul having taken over her body altogether. As frightening as that was, the other possibility seemed just as frightening. Any day now, the child would come out, and how easily it might be removed from her sight.

That was the new fear. While her plan to be discharged from the Lucys' house had not worked in the short-term, it seemed a likely possibility once she had the child. But what then? She had no inkling of their plans or inclinations, so she had to do something.

When she stepped outside of the Lucys' house to dump last night's chamber pots and slop jars, she kept on going. She went down farm first and started to knock on Patience's door, but she stopped herself. Isaac must have heard her on the steps for he flung open the door and allowed her inside. He said something to Patience in a tongue Serah didn't recognize. Patience laughed and answered him.

Serah felt the air in the room shift as she entered. She had breached something, she knew, but she went on with her proposal. "Going to see Mariah. Come with me?"

Patience squinted at her for a long moment and shook her head. "The woman's a fake."

Isaac spoke up again, the lilting consonants puzzling Serah. "What he say?" Serah asked.

Patience laughed again. "He say he thinks she's a fake, too."

"Why didn't he just say that, then?"

"He done with English. Says it like poison. Soils the mind."

"And you understand him?"

"More and more."

Serah looked at the two with bewilderment, before focusing her gaze on Patience. "Just come along for the trip. You don't have to see her."

Isaac answered again, in the same musical tongue.

"Nobody was asking you," Serah shot back at him. She turned to Patience, a pleading expression on her face.

Patience shook her head. "You be careful out there."

Isaac opened the door, and just like that, she was back outside on the steps, the door shut firmly in her face. She could still hear Patience laughing. What a unit they seemed to be now. She felt a pang of something, in the back of her throat, but ignored it and hurried on down the steps toward the creek.

At Mariah's, lucky for her, no one was waiting. Elias ushered her inside and she sat down across from the woman. Before Mariah could greet her or even say anything about her big belly, she smacked a handful of blue beads on the table. "Shore up the binding to Noah. And can you bind us to the child, too?"

The beads rolled off the table and onto the floor, but neither Serah nor Mariah moved. Elias picked up the beads, put them on the table, and left the room.

"Sorry. Can't really bind the child to you while it's in there. But if I shore up the binding between you two, maybe it'll help."

Mariah cut Serah's finger, adding blood to the frayed bracelet. The rest of the ritual was a blur. Serah grew light-headed, the busy patterns from the curtain spreading out into a hazy overlay of squiggly lines and circles.

Elias put her on his mule and carried her home. She was housebound again after that, for much of June, but when the cut on her finger ached, she wondered if Mariah was out there, somewhere, calling Noah back. And she'd join in, wherever she was, whispering words she didn't even remember Mariah saying. "Shake-a-canna, Rake-a-canna, bring Noah Dobson back to me."

CHAPTER TWENTY-NINE

July was a scorcher in ways we couldn't have imagined. The air was hot and suffocating, a wavy wall of thick heat that made it hard to breathe. It felt like putting one's face over an open flame. Crops withered and died; hapless birds rushed into dark houses and barns, breaking their necks. Even in the shade, it was a piping 110 degrees.

We spent those super-hot days in the loom, trying not to faint while spinning thread. The wavy hot air brought bad news that lay suspended in the haze.

Buildings were combusting. A series of fires lit up the state. Half of downtown Dallas went up in flames, and forty miles away in Denton, too. Not to mention Pilot Point, Ladonia, Milford, Sulfur Springs, Fort Worth, Honey Grove, and Waxahachie. All over the course of one long weekend.

We heard the Lucys talking about it, this alphabet of fires spreading like a song. In a matter of days, culprits were named.

The first: newfangled prairie matches. One man said he saw a whole box burst into flames before his very eyes.

Another theory soon emerged in the tense shadow of scorched buildings. A coerced confession from a slave near Crill Miller's farm outside Dallas became a siren call. A new vigilance committee was formed, and every Negro near Miller's farm was interrogated until the right answers were given, and the full view of a conspiratorial plot began to unfurl under a dense white sky.

Men we knew who ran the drays long distances, hauling cotton and timber and wheat, told us what they heard at the mills and the ports. Some were even interrogated and beaten, accused of collusion in a great plot with Northern abolitionists who aimed to destroy the state by fire and make way for insurrection.

We asked them more questions, but they were unwilling to tell us more, warning us how quickly word was spreading from county to county. How they could barely do their hauls without constant checks of their passes, how often they were relieved of their tools.

"Don't repeat what I say here," a drayman would say to one of us. "Of course not," we'd lie. It wasn't a big lie, because we'd only tell one another, under the tree where we still gathered sometimes. And in the dark, looking up at the web of branches under the moon, we'd piece together these bits until a strange thread emerged. A new panic spreading like the flu.

———

JUNIE HAD NO CHOICE: this time, she'd have to use the cotton root to make Lizzie's tea. It seemed likely that Lizzie might complain about the difference in taste, but she could make something up, about how this new ingredient was important at this stage. She set it boiling in the cookhouse and asked Serah to keep an eye on it, as she knew the girl wouldn't press her and would simply do what she was told.

During the morning meal break, she removed it from the heat and let it cool. Once the temperature had lessened, she strained the liquid and poured it into a small pitcher, before carrying it into the Lucys' house. She knocked on the bedroom door, where Lizzie was rushing around, packing some of Carol's things—diapers, booties, rag bibs. Junie set the small pitcher on the table, as she had done nearly every day for the last two weeks. "This batch may taste a bit different. Boiled it longer this time."

A quizzical look spread across Lizzie's face. Junie felt her legs stiffen, her mouth now dry. She wasn't sure she had answers ready for whatever questions were coming.

Lizzie went over to the pitcher and peered down inside it. She leaned over and sniffed, scrunching up her nose. She rose and gave Junie a pointed look.

Junie froze. Any day now, she was sure the white woman would turn on her. Lizzie would gag on the vile liquid and accuse her of trying to poison her. If not that, then later, when the tea worked, the woman would grow regretful and have her strung up for murder. And if the remedy didn't take, she'd be a liar, a godless root worker who tried to contaminate the woman's mind against Christ, and whatever burden the child became would somehow fall upon Junie's shoulders.

Every day, she pushed these scenarios from her mind, forced herself to only picture the large boat, rocking precariously down a narrow river. Only the hazy vision of her children kept her feet moving, her mouth lying. A stack of lies so tall she worried they'd soon topple over.

"I told you I'm supposed to go to the Suttons' for Emmaline's lying-in," Lizzie said. "But maybe I'll just send word that I don't feel up to it. It can't be safe traveling right now."

Lizzie sat down for a moment. She drank a few sips of the liquid. "Argh, it doesn't get better, does it?"

There was a loud crash in the front room of the house, followed by Harlow bellowing loudly, and the front door slamming. Junie couldn't decipher what he had been yelling, but it jolted Lizzie to her feet, muttering under her breath.

"Probably won't be back from the Suttons' until tomorrow, so I'll need more than that," Lizzie said, her eyes on the bedroom door.

"That's all I got now."

Lizzie rifled through the drawers. "No matter, I guess. I couldn't travel with all that liquid no way. Just bring me the clippings and I'll boil them myself while I'm over there."

Junie felt stunned. Like time had sped up and she was trying to catch up to it.

"Don't just stand there. Go get 'em. The Suttons' wagon will be here soon."

Her mind spun for an excuse, but Lizzie just waved her away. Junie left the room and went out of the house. Her options were few. She could ignore the ask and just return to the fields, or risk giving Lizzie what she requested, a risk that seemed less perilous the more she thought about it. The bigger question was another missed dose. While Junie may not have fully understood the workings of plants and how they affected the body, the one thing she knew for certain was that consistency was key. Like prayer, like tending crops, like raising animals, little worked without regular repetition.

She went to the cookhouse, where a sack of the roots lay hidden underneath the table. She had planned to soak another batch for Lizzie's next dose, but now she wondered what was the danger in handing some clippings over? It's not like Lizzie knew what they were by sight. Of all the tasks Lizzie supervised or tackled with her own hands, the planting of cotton wasn't one of them. Lizzie might know something about cooking or sewing, weaving or canning. And sure, a few times a year, she wandered down to a weigh-in and watched the seed cotton be sacked and measured, before being taken over to a neighbor's gin. Maybe she had even observed Harlow bringing in new seeds, opening pouches of the latest breeds to try, but from the house where she spent most of her days, they were only visible in full bloom. Without the wispy white heads or the spiky hard receptacles that attached them to reedy stalks, they looked like most anything else, like any twig littering the forest floor.

And so, Junie wrapped a portion of the roots in a rag after checking them first for any telltale signs, any remnants of the boll or the head, making sure it looked like nothing more than kindling. She made a tight fist-size bundle and took them into the house, where she placed them next to Carol's diapers. Lizzie nodded and went back to trying to iron the wrinkles out of her best dress.

—✦—

THE SUTTONS' DIM COOL house should have felt like a respite to Lizzie. More than a handful of women were there already, some gossiping over iced tea and lemonade, while others tended to Emmaline, sweating and uncomfortable in a thin nightgown. The women moved easily from bedroom to parlor and back again, while two house girls brought in iced water and coffee, hot water, and towels. Emmaline had in the galley a midwife *and* a doctor at her service. The doctor was some Harvard-educated thin wisp of a man who barely looked old enough to shave, while the midwife was a stocky older German woman with a thick accent and a collapsible chair she carried from room to room, as if it would disappear the moment it left her sight.

While Lizzie should have felt relieved to sit in the parlor, sipping ice water under the vigorous fanning of an adolescent house girl, all she felt was a familiar jealousy even she was tired of. She swirled the cool glass, marveling at the fantastic clinking sound the ice made and the cold shards that lay alive on her tongue. Emmaline still had ice, in this heat. Of course, the Suttons had their own icehouse, but after a month of this weather, she couldn't fathom how they managed to keep anything frozen. If the house girl had leaned over and said a magical fairy delivered it, Lizzie would have believed her.

Carol squirmed in her lap, sucking from a cold wet towel, but the child didn't scream. Even if she did, the Suttons were prepared for that eventuality. A wet nurse was on standby, Emmaline's sister assured Lizzie when she first arrived. "Ready whenever you need," the sister sang, as Carol bucked and shrieked in Lizzie's arms. Lizzie stretched her lips wide in the appearance of a smile, but once she was led into the breezy parlor, and offered a seat next to a mountain of pastries on a silver tray, she decided then that she would spend most of the lying-in opposite that fanning house girl, instead of near Emmaline's swampy bedside.

Lizzie told herself it was because of the smugness on the sister's face, but in truth, she walked in with the intention to do as little as possible. She had no interest in propping up Emmaline in one uncomfortable position after another, while the woman panted and heaved in her face. She didn't want to mop down Emmaline's sweaty limbs with a fresh washcloth or offer middling advice about "bearing pains," or any of the other hundred tasks women came to do at these affairs.

She could hear them now down the hallway, a rising nervous chatter that permeated the house like the drone of a beehive. It wasn't a selective group of women. Any woman nearby was invited and probably a handful more than usual, as it was expected that some would be too fearful to make the trip.

She let herself doze off, only waking when the other women began filing into the parlor and taking seats alongside her. The doctor had chased them out of the bedroom, complaining about how he couldn't do his job with a bunch of meddling biddies in the way. "You shouldn't have come," he told them.

If they were upset in the moment, they were no longer. Now, in front of Lizzie, they mocked him. His flustered, blushing face. How he was downy like a baby, a veritable coating of blond fuzz on his face and neck. How he asked them to help Emmaline back into her clothes, instead of the sheer nightgown she was in when he arrived.

"Modesty is of the utmost importance," he told them, before stepping outside and fastening a long white cloth around his neck.

"What he need that bib for?" A brown-haired woman asked the group.

"Decency. He's supposed to touch without looking, you know."

A few of the women tittered.

"Well, he *is* a child. I declare I got girdles older than him."

"He probably never even seen one up close. Just them scary drawings in dusty textbooks."

"Fancy college or not, I do think it's improper. Some strange man that ain't her husband down there rooting around."

Another woman nodded vigorously. "And wasn't it a school way up north? Don't seem like Sutton to let some strange Northerner in his house, let alone mess with his wife."

"You sound like those nuts in Dallas."

"You must not read the papers."

"I read plenty. Since when every Yankee John Brown? Ran

that last cobbler out of town over an accident of birth. I paid him good money to fix my best pair of boots and now I'll never get them back or the cash I gave him."

"Ladies, I do think we have a bona fide abolitionist in our midst," a blond woman said, letting out a low whistle.

"You take that back, Amelia."

A loud cough from above interrupted the growing hubbub. The doctor stood in the doorway. "Would one of you ladies mind coming in for a spell? It's not proper for me to be alone with Mrs. Sutton."

No one moved, as everyone was eager to see how the two women would resolve what was now fraught and heavy between them.

"Go on, Lizzie," another woman piped up. "You've been hiding out here all afternoon."

All eyes turned to Lizzie, and she directed her gaze to Carol, asleep on the floor, a blanket spread out underneath her.

"She's fine. We'll call you if she wakes up."

The intensity of their pointed gaze pushed Lizzie to her feet, and she nodded, suddenly wanting nothing more than to get away from them all. She followed the doctor to the bedroom.

LIZZIE MADE A HORRIBLE witness. She sat in the corner, with her face turned away most of the time. She didn't talk to Emmaline much, didn't hold her hand or mop the sweat away from her face. She didn't even watch the doctor really, stiff and kneeling, one hand wandering around under a puddle of fabric with Emmaline turned on her side, so the two didn't have to look at each other.

In between questions, he rambled on, about the weather and

heat, about a new mill being erected in the county. A stream of inane conversation, about building materials—pine, white oak, cottonwood, and the rumor of a coming railroad, while the woman grunted and panted, sometimes crying out in pain.

Lizzie couldn't keep her thoughts together, and she made an excuse to escape, to send another woman in to take her place. He nodded and she sprung up and bounded toward the door. For a moment, she was ashamed that she couldn't even hold up her end of the bargain. She should at least be able to play the role, to dither and help and gossip and sew. Or even better, to get closer, to assist the man, to unleash a stream of chatter that might assuage the redness in his face and loosen up some free medical advice. Was she bypassing an opportunity to solve her most urgent problem?

The ice water and cooling fans were just a bonus. What she really needed was some medical know-how. Whatever Junie had given her wasn't working. There were moments where she felt grateful, as she knew this time everything would be easier. Serah would wean hers early and she'd finally have a wet nurse of her own for as long as she needed. But she couldn't shake the feeling that it was too soon. She was still apprehensive, though she felt like she shouldn't be. After all, there were women she knew who had a baby every eighteen months, like clockwork. But she didn't feel like she had the constitution for it. After four deliveries, her body already seemed so different. There were all kinds of changes she didn't know how to explain or who even to explain them to. The women in the parlor still felt too far away for that. It was at these times she missed her mother and sisters most. Were these strange fatigues and fevers common? Was it normal to have a bladder that leaked like a sieve or seemed to hold no more than the smallest cup of water? Or for her uterus to slide so low she swore she could feel it peeking out when she peed?

Not to mention her breasts. She feared another babe barreling through would split her in half. Somedays, the fear was muscular. So much so that when Charles moved against her at night, her whole body snapped shut.

She sucked in some air and settled herself back on the chair. "Dr. Coleson?"

He shushed her, fumbling with his pocket watch, Emmaline crying out in great pain again.

"Ah, that's it. About seven minutes apart, it seems."

"Oh, I can keep time for you." Lizzie gave him a weak smile and offered her hand. He gave her the watch, and she moved her chair a bit closer to the bed.

With a bit of delicacy, she moved the conversation ever closer to points of relevance. Never mind about the pine and white oak of the new mill, or the precise probable location of the railroad post. Instead, how long had he been man midwifing? And if a woman did find herself caught, but she worried her constitution was too weak from the last birth, was there something she could do, to stave it off awhile? Weren't there such methods? Midwives said there were, but he must know better than them old grannies and such. A learned man of science such as himself, more astute, with more knowledge in his left foot than all of them put together.

He blushed, but this time, a different kind of blushing. He puffed his chest out, wiped his damp hands on a rag, and looked her in the eye. "Midwives can't do what we do. They're alright in a pinch, I suppose, but if there's a breech or a more complicated matter, they aren't much use."

"I had this case once"—he leaned toward her now—"where the uterus closed around the fetus like a vise. Everything stopped. The patient was in labor, I could hear her, whenever I stepped outside to talk to her husband, but soon as I came back in, the

uterus tightened like a tobacco plug. What's an old midwife going to do with that? But you see, I got a whole bag of tools at
my disposal." He leaned over and pulled out a metal tool with a
twisted head. He dropped his voice to a whisper, "I had to pry
her open like a walnut. But after that, smooth sailing. Baby came
right on out."

Lizzie couldn't remove her eyes from that metal tool, how
much it resembled cutlery, something used to carve a slice of ham.
She felt her body grow heavy and she sat back firmly onto the
chair, as if it was threatening to slide out from underneath her.

"It's all a matter of balance. Midwives don't understand that,"
he went on. "The four humors: phlegm, black bile, yellow bile,
and blood are the keys to good health. And in females, restor-
ing the menses will solve most problems. Its disappearance is a
telltale sign of imbalance. The human body is more complicated
than we realize, I always say. More delicate, too."

He turned back to Emmaline, who was breathing heavily,
her eyes shut tight.

"What time is it?" he asked Lizzie.

Lizzie shook her head, counting. "Eight minutes?"

"That can't be right."

She handed back the watch and stood up.

He was still fiddling with it when she moved toward the
door.

"Need a break? Send in another, won't you?" he hollered as
she pulled the door shut behind her.

The hive energy of the women was farther down the hall.
Lizzie turned and went the opposite way, back out the front
door. It was dark now, but the moon was bright. It was still unearthly hot, a gust of heat smacking her in the face.

The German midwife, who was sitting in a rocker, jumped
up as Lizzie stepped onto the porch. She was short, with unruly

gray hair she wore tucked in a loose bun. The collapsible chair leaned against the front of the house.

"It's just me," Lizzie said, waving the woman to sit back down.

The midwife settled back into the rocker, smoothing down her long skirt. "How is she?"

"Alright, I guess. She'd probably feel better if you were in there."

The midwife shook her head. "With him?" Her bottom lip turned up into a nasty sneer. "*Nein danke.*"

Lizzie sat down in a rocker next to the midwife.

"She wants me, but husband wants flashy doctor. He win."

Lizzie laughed. "That sounds familiar."

For a long moment, they were quiet in the dark of the porch, watching the wind shift the dry shriveled stalks of what was left of the Suttons' garden. It was even more haunting in the dark, the loose pale sprigs waving like bony figures from the beyond.

Dogs howled, followed by shouting and whistling.

Both women sat up on the edge of their chairs. The patrol was out, circling the area.

"She pushing yet?" the midwife asked.

"No, seemed like the bearing pains were getting further apart."

"Hmph."

"I may have got the timing mixed up, though."

"No, you're right. I've been listening the whole time." The midwife knocked on the wall behind the two rockers. "When your countrymen are quiet, I can hear her just fine." She pulled a folded cloth out of her pocket and unraveled it in her lap, revealing a tangle of dry reedy twigs.

"What's that?"

"Cotton root. It speeds up the bearing pains."

"Oh, like from a cottonwood tree?"

The midwife shook her head. "No, from the crop. If you find yourself troubled and you need to bring on the red king, it works for that, too." She separated a fistful of twigs out and wrapped up the rest, sticking the remainder back in her pocket.

Lizzie cocked her head to the side and stared.

The midwife laughed at the look on Lizzie's face. "I hear the *schwarzes* swear by it. All the time, they chew and chew. It's a wonder y'all have any left." She stood up and moved closer to the house. "She's too quiet."

But Lizzie wasn't listening. She was still following the bundle of twigs in the midwife's fist, her mind spinning a million incoherent thoughts. In a rush, she had tucked the clippings Junie had given her in a sack with Carol's clothes. Maybe here was a better solution.

The midwife pulled open the door.

"Wait," Lizzie said. "Can I have a little? Of the cotton root?"

The midwife nodded. "Once I get Mrs. Sutton on her way, you can have whatever's left."

⚺

A PICTURE WAS FORMING in Lizzie's mind, but it didn't crystallize until hours later. Until after the midwife had muscled the baffled doctor out and reinstated the party of women. After Emmaline squatted on the collapsible chair, a half-moon cut out of its base, her sister holding one arm, the blond woman holding the other. A slimy head emerged from the fleshy opening and into the midwife's ready hands. An audible cheer went up in the room. Lizzie watched it all, disinterested in the corner, waiting for the moment when the tangle of roots would be handed over to her.

Once Emmaline was cleaned up and the bedding changed, the baby cleaned and dressed, the bundle of twigs was finally hers. She thanked the midwife and slipped off to the empty parlor, where she opened the bundle and compared them against the clippings Junie had given her.

They were identical in color, in slimness, plus similar indentations and discolorations where the limbs had been broken off. She stuck one of the bony twigs from the midwife into her mouth and chewed it, as if it were a delicious dessert she had been waiting for all day. She chewed it over and over until the tough stem broke down into a soft grainy pulp, then spit the mass into her hand. The smell that wafted from it was musky and slightly nauseating. She did this again with a twig from the tangle Junie had given her. They tasted the same, smelled the same.

And more than that, she couldn't shake how familiar the scent was. Serah smelled like that, as did Patience and Lulu. Junie sometimes, but not all the time. She assumed it was a shared bodily odor among them, some mixture of sweat and soil. With her tongue, she could feel a chalky film covering her teeth. She scraped a front tooth with her fingernail, and buried underneath was a yellow substance.

She moved closer to the table, where she pulled the pitcher and plates off the tin tray, and then held up the tray to look at her reflection. She opened her mouth wide and saw her teeth speckled with yellow grit. The tray slipped from her hands.

That speckle of yellow grit. That, too, was familiar. A strange interaction in the yard one summer. She had seen Serah outside, hanging the family's laundry, and she had caught the girl chewing yellow clay. She remembered the girl had said it was to stave off hunger and she never forgot it, because the answer always unnerved her. Sure, she could write off pica as just another childish trait of the people she and her husband owned. Another way they were fit for their place in their world and she hers. But, in a sea of red balance sheets, the pica said something more about she and Harlow and the enterprise they were running. That not only were they a small farm with fewer than ten slaves to their names, but those few people were so poorly fed that they chewed on dirt and clay to satiate their hunger. She would've happily given the girl twenty lashes for stealing food from the cookhouse, without looking into it any further, but this wasn't neat in the same way. And she hated that. It stung. Another piece of evidence of their mounting failure.

That old feeling washed over her. And it wasn't fair, to say it was old. It was always there, a shadow in the corner, a fly drowning in the cream. She had barely moved, a portion of her face visible in the silver tray, crooked on the table. She picked it up and walked outside with it. With both hands, she hoisted it low between her knees and flung it out toward the dead garden among the waving dead tendrils. It fell to the ground with a sharp, clanging thud. A glorious sound.

She had the mind to walk home, but there was Carol. And the moon had moved. It was darker now, too dangerous to walk. She'd have to wait 'til morning. She turned back to the house just as Emmaline's sister appeared in the doorway, wide-eyed, a shotgun in her arms.

Emmaline's sister lowered the weapon when she saw Lizzie. "You alright? What was that?"

Lizzie turned to look at the woman standing on the porch, the Sutton's large Greek Revival–style house towering against the dark sky, its paint so white it looked illuminated.

"Nothing," Lizzie said slowly. "I just came out for some air and knocked something over."

"C'mon back in. It's not safe."

Lizzie nodded and followed Emmaline's sister inside. She

went back into the room, where Emmaline and most of the women were asleep. Two women sat in the corner, whispering, and sewing.

"Where's the midwife?" Lizzie asked.

"Back in the kitchen, I think. C'mon, we saved you a space next to Carol. She was an angel. Does she normally sleep that long?"

Lizzie didn't answer. She scrunched down next to Carol, balling a blanket underneath her head.

If she had thought she would be getting any sleep, she would have complained. She would have extracted Carol from the mess of doting sleeping women and moved to the parlor. Instead, she just lay down. She needed the hive energy of the women to counteract what was congealing in her mind. The years in Texas. The nonexistent birth rate. The book of names that went nearly unchanged from year to year, without additions or increase. The needed wet nurse. How the only surviving children came from her womb. They all knew that myth of a plantation overrun with pickaninnies, fruitful mothers with litters of children. She had the plumb opposite, and for years, it plagued her. And now she knew why.

For so long, she wondered if they had been cursed. The fruitless soil, the perpetual bad weather—from strange freezes to hellish droughts, not to mention the death of young William. But all along there had been another reason for their mounting failure. Why, the answer had laid itself out before her so plainly, and she'd do with it what any Old Testament God worth his salt would do. Rain down hellfire until the angels saw fit to intervene.

CHAPTER THIRTY

THE NEXT MORNING, A HAZY fog greeted us. We welcomed it, thinking it might finally be the end of this perilous heat wave. Rain was finally on its way, we figured. The whole of Texas had been waiting on such rain for two months at least. All morning, we worked slow, trying to salvage what corn we could, sniffing the air for sign of a storm. The salvaging was a fool's errand, as most of the corn was withered and desiccated, but we tried anyway. For the first time in a long time, we were out there all together, with Nan and big-bellied Serah among us, trying to squeeze a full day of farmwork into the few tolerable hours of daylight, while Monroe and Isaac were off with Harlow on an errand.

We weren't out there long before the fog burned off and the sun's gaze grew in intensity.

"C'mon, Patience, make it rain now," Serah teased.

"That ain't what I said."

"You didn't deny it," Nan added.

We laughed, all except Junie, who just nodded, with a small closed-mouth smile.

The air grew warmer, a hot wind barreling through, clogging our noses, and making it harder to breathe. The sun bore down harder, a seething inescapable eye. We traded straw hats, draped our aprons around our heads and necks, but the sun and wind pushed in anyway, stinging our eyes, erupting in heat rashes up and down our arms and backs.

When we were done, with barely a bushel to show for the effort, we trudged over to the loom, where we'd normally spend the hottest portion of the day spinning, but it was padlocked. The riverbed near it was waterless, just a winding bed of pale stones.

Stiff-legged and parched, we headed back to the quarters, but the well over there was barricaded now, covered over with a flat piece of wood and a large block of stone we couldn't move. Something was surely awry, but we couldn't think past our thirst or the tingling heat engulfing our limbs. We plodded to the cookhouse, but the mile-long walk felt thrice as long. And by the time we reached the doorway to the small dark building, heat sickness felled us all. We stumbled in, dizzy, so beset with headaches and stomach cramps we could barely move. Patience, Lulu, and Junie were sweating profusely, wiping their faces and necks with the damp sleeves of their blouses, while Serah and Nan complained of feeling dried out, so flush with heat their insides felt aflame.

On the floor, we laid out, grateful to escape the sun. We passed around a small tin of water until there was none left. It clattered to the ground with a most accusatory sound.

"Go get more."

"Why me? Send her."

"You drank the last of it. You go."

Patience dragged herself up and stumbled back outside. She made her way to the new cistern fixed to the side of the Lucys' house. With small hobbling steps, she passed by the side of the house and peered into the window. No one was there. That was strange. She couldn't remember there being a time when no one was ever inside it.

She reached the back of the house, where the cistern towered over the roof. She stuck the pitcher underneath the spout and grabbed ahold of the handle, but before she could turn it, the hot metal scalded her.

She jumped back, cursing to herself, shaking her burned hand, the pitcher rolling away in the dirt. Grabbing hold of the pitcher, she positioned herself back underneath the spout, using the tail of her skirt to protect her fingers.

The spout seemed stuck. She grunted and heaved until it loosened, but nothing came out. It was completely dry.

THE HEAT SICKNESS AND the thirst were deliberate, part of the plan, we realized later. We awoke to Lizzie playing nurse, providing water, and dabbing faces with a damp, cool cloth. She even sent Ollie out to empty the buckets of vomit, and one by one, she had Monroe carry Lulu, Patience, and Serah back to the quarters. Where Isaac was, no one knew.

For Junie, consciousness came and went, until finally she woke up on the cookhouse floor, dizzy and unsure of where she was or how she got there. All morning, she had been a ball of worry, wondering when Lizzie would summon her to the house, to ask for more of the tea, or complain about having missed last night's dose entirely. Those were the scenarios she hoped for.

What really worried her was the idea of the tangle of roots lying about somewhere in the Lucys' house. She bolted upright but felt immediately pulled down by the fatigue of her body. She coughed, her throat dry. A blurry figure handed her a tin of water, only a quarter full. She gulped it down and held out the cup for more.

The morning's dread surged back to her. She had to retrieve whatever Lizzie hadn't used. What if Nan or Serah saw it? Or even worse, Harlow. He'd know exactly what it was.

A trickle of water dribbled into the tin cup and stopped. She reached for the pitcher, but the hands holding it, pulled it out of reach. Junie stared, trying to get her eyes to focus in the dim room.

"No. Not until we talk."

The figure's features slowly grew sharper. It was Lizzie, her limp hair uncombed, a ribbon askew, a strange glassy look in her eyes, sitting at the small table in the corner.

Junie sat up taller, trying to get her bearings. Dusk was falling, but there wasn't enough light to read whatever was flickering across Lizzie's face. Instead, she noted the weird angle of the woman's shoulders, the continuous bouncing of her right leg, almost independent of the foot connected to it.

"You make the tea?" Junie asked slowly.

"No, but I will . . ."

"Your blood come down yet?"

"No, but it will . . ."

"You don't seem worried."

"Well, it worked so well for you and the others. I need not fear, shall I?" Lizzie said, her voice shaking.

Panic rose in Junie's stomach. "What you mean?"

Lizzie sighed. "Don't insult me."

"Miss Lizzie, I don't know what you talking about," Junie said, slowly, trying to keep her voice calm.

Lizzie tittered. "Now, I know you're lying. I can count on one hand how many times you have ever referred to me as such. I must really have your attention now."

The two women looked at each other, unseeing. Clouds passed over, blocking what little light was left in the sky. Dark fell over the cabin, but neither woman moved for a long time, the air growing thick between them.

"How'd Miss Emmaline do?" Junie ventured. A test question.

"Oh, she did just fine. Had a bitty baby boy. What in Hades we need with another one of those, huh?" Lizzie said, laughing at her own joke. A strange cackle that bounced around the walls. "How's your head?" she said after a while.

"It hurts something awful," said Junie. Time seemed to be off-kilter, warped by some strange dullness she felt clouding her mind, soddening her limbs.

Lizzie struck a match. "The men in town think this bitty old match can start a fire by its lonesome. Isn't that something?" she said as she lit a candle. She sighed and offered Junie a scant bit of water. "Here."

Junie gulped it down and held out the cup. "Is there more?" The image of the well came back to her. Covered over and barricaded. "We couldn't get any from the well."

"Oh, just some foolishness with the patrol. Never mind all that. I want to talk about these twigs you gave me." Lizzie pulled out a bundle of cotton root from her dress pocket and dropped it on the table, causing the flame of the candle to flicker.

Junie stiffened, the throbbing in her forehead spread out, a small vise tightening around her skull. "Need me to boil it for you?"

Lizzie pulled free a short brown stalk and put it her mouth. She began chewing, her eyes never moving from Junie's face. "No, I wanna know how long y'all been unsticking the pig," she said, her mouth half-full. "Is that what y'all call it? That is how you put it, remember? 'Can't the pig be unstuck?' I haven't been able to get it out of my head since."

"Ma'am?" Junie breathed. *She knows.*

Lizzie chewed a minute longer, then blew the thick mass of cotton root out of her mouth. Bits of the chewed root flew into the air, onto the floor, onto her dress. "My whole damn life, you've been by my side. Like family, I'd tell anyone who asked, but maybe I was just blind to what you are, what you've always been."

"I don't know what you mean," Junie said quietly. She kept her body still while scanning the room. How many steps lay between her and the door? How far was the rack of pots and pans? Which one was closest? Heaviest? Where were the hearth's poker and shovel? They were usually right there on the left side.

Above the hearth, Junie could see an image forming. The same visual that had been playing in her mind ever since she first saw the steamboat tickets. A large boat barreling through dark gray water, before stopping at a rickety port where her two children stood.

"I hate it when you pull that dumb slave act with me. It's insulting. Now, I'm giving you the chance to explain yourself. Most people in my position wouldn't be as generous. You know that. But then, you always have taken my kindness for weakness. You and Charles, two birds of a feather that way."

"What you asking me?" Junie said, unable to keep the harsh edge from creeping into her voice.

"I want to know how long y'all been using the cotton root? Emmaline's midwife told me all about it. How y'all use it and for what purpose."

Junie felt her stomach seize up. She searched for an explanation just plausible enough to buy her more time to think, but her mind felt plodding and slow. "Who—"

"And before you play dumb, I should tell you I wrote to Mason this morning and told him we should talk seriously about the fate of your offspring. We could use them here . . . but maybe it's best he sell them. The markets in Louisiana are always hungry this time of year."

The large visual on the wall began to darken in spots, as if it was suddenly splattered with a dark, viscous oil. Junie watched as the oil spread and congealed, until it seemed to soil everything. When she could no longer see the boat, no longer see Patrick's and Hannah's small faces, she turned to Lizzie. "You want me to beg you? Is that what you want?"

Lizzie shook her head.

"What then? What we trading for?"

"I want to know everything," Lizzie said, that glassy desperate look appearing in her eyes again.

"And you'll do what? Write Mason?"

"Yes, I give you my word he won't sell them, but you have to tell me everything."

"Pssh . . . I'd be a fool to believe anything that come across your tongue."

"Well, that would make two fools then, 'cause I've never lied to you and you've been lying to me for God knows how long. I expect nothing less from the rest of them down there, but you?" Lizzie stood up and began pacing. "Just how long y'all been using it? Three years? Five? The entire damn decade?" she said, slamming a hanging pot down to the floor, with a loud crash.

Was this the day of Judgment old folks back home used to sing about? Junie tried to remember the hymns, what guidance they offered, what peace . . . but there wasn't any. Just the sick feeling of oil on her stomach, on her tongue, the inky trail of that boat and her children sliding farther away into whatever plane they were fixed to. *May they be protected. May they be safe.*

A cold steeliness came over Junie. "Off and on, we used it. Whenever we needed to."

"Needed?"

"Yeah, needed. Whenever the pig didn't want to be stuck. Like when somebody put a buck to you like you wasn't nothing but an old sow."

"I already told you that was Charles. You can't still be upset with me for that."

A long pause filled the room, the sound of night pushing in. Whirring mosquitoes and cricket songs. A dog howling in the distance.

"And you know what trouble I had breastfeeding," Lizzie went on. "I needed help. If Charles went about it improperly, it's 'cause we were desperate. I was desperate."

"So were we."

Lizzie stared at Junie and Junie stared back. Met the woman's eyes without shielding any emotion or thought inside her, for the first time she could remember.

Lizzie blinked, averting her eyes as if struck. "I'll advise Mason not to sell your children, but I can't save you from the lash. Not this time."

Junie dragged herself to her feet and stepped into the doorway. That black oil seemed to be above her now, covering the sky. She looked for the moon, for the stars, but couldn't find them. She turned back to see Lizzie still watching her, the woman's mouth drawn into a thin frozen line. "Little sister," Junie sang, "when have you ever saved me from anything?"

Junie stumbled down the steps, deeper into that dark, viscous night. She heard Lizzie behind her, tumbling down the cookhouse steps. "You ungrateful wretch," Lizzie yelled. "By and by, you'll soon know what it feels like to go out into the world without my help."

CHAPTER THIRTY-ONE

THEY HAILED FROM HENDERSON, ANDERSON, Freestone, and Ellis counties. They were boys, big and small, the youngest a scrappy ten-year-old and the oldest just turned seventeen, a ragtag gang making its way to Navarro.

They had been riding all summer. These boys, their number growing with the heat. At first, it had just been three or four farm boys from Henderson, ditching work to go to a hanging in Dallas. But one could say it started way before that. Back in their own counties, they each caught the bug.

In the slow winter months leading up to that long hot summer, they had begun ditching school to go to any dustup nearby, and each county had a few. Even before John Brown's execution in December, folks had been prickly. The old preacher's half-baked raid on Harpers Ferry was considered a joke, but the reaction to his death is what got stuck in white folks' craw. In two short months, Brown went from being a certifiable loon and laughingstock to a saint and martyr now that he was on the verge of execution. Had people all over the North singing his praises, over his mettle, his holy conviction, his willingness to die for abolition. The day he was hanged by the state of Virginia, northward church bells were rung in his honor, guns set off in precarious salute, and preachers ministered to solemn congregations. The feeling in the North seemed to be that Brown had been crucified. The line from then on was clearly set. Anyone who didn't boldly declare slavery a blessing was an enemy, anybody from the North was suspect, likely to be a John Brown copycat or an emissary of abolitionist causes.

When the Chapel Hill committee gathered outside the yard of old man Willis, seen talking behind closed doors with Negroes, the boys were there. They were among the crowd when the man was served his "walking papers" and run out of town.

They were there, in Marshall, when a minister accused of being an abolitionist was charged with treason and barely escaped with his life. That one was a sight to see. When the mob pursued the minister and his family and finally caught up with them twelve miles from town, the boys were among the procession that walked the man to the jailhouse. Some of the bigger boys pushed into the middle of the fray and got to lay hands on the preacher, got to pinch his arm and punch him in the back before he was stripped, whipped, and robbed, before being locked away in the calaboose.

For weeks afterward, the boys bragged about it in class, or on the farm, to all the boys who hadn't been there, whose mothers had managed to keep them home. They rubbed it in. All the fun they'd had and how they couldn't wait for the next one.

They were not disappointed. Come spring, there were more events to go to, and the boys blew off school, blew off chores, to travel in rollicking packs to the site of one great affair or another.

In May, they rode all the way to Fannin to see the hangings of Emma, Ruben, and Jess—three slaves hanged for killing their master. The boys outshouted men twice their size in the tussle for souvenirs—a scrap of a shirt or dress, an ear, or a finger. These mementos would go in the small metal box they carried with them the entirety of that summer.

And once the fires began in July, they didn't even bother going home. They traveled as far as Fort Worth to see another accused abolitionist tarred and hanged. And then back to Dallas, where they camped out the night before an execution to secure a good place in the clearing. That morning, the boys feasted on biscuits and ham, drank bitter coffee, and passed around a bit of whiskey, and were woozy with heat and drink by the time Patrick, Sam, and Cato were hanged—the three slaves the Dallas County mob identified as ringleaders of the fires that scorched and decimated the downtown area.

Newspapers warned Texans of a large, detailed plot of insurrection, scheduled to happen on election day in August. All-out war was on the horizon, one editor wrote, detailing a vast conspiracy of Northern abolitionists who had planted emissaries all over the South, who were working in concert with Black people.

Local papers reported of nearby towns being burned to a crisp, mobs discovering stockpiles of guns and strychnine in slave cabins, interrogations ferreting out hit lists of prominent citizens, and more lurid details of the unseemly plot. That day, while the men were out voting, Black men would poison their wells and take their wives. And a murderous few would lie in wait to slaughter the husbands once they returned home.

As hysteria increased, the boys' attentions grew scattered. It was hard to know which events would turn into the large festive parades of the early part of the summer. They could always ride with the local patrol and see what turned up, as it wasn't unlikely for a raid to turn into a small quiet hanging now and then. But those events happened suddenly and rarely made the papers. And often, by the time word spread of a such a hanging in progress, the boys didn't reach the site until it was all over. Sometimes, they could still grab hold of something for the souvenir box, but it just wasn't the same if they didn't see it with their own eyes.

And that created another issue, with the boys being spread so thin. They fought over the box more and more. Who got to keep it and for how long? It got so the boys didn't even want to share what they obtained with the rest of the group.

By the time they heard about an event in Navarro, it was tacitly understood that any boy who wanted a souvenir would have to secure it himself. That morning, they got on the road at first light, in hopes they'd get a good spot before the festivities happened around noon.

—✦—

WHEN THE LOOM WENT up in flames, we didn't wait to be questioned. Some of us tried to disappear, but there was nowhere to disappear to. The woods were scorched and barren, most of the trees undressed, as if in the midst of a harsh northern winter. The creek was a memory, dry as bone.

The patrols were everywhere. One of their number seemed to be posted every hundred yards. We wondered if these white men even pretended to work anymore, if they had livestock to tend to, crops to water.

We knew about Dallas and Pilot Point and Denton. We knew they'd look to us and ask about the origin of the loom fire, but only one answer would be accepted. Monroe made his claim early. He zipped around, helping Mr. Lucy put the fire out, kept it from spreading, in hopes that his presence would alleviate any question of guilt. A foolish strategy, we thought, but it seemed to work.

They only looked at us. They only sought us. And when they'd caught and penned us all, we saw Mrs. Lucy up ahead, her face a hot red streak, her mouth a twisted spoon. "I know it was them. Those wenches have been plotting against me since creation."

Any other time, we might have been tickled by her turn of phrase, to hear her channel us this way, but the horrible men surrounding us, their wide faces, and grubby roaming hands, made it hard to hear clearly. Without them, maybe we would have realized what she was saying, what she believed was the true crime, the fire itself merely a ruse of her own making.

We were harried and confused while Junie stood still as the trees, locking her eyes on Lizzie.

Lizzie stared back, her face flushed. She pointed a crooked finger at Junie. "No, just her! She's the ringleader!"

The men seized Junie first, before tightening their grip on the rest of us.

"She the ringleader?" they asked us.

Some of us shook our heads no, others remained frozen.

"Just what I thought." One of the men sniffed. He pushed his face close to Patience's. "You look like the ringleader to me."

"Nah, I think it's the old woman," another man answered.

"I said I'm dealing with the rest of them. Just take *her*!" Lizzie screeched.

"Now, ma'am, the Navarro Vigilance Committee has the authority to handle these threats as we see fit," a redheaded man said. "We're taking these wenches to jail. If Charles wants to file a motion, he can do so down there."

The vise around us tightened. We fought, but there were many.

A loud gunshot startled us all. One round, then two. We all turned and saw Harlow firing into the sky. He lowered his revolver and moved slowly toward us. "Paul, you son of a bitch, release my property," he yelled. "Now, goddamit, or this next ball will be in your throat! You, too, Wendell."

Several of the committee men raised their rifles in Harlow's direction. "You step back," a bearded man barked. "You don't like it, you take it up with the council."

"Yep, you agreed just like everybody else, Harlow. Arsonists will be dealt with no matter who they belong to," the redheaded man added.

The bearded man moved close to Harlow until his rifle was inches from Harlow's chest. "You hang back and collect yourself," the man said quietly. "And once we're gone, you go see Reynolds."

"Charles, you bastard," screamed Lizzie. "Are you just going to let them take everything?"

"Shut it, Lizzie," he yelled back.

The bearded man kept his rifle aimed at Harlow's chest, while the rest of the men hauled us away.

They took us to jail, with gleeful words on their lips. We heard ourselves condemned. Damned. However one considers going over, this felt different. Who among us hadn't considered self-destruction? Who hadn't washed clothes at the edge of a river and one day found herself walking deeper and deeper into the throat of it? Who hadn't considered the bottom of a well or any of the other numerous possibilities that might present themselves in a single day?

On the way to the jail, Serah was separated from us. Her pregnant belly deemed her capable of being reformed, and if not reformed, then just valuable enough to be spared.

Inside the calaboose, some women tried bargaining with the

guard, how they could pick more cotton or drive a plow better than any full hand in the county. They were super women, they promised. If their lives were spared, they could do it all. Split rails, have babies, pick a hundred bushels by their lonesome, and cook up a fantastic plentiful meal with nothing but corn, lard, and whatever scraps one could muster.

Junie may have been the only one who didn't bother with any of the above strategies. All her energy was set upon one thing, speaking to her children on this plane. And if it went the way it appeared to be going, maybe at the critical moment, she could fling herself beyond. Her soul could leap toward Georgia and bypass the otherworld altogether.

The march from the jail to the site couldn't have been more than half a mile, but it felt much longer. The sun was high, its furious glare singeing our skin. We walked single file, bounded together by the wrists, past a graveyard of desiccated trees, out to where a large oak towered above.

A cheer went up in the crowd. A sweaty mass of pink swollen faces. They taunted and heckled us.

Together, we sang. "I know moon-rise, I know star-rise. I'll lie in the grave and stretch out my arms. Lay this body down."

Two limbs of the tree were already roped, made to do the crowd's bidding. Those of us who could talk to trees tried to reason with it, accuse it of complicity.

"I'll lie in the grave and stretch out my arms. Lay this body down."

Past those horrible faces, there was a high fluttering in the trees north of us. The dry branches clacked, the dead leaves rustled, our song now stuck in their boughs. "I go to the Judgment in the evening of the day, when I lay this body down."

"Shut up that racket!"

"They singing in code!"

The song rose higher. "And my soul and your soul will meet in the day, when I lay this body down."

Junie. Lulu. Patience. Nan. Each one adding to the song. The melody then breaks, breaking open, rising higher, before adhering itself to the slow movement of clouds passing over.

—≤—

TWO OF THE BOYS secured souvenirs, which included: a scrap of Junie's gingham trousers, a lock of Patience's braid, and one toe, but from which woman they cannot remember.

Come September, after the hysteria has died out, a couple of newspapers will run retractions, noting fires reported that never actually happened, wells declared poisoned that were in fact untainted, and substances thought to be strychnine that turned out to be harmless. Some people will begin to wonder if there was ever a plot of insurrection at all. The box of souvenirs will then lose its luster and later be forgotten about, when Texas joins South Carolina and the rest of the South in the call for secession.

—≤—

SERAH COULD HEAR THE women's song from the yard of the auction house, where she remained alone. The small building was only a few paces from the jail, as people were often moved between the two structures.

From where she paced, she tried her best to ignore the lower half of her body, cramping in pain, and focused on the sound of the song starting up, then stopping, taken up by the next pair of women, until there was no song at all.

She squatted in the dirt and was surprised that the baby

slipped out easy, as if it had been waiting on her to just stop pacing long enough for it to descend.

The child was alive, a wrinkled baby girl, not much bigger than her hand. She cleared its mouth, as she had seen Nan do, and the baby began to cry. She ripped off a portion of her skirt and wrapped the baby inside it.

Something else was coming. With the child in one arm, she squatted and watched the slimy afterbirth fall into the dirt. She searched around for something to wrap it in. She didn't want her child to be anchored here, not in the yard of a trader's house, or in Navarro County itself. She wanted no link between her family line and this terrible place. She let it dry out in the sun; the husk of the thing would have to go with them. She had nothing to cut the cord and it seemed most reasonable to her to never cut it, to never be more than an arm's length from each other.

A decade or so later, when Serah will give birth for the third and final time, in the white clapboard house she shares with her family, her oldest daughter, born in the trader's yard, will be the one person she wants bedside. Though the midwife will frown at the child's presence and send the little girl off to fetch one thing or another, Serah will remain steadfast in this one request. Outside, Noah will pull the plow slow within earshot, tracking the rise and fall of sounds coming out of the small pulsing house. If it's a girl, he'll burn a piece of tobacco and indigo, and if a boy, tobacco and corn. When the pain thickens, Serah will summon the little girl by her bedside once more and tighten her swollen fingers around the child's tiny hand. And it'll be hard to say which one is the anchor affixing them to this new world, lest they be suddenly wrenched back into the old one.

Back in the trader's yard, the newborn hollers, taking up the women's dirge. Serah can hear the women singing again, a chorus embedded inside the baby's sharp cries.

ACKNOWLEDGMENTS

A first novel is often a marathon and as such, I need to thank those at both ends of the journey. An extremely special thanks to Henry Dunow and Arielle Datz; Sara Birmingham, TJ Calhoun, Shelly Perron, Caitlin Mulrooney-Lyski, Jin Soo Chun, and the rest of the amazing Ecco team; along with Ore Agbaje-Williams of Borough Press. I'm deeply grateful to you all for making this dream come true. An additional hearty thanks to Kiese Laymon and Margaret Wilkerson Sexton.

A big thank you to the Michener Center for all their support. Thank you, Billy Fatzinger, Holly Doyel, and Bret Anthony Johnston for everything and then some! Heart-filled thanks to Elizabeth McCracken, Roger Reeves, Daina Ramey Berry, and my Michener/NWP community of kickass writers, with particular thanks to dear friends/early readers Rachel Heng, Shaina Frazier, Rickey Fayne, Nathan Harris, Desiree Evans, and Shangyang Fang.

I also want give thanks to all the writing institutions and communities that supported me and earlier iterations of this project: VONA, Callaloo (shout out to Ravi Howard); Hedgebrook, Saltonstall, Sackett Street (with immense thanks to Heather Aimee O'Neill, who read early drafts of this novel); CUNY Writers' Institute (special thanks to Andre Aciman, John Freeman, Patrick Ryan, and especially Matt Weiland, who believed in this book when it was just a first chapter); Paragraph Workspace; and Tinhouse (enormous thanks to Alexander Chee, whose insightful feedback set this book on a different trajectory).

This book owes a great debt to the work of black women scholars and historians of African American history, at large. Paula Gidding's *When and Where I Enter: The Impact of Black Women on Race and Sex in America*, Stephanie M. H. Camp's *Closer to Freedom: Enslaved Women and Everyday Resistance in the Plantation South*, and Herbert G. Gutman's *The Black Family in Slavery and Freedom, 1750–1925* are cornerstones of this text. Other important sources include: Anthony Kaye's *Joining Places Slave Neighborhoods in the Old South*, Yvonne Chireau's *Black Magic: Religion and the African American Conjuring Tradition*, Sharla Fett's *Working Cures: Healing, Health, and Power on Southern Slave Plantations*, Deborah Gray White's *Ar'n't I a Woman?*, Stephanie Jones Rogers' *They Were Her Property: White Women as Slave Owners in the American South*, Marie Jenkins Schwartz's *Birthing a Slave: Motherhood and Medicine in the Antebellum South*, Michelle Lee's *Working Cures*, Zora Neale Hurston's *Mules and Men*, Ann Patton Malone's *Women on the Texas Frontier*, Thavolia Glymph's *Out of the House of Bondage: The Transformation of the Plantation Household*, Tera Hunter's *Bound in Wedlock: Slave and Free Black Marriage in the Nineteenth Century*, Michael A. Gomez's *Exchanging Our Country Marks*, James McPherson's *Battle Cry of Freedom*, Nikky Finney's *Rice*, Everett Gillis's "Zodiac

Wisdom," and Donald E. Reynolds' *The Texas Terror: The Slave Insurrection Panic of 1860 and the Secession of the Lower South.* The dissertations of James David Nichols and Mekala Audain on the travels of enslaved African Americans to Mexico were vital. And, of course, the testimonies of enslaved African Americans themselves, including Harriet Jacobs, Charles Ball, Katie Darling, and Rose Williams. The lullaby in the book is from Sea Island singer Bessie Jones' album, *Get in Union.* The author of the spiritual at the end, "I Know Moon-rise," is unknown, but documented in an 1867 edition of the Atlantic Monthly.

Last, but not least, tremendous thanks to my family—Mom, Dad, Damon, and the entirety of the Rose and Atwater clans, both those still here and those in the hereafter. I'm eternally grateful for your presence in my life. Deep gratitude to my crew—Carla, Kihika, Beverly, Kimmie, Akiba, 'Drea, Jackie, Maleda, and my All of We sistren, whose unwavering belief in me over the years makes this possible. And special thanks to my Howard film community, whose communal study over the years informs this work—Haile, AJ, Brad, Daniel, Frank, etc.